It is only to be expected t[...] spirited Miss
Cherryanne Devenish will embroil herself in a scrape
when she takes her place in gossip-loving Regency society.
But not even she can foresee the circumstances of her first
meeting with the notorious Marquis of Shalford – when he
bursts into her bedchamber at a wayside inn, seeking a
vantage to shoot an escaped lioness!

After that encounter, Miss Devenish wants nothing more
than to put the adventure – and the Marquis – out of her
mind. Besides, he is destined to marry the rich and charming Honoria Winton, in order to repair his fortune.
Circumstances, however, continue to throw the Marquis
and Miss Devenish together, and more decorous court-
ships have lost their savour for her . . .

By the same author in Masquerade

The Elusive Marriage

Patricia Ormsby

MILLS & BOON LIMITED
London · Sydney · Toronto

First published in Great Britain 1979 by
Peter Davies Limited, 10 Upper Grosvenor Street,
Mayfair, London W.1.

© Patricia Ormsby 1979

Australian copyright 1980
Philippine copyright 1980

This edition published 1980 by
Mills & Boon Limited,
London W1

ISBN 0 263 73222 3

Made and printed in Great Britain by
C. Nicholls & Company Ltd,
The Philips Park Press, Manchester

For P.C.K.
because he likes it

AUTHOR'S NOTE

The tale of the lioness attacking the Exeter Mail is a true one and, in fact, took place on 20 October 1816. Subsequent events as related in the following pages are, of course, largely fictitious.

CHAPTER
ONE

The travellers were within sight of the inn when the offside grey went lame. At once the window of the light chaise was lowered and a modish deep-brimmed bonnet of *gros de Naples*, surmounted by a great bow of satin ribbon, was thrust forth.

'Whatever can be the matter now, Kenyon?' the owner of this elegant example of the milliner's art wished to be informed.

The groom, who was acting as coachman, descended ponderously from his box and went to inspect the grey's right hock.

'Like as I said, miss,' he proclaimed gloomily. 'Strained, it is. He'll go no further today.'

Instantly the door was flung open and the lady descended to inspect the damage for herself, despite audible protests from inside the carriage to the effect that it was coming on to rain and would Miss Cherryanne have the goodness to remember that she was wearing her new kid half-boots, to say nothing of her new bonnet, which was not what the speaker had approved of in the first place, and now see how right she was shown to have been.

'Oh, do be quiet, Bridie, if you please,' begged her mistress, bending down to feel the injured hock with complete disregard for any possible damage to her high-collared velvet pelisse, let alone her footwear. 'Yes, Kenyon, I am persuaded you are right. Oh, fiddle! And I was set on reaching Amesbury today.' A sharp flurry of rain from the scurrying clouds brought another impassioned appeal from the interior of the carriage, but the young lady ignored it. 'What to do? What is that building ahead of us?'

'I take it to be the Winterslow Hut, miss. A respectable establishment, or so I've heard. Chance they'd have a change of horses.'

'No.' She shook her head firmly. 'I am not leaving poor Remus here. You know her ladyship has declared she will trust her horses to none but your brother at the George at Amesbury. It would mean leaving Romulus too, for he'll not pull with any other. If we rested Remus until tomorrow, do you think he would be able to continue to Amesbury?'

' 'Tis possible, if I poulticed him through the night. And once at the George,' Kenyon's eyes lit up with delight at so agreeable a prospect, 'we can bide there awhile so that he may make a good recovery before continuing on our journey to Bath.'

Miss Charity Annabelle Devenish, knowing her groom's predilection for comfortable inns, barely repressed a smile. 'Let us go on to this Hut place, then,' she commanded him, 'else we are going to get very wet indeed.'

She climbed nimbly back into the carriage and it proceeded at a pace in keeping with Remus's halting gait, until they drew up in searing rain outside the Winterslow Hut. Here they were made welcome and the horses taken to the stable, where Kenyon was at once in deep consultation with the head ostler over the strained hock, while a handsome bedchamber was placed at Miss Devenish's convenience by an attentive landlord. Being somewhat out of temper she merely nodded her acceptance and required him to set aside a small room for her maid's use.

'No need for you to put yourself to that expense, miss,' declared Miss Bridget Hanrahan, removing her young mistress's pelisse and shaking it free of any lingering raindrops. 'I can sleep on the truckle-bed in here with you. 'Tis a fine big room.'

Miss Devenish, while entertaining the warmest affection for her devoted abigail, had on former occasions been forced to lie awake listening to her resounding snores and had no intention of incurring such inconvenience again, so she merely smiled and said it would be nicer for Bridie to have her own room.

'But you will keep your door locked, will you not, Miss Cherry-anne? It all seems very respectable, but it isn't the George at Amesbury, and we don't know, do we?'

The excessive gentility of accent in which this warning was pronounced alerted Miss Devenish to her maid's opinion of the gravity of the situation and, promising to do everything that was prudent, she removed her bonnet, revealing a head of glossy, near-black locks, dressed *à la Madonna*, which framed an enchanting little face, blessed with an exquisite cream-and-roses complexion, and dominated by a pair of fine blue-grey eyes, set 'with a smutty finger', inherited from her Irish father.

'But mind me, Bridie,' she said, turning to shake an admonishing finger at Miss Hanrahan, 'do not you be coming to see if I am secure six times in the night! There is no harm likely to befall us in such a peaceful place – Bridie! Your poor face has swelled up again!'

'Aye, 'tis that dratted tooth, bad cess to it!' confessed Miss Hanrahan, lapsing under stress into her native idiom. 'I'm not like to get much sleep tonight with its aching.'

'That you will!' promised Miss Devenish. 'A James's Powder and a glass of rum when you go to bed is the very thing. Or, if that doesn't answer, a few drops of laudanum.'

'You bid Kenyon to fetch me a glass of rum from the tap and he'll have the whole bottle and put it on your tally, sayin' 'tis somethin' for the horse!' declared her henchwoman forcefully, shaking out a handsome shawl of flowered French silk with unnecessary vigour. 'Well did he know that Remus was not bang up to the mark – or should ha' done if he was any sort of a groom, at all, at all!'

'He did warn me yesterday that he suspected the hock to be rather heated,' admitted Miss Devenish.

Miss Hanrahan sniffed and was understood to say that, in her opinion, Kenyon was a shabby fellow who would avoid doing anything that did not suit his convenience and, if he had fault to find with his situation – well, he had the solution in his own hands. Furthermore, she would bet a pea to a pound that he was in the taproom this very minute, taking the lining out of a pot of porter and adding another nail to his coffin.

Miss Devenish, who knew well the state of smouldering hostility that existed between Lady Harpendene's groom and her maid, took scant notice of these animadversions. 'Well, you must confess it was prodigious kind of grandmama to send him with us and allow us to travel in her chaise to Bath. I had far rather he than John Coachman. We would never have exceeded eight or nine miles in the hour with him.'

'Aye, Kenyon pushes them along, I'll give him that – but see

what comes of it! Like as not, we'll be finishing the journey by
stage from Amesbury.'

Further gloomy forebodings were interrupted by a knock on
the door and the entry of a rosy-cheeked maidservant who desired
to be informed at what time the lady would care to partake of
dinner and would she be wishful of having it sent up to her room.

'That she would!' decreed Bridie before her mistress could
make reply. 'She'll not be going down to the coffee-room to be
ogled by any young sprig that calls in off the road!'

Miss Devenish, ignoring this outburst, admitted to being sharp
set and said she would eat at five o'clock. 'I suppose', she added
as the door closed behind the bobbing maid, 'five o'clock is an
unfashionable hour to eat in these parts? I've heard they don't
dine in Bath until seven or eight at night.'

'What's good enough for Lady Harpendene should be good
enough for the likes of them!' snorted Bridie, getting up off her
knees from beside the valise. 'An' if I remember aright, your auntie
was ever a great one for her food, so *she'll* not keep us waiting.'

A slight frown creased Miss Devenish's smooth brow as she
wondered, not for the first time, what had prompted Mrs Marsden
to invite her niece to make a long stay in Bath under her protection. Had grandmama suggested it, feeling that the company of
one rather infirm elderly lady was not quite the thing for a spirited
girl of twenty-two? Still pondering, she moved to the window and
looked out at the rain-washed prospect.

'What can be the purpose of all those caravans and wagons
across the road?' she asked. 'A circus, d'you think?'

Bridie gave the huddled vehicles a cursory glance. 'Aye, bound
for some fair, I daresay. There's a cage or two there as well – like
as not they've got some wild beasts with them. It's to be hoped
they are under good restraint.'

'Depend upon it, they will have keepers to handle them,' Miss
Devenish assured her. 'Oh! What a spanking turn-out! Come,
look, Bridie! That curricle-and-four just swinging into the yard –
and the gentleman handling the ribbons! Quite the swell, I do
declare!'

'An' a good thing it is you'll not be descending to the coffee-
room if there are more of his sort about the place!' announced

Miss Hanrahan trenchantly. 'Come away from that window, if you please, miss!'

But Cherryanne stood transfixed, gazing at the tall, lithe figure that sprang easily down from the curricle and, tossing the reins to his groom, stood looking about him with such an air of unconcerned consequence that she was forced to smile. As if aware of her scrutiny, he looked quickly up at the window and, as his eyes met hers, his lips pursed in a soundless whistle. Then he swept off his high-crowned beaver and made her the most elegant bow, revealing fashionably cropped chestnut locks and a classically handsome countenance. The sight of him, standing there in the rain, his many-caped drab riding-coat flung open to reveal his well-made person, struck her as being so ludicrous that she burst out laughing. Then the scandalized Bridie was pulling her away from the window, but not before she had seen the smile dawning on the striking face looking up at her turn into a scowl, and the brilliant eyes, the colour of which she could not ascertain at such a distance, flash with anger.

Oh-oh! she thought, so my fine gentleman does not care for being laughed at? Some out-and-outer of the ton, no doubt, who has but to drop his handkerchief to have the ladies fall over themselves in their eagerness to snatch it up.

'Now, miss, if you please, off with those dusty clothes and into a fresh gown.'

'It scarcely signifies what I wear if I am to spend the rest of the day here in my room. A robe-de-chambre will do.' Miss Devenish's tone was of supreme indifference but her sapient abigail was not deceived.

'You'd like to be below stairs, I daresay, being paid pretty compliments by that fine gentleman!'

Her mistress swung round upon her, eyes sparkling with mischief. 'Bridie, dear, do something for me! Find out who he is! I am persuaded he must be a nobleman of the first stare.'

'We-ell,' said Bridie, relenting slightly. 'There's no harm in that, I suppose, just so long as he doesn't start asking questions about you. Now, slip into this old merino gown. 'Tis a chilly evening and with your green velvet spencer atop 'twill keep you warm.'

Unresisting, Cherryanne allowed herself to be fussed over, the while her thoughts dwelt upon her not altogether happy situation. After seven years of widowhood, her mother had permitted herself to be enticed into marriage with an Irish squire. Mr FitzGerald Cunningham had been all easy affability during the days of his courtship, but once wed to the lady, he allowed it to be plainly understood that he had neither the desire nor the intention of maintaining an able-bodied stepdaughter of twenty-two. If her finical ladyship could not bring herself to accept any of the flattering offers made her by several gentlemen of standing and substance, then he would be obliged if she would keep in mind the fact that it was his roof that sheltered her and his money that paid for the food she ate, and that such a state of things could not continue indefinitely.

It did not continue above three months, for Miss Devenish wrote to her maternal grandmother in such terms as to bring a scathing set-down from that formidable lady upon her mother's head, and an invitation to her granddaughter to make her home with her in England.

Despite Mrs Cunningham's tears and her amiable spouse's comments that he had known all along how it would be, the chit would ingratiate herself with the old lady and cut her mother out of her rightful inheritance, Cherryanne packed her bags and, with aching heart, left her parent, her friends, and her beloved homeland for an alien shore, accompanied only by her maid. Her memories of her father, that gay, irresponsible cavalry officer who had swept her mother off her feet and over to his native Ireland, and then had died gallantly and with great panache in the Peninsula, she kept locked in her breast. But for her grandmother's practical support their lot would indeed have been a desperate one in the charming but ramshackle old house in Lucan to which Mrs Devenish had been brought as a bride.

Lady Harpendene had received her with bracing lack of sentiment, and demanded to be told what she had done to deserve such a nodcock of a daughter, who must be for ever marrying unsuitable Irishmen.

'And whatever for, pray? Are there no English gentlemen worthy of her attention?' She then adjured Cherryanne to make the best of the situation and they would rub along very well together.

Her granddaughter nobly resisted the temptation to speak up in defence of her father and to point out that, as her mother had chosen to live in Ireland, she was most likely to meet Irish gentlemen rather than English, but as this seemed probable to put her in the position of having to defend her parent's second marriage, she easily refrained.

She found Lady Harpendene to be an astringent autocrat, but not an unkindly one. She had a genuine concern for her granddaughter and only wished that her years and indifferent state of health did not preclude her from presenting the girl to London society as befitted her station.

'I had great hopes that Amelia Caldwell – she's daughter to an old friend of mine – would take you on. She has married off her eldest girl most successfully and the younger ones are not ripe for society yet, but her husband has whisked her off to Brussels and there's no knowing when they'll return. Bath is all very well, but it ain't the hub of fashion any more, and Maria will not exert herself above what is ordinary to push you forward. Now if Ariadne or George had been at home, that would be a very different kettle of fish, but she was wed to a Scottish laird last year and has not set foot south of the border since, while the on-dits have it that George is racketting around London, throwing away his blunt on every sort of frivolity.'

Miss Devenish thought her cousin George sounded to be a most interesting sort of young gentleman, but judged it prudent to refrain from saying so. She remembered him as a rather lanky lad, a few years her senior; his sister Ariadne as a lively child of her own age; and her aunt and uncle hardly at all, for there had been small contact between the two families since long before her father had died.

Her wandering thoughts were recalled sharply to the present by a little moan of pain from Bridie, who sat back on her heels, nursing her swollen face.

' 'Tis no good, miss. 'Tis drivin' me clean out o' me wits.'

'Bed for you, and a warm brick to your feet!' Miss Devenish agitated the bell-pull violently. 'Now where did you pack those

James's Powders? No, Bridie, I'll not hear another word. And when we get to Amesbury, you'll have that tooth drawn.'

The next hour was spent in settling the sufferer into her room, having a fire lit, dosing her liberally and soothing her fears, by which time it was well past the hour set for Miss Devenish's dinner. When she was satisfied that her patient was fallen into a sound sleep, largely induced by rum and laudanum, Cherryanne went back to her own bedchamber to find the maid awaiting her instructions. 'Yes, bring the meal up at once. I'm to blame if it is spoiled.'

' 'Twon't be that, miss, I promise you.'

The girl had made up the fire and lit the candles so that the room glowed warmly in the deepening dusk. Cherryanne sank into a chair and looked about her with some satisfaction. For a moment she had been tempted to countermand her order to have her dinner brought up and thought to brave the dangers of the coffee-room, but a number of carriages had pulled in off the road and the rising sound of male voices assured her that the company belowstairs would not be at all suitable for one unescorted and attractive young lady.

Being excessively hungry, she did full justice to the lamb cutlets, the duck roast with honey, the broiled mushrooms and creamed spinach, finishing off with Loundes pudding and a gooseberry tart. After the remains of this repast had been cleared away, she tucked herself up in her chair by the fire and straightaway forgot all about her surroundings and equivocal future in reading one of Mrs Radcliffe's Gothic tales which she had slipped into a valise away from Bridie's disapproving eyes.

After a while her head began to nod and her eyelids to droop, which was not to be wondered at since she had set out from her grandmother's house at Chilcomb, near Winchester, before ten o'clock that morning. But for poor Remus, she mused sleepily, they could easily have been in Amesbury before dark. The thought of Remus put her in mind of her afflicted maid and, guiltily, she set down *The Sicilian Romance* and started to her feet.

Bridie, as was evident by the sounds that assailed Cherryanne's ears before she even opened the bedroom door, was enjoying a profound slumber and, after one glance, Miss Devenish left her undisturbed, only uttering a prayer that those occupying adjoining rooms might survive the battery of snores that followed her defiantly as she retreated along the passage. She had arrived back at her own door which was close to the head of the stairs when the little maid came scampering from the opposite direction.

' 'Tis the mail, miss! I seed the lights come over the rise.'

'What mail? Do they change horses here?'

'Oh, no, miss. 'Tis the Exeter mail a-goin' up to Lunnon. They only cast off the mail-bags and are away again in a trice. If you go to your window you'll have a fine view of it.'

Obediently Cherryanne hurried into her bedchamber and, not even troubling to close the door behind her, ran to the window to draw back the curtains and look down into the pool of light cast by the outside lanterns and the undraped taproom windows. There, indeed, up the long straight road came the mail, its lights twinkling, sparks striking off the horses' hooves as the coachman reined them in and swung the whole equipage into the forecourt of the inn.

Then the unbelievable happened. As the guard was preparing to throw out his mailbags a huge yellow creature seemed to rise from the ground and hurl itself towards one of the leaders. The horse kicked and plunged violently but the lioness, for such it was, fastened the talons of her forepaws on each side of his neck while the talons of her hinder legs were forced into his chest. The ostlers, who had come running at the approach of the mail, stood transfixed in horror, the passengers were shouting and screaming in alarm, while the unfortunate horse which had been attacked fought with great spirit but, in plunging, embarrassed himself in the harness.

The coachman drew out a knife and was proposing in the most gallant manner to alight and risk his life in attacking the beast, but was restrained by the prudence of his guard who held him back from so ill-advised an attempt.

Cherryanne, hands pressed to cheeks, eyes dilated in terror, was staring at the awesome scene when a hand grasped her shoulder roughly, thrusting her aside. The next moment the window was flung open and a man was kneeling beside it, levelling a pistol at the lioness.

'Your pardon, ma'am, but you have the best view of any – devil take it!' He lowered his weapon as, from the back of the inn, there bounded a large mastiff who hurled himself upon the lioness. She, enraged by such interference, quitted the horse and turned upon him. The dog, dismayed at its own temerity, fled, but she pursued him into the darkness and there slew him at her leisure.

'Oh, dear God, the poor brave creature!' Cherryanne hardly knew that she had cried out in her anguish, but her companion, rising to his feet, set her none too gently upon a chair.

'This is no time for a fit of the vapours,' he rapped out. 'Sit there and close your eyes if you cannot stomach what you see, for if the beast comes again within my range she is as good as dead.'

His curt dismissal of her did more to restore Cherryanne to her senses than a kinder treatment would have done. For a moment she glared at him angrily as he dropped again on to one knee by the open window, and recognized for the first time the thick chestnut curls, the proud, clear-cut profile, the whole elegant person of the gentleman whom she had observed descending from his curricle a few hours previously. Then the urgency of the moment overcame her resentment.

'Oh, shoot her, sir, I beg of you, before – before she kills again!'

'I cannot,' he ground out furiously. 'She has gone too far away. Besides, the place is overrun with people. They are – yes, they must be keepers. She'll have escaped from the menagerie yonder that is on its way to Salisbury Fair.'

'M-menagerie?' stammered Cherryanne. 'I th-thought it was a circus!'

He grimaced slightly. 'The inn folk were not too happy about it resting there, I can tell you, and rightly so it would seem. How would it have been, I wonder, if she had escaped at the very moment I was making my bow to you this afternoon?'

'Oh, don't speak of it!' she whispered, covering her face with her hands, but his interest was again taken by the activities outside and he paid her no heed. After a moment she dared to join him and look fearfully at what was happening below. But the moment of high tension had passed, the keepers had rallied around and were driving the lioness away from the inn, the injured horse had been loosed from the harness, the alarmed passengers, though not yet daring to dismount, had ceased their outcries, the body of the unfortunate dog had been dragged away – indeed, Cherryanne was tempted to wonder whether she had not imagined the whole terrifying episode.

The gentleman straightened up and closed the window. 'And that, I collect, is that!' he remarked almost regretfully. 'A most unusual occurrence, to be sure, do you not agree, ma'am?'

It was at that moment that Miss Devenish realized she was alone in her bedchamber with a strange man and he was smiling down upon her in the most disturbing way, very much at his ease and seemingly in no hurry to quit her company.

''Pon my soul, an even prettier little pigeon than I had supposed,' he remarked in a reflective sort of way, tilting up her chin with a careless finger. 'I allow our introduction to have been a trifle informal, but in such circumstances that hardly signifies.'

And before she knew what he was about, he bent and kissed her swiftly upon her parted lips.

CHAPTER
TWO

The distressing scenes she had just witnessed and the utter impropriety of her situation had not rendered Miss Devenish totally incapable of movement. At once she flung up a hand to strike at the vivid, mocking face so close to hers, but it was seized in mid-air, as if in a vice.

'Oh, no, you don't! I'll have no chit slapping my face because I have offered her the civility of a chaste salute.'

His eyes glinted down at her, alight with malicious amusement, and, even in her outraged confusion, she saw them to be heavy-lashed and deep-set and of so dark a hue as to be almost black. Then a sound from outside the still half-open door distracted him. Tossing her back into the chair with no more effort than if she had been a child, he strode across the room and slammed the door shut. Cherryanne who, besides having inherited from her father his laughing Irish eyes, had also been endowed with his impetuous Irish temper, bounced up again in a fine fury. With some vague notion of throwing it at his head, her hand went out to seize the branch of candles on the table beside her. Then her eye fell on something much more suited to her purpose – his pistol, lying primed where he had put it down the more conveniently to embrace her. With a swift movement she concealed it in the folds of her skirt and stood defiantly facing him as he came back across the room.

'And now, Miss – Devenish, I believe it is? Shall we continue to improve our acquaintance?'

So he had been making enquiries about her! As he stood, hand on hip, looking her up and down with insulting particularity, her indignation at such treatment overcame her alarm.

'Stay where you are, sir, or I vow I'll put a bullet through you!'

'What? My own pistol? Gad, that was quick of you!' There was a hint of admiration in the lazy, well-bred voice. 'But you'll not pull the trigger, will you, my dear? You'd not have the resolution for it.'

. 'Just come one pace nearer and you'll have your answer, sir!' she got out between clenched teeth, praying that he did not see the trembling of her hand holding the heavy pistol.

'But I *am* coming nearer!' His tone was light and amused as if he had not the least expectation of her fulfilling her threat. 'Give it to me, you silly child. I ain't going to hurt you.'

He stepped forward confidently, hand outstretched, but Cherry-anne, understandably distrustful of such advances, cried out desperately: 'Go back, sir, or I shall fire!'

The last word was drowned in the noise of the pistol going off and in a great shattering of glass. Then he was removing the weapon from her limp grasp.

'Not bad for a beginner,' he said coolly. 'I confess I did not believe you would do it.'

She scarcely heeded him for her eyes were fixed upon the mirror hanging upon the wall behind him. 'Great heavens, I have smashed it to pieces!'

'Yes,' he agreed, 'and brought seven years' bad luck upon your-self if the old wives' tale is true. Now, lest anyone should have heard the shot – which, I confess, I think to be unlikely as there is still an almighty uproar going on below – I shall open the door again and we must explain that it was an accident, you, never having handled a pistol before, were merely giving it back to me with your compliments on its admirable workmanship.'

In the taproom, Mr Joseph Pike, the guard of the mail coach, fortified by innumerable flashes of lightning to restore his agitated nerves, was recounting to those who had not been fortunate enough to witness the attack upon his vehicle just how it was the coachman was still alive, thanks to his restraining influence; while the coffee-room was filled with passengers and the many persons who inevitably spring from nowhere when any catastrophe occurs, so that nothing less than the roar of a cannon could have pene-trated the din in these apartments. The landlord, however, passing by the foot of the stairs, heard the pistol shot quite clearly and checked his stride, his arms full of bottles, to listen.

'Why that be – 'tis from the front room! Here, Will, take these!'

Dumping the bottles unceremoniously into the astonished tap-room lad's arms, he mounted the stairs two at a time and rapped smartly upon the door of Miss Devenish's bedchamber. To his surprise, it swung open to his touch and he perceived the lady standing in the middle of the room, looking somewhat discomposed.

'Landlord, I fear I have destroyed your mirror,' she said flatly.

The landlord, who had anticipated a worse calamity, received this intelligence with a certain amount of irritability which was hardly to be wondered at in view of the trying events of the evening.

'Indeed, that you have, miss, and a pretty penny it'll cost you!' he began truculently. 'And may I ask just what you was doing with firearms in – ' He stopped abruptly, becoming aware for the first time of the presence of another. 'M-my lord!'

'Rushed up to have a pot-shot at the beast from this window, being the best viewpoint,' explained the gentleman languidly, all his attention apparently given to polishing his quizzing-glass. 'Too late, though, the dog had drawn her away. Then the lady here had a fancy to look at my pistol – unfortunate accident. Put it down on my shot. And send up a bottle of brandy, if you please. All this has been very upsetting for Miss Devenish.'

'Yes, m'lord. Certainly, m'lord.' The landlord bowed himself out in some haste while Cherryanne was still wondering why she had not claimed his protection and told him the true story.

'I – I have no need of brandy, sir – my lord,' she began tentatively and stared at him in surprise when he dropped into a chair and smiled up at her.

'Have you not, my dear? Well, to tell truth, I think I have! Your aim was not so very bad, you know!'

Then she saw the dark stain spreading on the shoulder of his blue coat and cried out in dismay.

'I did hit you! Oh, dear God!'

'Don't despair, ma'am, it is only a flesh wound. But I am bleeding like a pig – I always do, I'm afraid. I hope the sight of blood doesn't send you off for you'll have to tie it up for me!'

Though he was still grinning impudently at her, she perceived that his face was very pale and a faint sheen of moisture showed on his forehead.

'You are in pain – let me help you off with your coat.'

'No.' He took her hand and pressed it lightly. 'For I must be on my feet when the landlord returns. Tell me, Miss Devenish, why did you not disclose to him the fact of my having forced my attentions upon you?'

'I – I don't know,' admitted Cherryanne candidly. 'I am aware you are a very forward and – and presumptuous young man, but I did not believe you would do me any real harm.'

'You took me for a gentleman, did you?' There was a strange note in his voice which she failed to recognize as self-mockery. 'You have much mistaken the matter, poor child! While my intentions are often good, I cannot promise you to keep to them! But as for you, Miss Devenish,' he went on, the amusement back in his eyes, 'it would seem that I also have been mistaken, for how could I suspect that the lady who smiled so enchantingly upon me this afternoon could shoot me down so ruthlessly tonight?'

Much mortified, Cherryanne blushed and hung her head. 'My – my conduct was most misleading, I confess,' she whispered. 'But you looked so – so – '

'So what?' he prompted her.

'So interesting!' she confessed. He flung back his head and laughed.

'Oh, Miss Devenish, such improper notions will never do for Bath!' he quizzed her.

She gasped. 'How do you know so much of my affairs?'

'You have a loquacious groom and mine is very expert at extracting information.'

'I go to stay with my aunt who will, I am persuaded, put me in the way of being accepted into the polite circles of Bath society,' said she, all dignity.

'You will find it uncommon dull, I promise you!'

'Since I cannot aspire to the London whirl, sir, I must be content, must I not – oh, sir, my lord – oh, where is that landlord?' cried she, perceiving his increased pallor and the sudden tightening of his lips.

'Sssh! Here he comes. Your arm, ma'am.'

Anxiously, she assisted him to rise and when the landlord entered bearing the brandy, it was the gentleman who was bending solicitously over the lady, enquiring how she did. When, at last, their host had left them and the maid had swept up the broken glass, Cherryanne urged her companion back into a chair and watched him drink down a fair measure of brandy before helping to ease him out of his well-fitting coat. To her horror, his fine silk shirt and embroidered waistcoat were both saturated with blood, and there was nothing for it but to remove them and his neckcloth before she could attend to the wound in his shoulder.

She was bathing this and endeavouring to pretend that it was nothing out of the way for her to be tending half-naked and unknown gentlemen in her bedchamber, when a timid tap sounded upon the door and, before she could utter a word of warning, it opened to admit Miss Bridget Hanrahan.

The sight that met that damsel's somewhat befuddled gaze was sufficiently alarming to shock her into complete sobriety.

'Miss Cherryanne! Whatever are you at?' Her voice, rising higher with every word, would most likely have escalated to an outraged scream, had not Miss Devenish, moving very swiftly, dragged her inside the room and shut and locked the door.

'The very person I need!' she said briskly. 'This gentleman has been wounded, Bridie, and I need your assistance to put him to rights.'

Thereafter Miss Hanrahan found herself to be fully occupied in tending to the gentleman, the while Miss Devenish regaled her with a lively account of the incredible happenings of the evening.

'An' to think I never heard a thing!' marvelled Bridie, placing a thick pad of towelling over the wound and casting an eye around the room for something to hold it in position. 'Tear me a strip off a sheet, miss – best do it at the bottom so they'll not find out until we've gone in the morning!'

Miss Devenish, with a lofty disregard for any such precaution, flung back the covers and tore the top sheet clean in half. 'There!' she said grandly. 'You will be able to swathe him like an Egyptian whatever-it-is!'

'Aye, an' he could do with swathing!' muttered Bridie darkly, eyeing the gentleman's smooth bare torso. 'Another sup of brandy, Miss Cherryanne, or we'll have him going off. Oooh!'

She clapped a hand to her swollen cheek and he watched her with sympathetic interest. 'Toothache, is it? You'd best have some brandy yourself, ma'am.'

This Bridie was easily persuaded to do, and the powerful spirit, taken on top of rum and laudanum, speedily reduced her to a state of near insensibility.

'You are going back to your bed, Bridie,' stated Miss Devenish, seeing how it was with her henchwoman, 'and you, sir, had best take yourself to your chamber.'

So saying, she swept Bridie off to her room and there remained until the now completely foxed Miss Hanrahan was tucked up and snoring soundly. Then she returned on tiptoe to her own chamber, quite expecting to find it empty.

Such, however, was not the case. His lordship – and just what manner of lordship he might be she proposed to discover without loss of time – sat slumped in the chair where she had left him. His shirt lay on the floor at his feet, which seemed to postulate that he had made an attempt to clothe himself, but clearly it had proved beyond his powers for he looked to be quite insensible.

'Oh, la!' stormed Miss Devenish, stamping her foot in justifiable irritation. 'If you must swoon, sir, could you not reserve it for the privacy of your bedchamber? I declare I am at my wits' end what to do for the best!'

'Just hand me the brandy bottle, ma'am, and don't put yourself in a taking. When all's said, who's to blame for my sad plight?'

Perversely, the relief of hearing him speak only served to send Miss Devenish further up into the boughs.

'We don't require you to be completely cut!' she snapped, thrusting the brandy at him. 'Nor is it my fault you are in so sorry a state!'

He threw back his head and tilted what seemed to her to be half the contents of the bottle down his throat. 'If you are to clothe me and escort me to my bedchamber,' he said sweetly, handing it back to her, 'you'd best fortify yourself, ma'am.' Her outraged expression caused him to raise a quizzical eyebrow. 'What else to do, my dear? I can hardly totter along the passage clad only in breeches and boots, nor can you go downstairs and drag my groom out of the tap without arousing adverse comment.'

Miss Devenish was forced to acknowledge the good sense of this argument. 'I could ask the maid to fetch him,' she began and then stopped, realizing that such a request would be equally certain to arouse the speculation she most earnestly wished to avoid.

'You see?' he murmured, the malicious mockery dancing again in his eyes. 'But once in my own room I can summon the fellow and no one need be any the wiser!'

'Very well.' Miss Devenish, her pretty mouth set firmly, picked up his shirt from the floor. 'Can you get your arm into the sleeve of this, sir?'

Despite the strong aroma of brandy which slightly nauseated her, she went about her task in a downright ruthless manner, her ruffled sensibilities in no way soothed by his obvious enjoyment of her predicament. When shirt and waistcoat were on and his cravat re-tied after a fashion, she found that to replace his admirably cut coat was clearly impossible.

'No matter,' he assured her. 'I'll get my good arm into it and if you will tuck the empty sleeve into my pocket I daresay no one will notice anything out of the ordinary should we encounter anyone on our way.'

The next few minutes were the longest Miss Devenish ever remembered having had to endure in her life. The gentleman's room was situated in the corner position at the end of the passage from which the bedrooms opened off, and they proceeded slowly along, she clinging to his sound arm and praying that no door would fly open as they passed and some curious resident emerge to view their uncertain progress.

'Have no fear, ma'am,' he comforted her. 'Anyone coming upon us now must surely assume that I am a trifle on the go and you, my dutiful wife, are escorting me to our nuptial couch – there, no doubt, to read me a curtain-lecture on the evils of over-indulgence!'

This impertinence caused Miss Devenish to be doubly grateful for the indifferent lighting which concealed her blushes as well as her companion's unsteady gait.

'Here we are,' he went on, removing his arm from her clasp in order to open the door. As he did so, the sound of someone ascending the stairs caused him to thrust her in front of him into the room and close the door quickly behind him. 'My apologies for the disorder, but I never take my valet with me on brief journeys. In return for which consideration I have to suffer his mute reproach for several days after my return while he puts my apparel to rights. Why is it that persons who have known one since childhood can never be convinced that a certain degree of maturity is to be expected with increasing years?'

Miss Devenish agreed whole-heartedly that nothing could be more lowering than to be treated as if still in shortcoats when one was sufficiently stricken in years to be termed adult.

'Now, sir, if you will be seated I will light more candles and draw the drapes.' This she did with a brisk competence that hid her understandable shyness at finding herself alone in a gentleman's bedchamber with him. He watched her, a half-smile on his rather hard mouth. 'There!' she said, tossing a few small logs on to the fire, 'that will burn up famously in no time. So, if you will permit me a few moments to reach the sanctuary of my room before summoning your groom, I will take myself off.'

'Come here, Miss Cherryanne Devenish!' He was standing, supporting himself with one hand on the mantelshelf, and, as she turned to him in surprise at the peremptory command, he stepped forward and clasped her to him with his good arm. 'Cherryanne!' he repeated, as if savouring the word on his tongue. 'Now what combination of names could produce so delightful an outcome?'

Miss Devenish, who held no great opinion of the name, was surprised to hear how well it sounded when pronounced by his lordship. Her mother had thought it such a pretty notion when Lord Byron had married Miss Anne Isabella Milbanke that the lady should call herself Annabella, and she was moved to contract her daughter's given names in like fashion, nor did the subsequent disastrous collapse of the Byron marriage discourage her from continuing to call her only child Cherryanne. That young lady, for her part, just so long as she did not have to answer to the name of Charity – which she considered to be beyond anything and fit only for a foundling brat – was quite indifferent as to what she was called, but felt that the present situation hardly allowed for a discussion upon the matter.

'Sir!' she protested, endeavouring to free herself yet fearing to struggle lest she should hurt him.

'Cherry Ripe!' he muttered thickly. 'For so you are, my innocent little girl! Ripe for picking!'

'And you, sir, are ripe for nothing but your bed!' she informed him severely. 'Now sit down, if you please, for I cannot stand here holding you up all evening and I am persuaded you will fall flat upon your face if I withdraw my support. All that brandy taken on top of so great a loss of blood has quite intoxicated you.'

He chuckled. 'I must confess to being a shade castaway,' he admitted. 'But am I to be offered no further recompense for the wicked thing you did to me?'

'What can you mean, sir?' For all her assured manner, Cherry-anne's heart was fluttering wildly.

'This!' he said, and kissed her again, very much more soundly than before.

Miss Devenish had, on occasion, received the salutes of her father's numerous male relatives in Ireland, but none of those decorous tributes had prepared her for so warm an embrace from so personable a young man.

'If – if you please,' she faltered bravely when she could draw breath, 'though you may deny yourself the title of gentleman, I beg you to remember that I – I aspire to be called a lady!'

'And so you are. Forgive me.' He released her at once and raised her hand to his lips. 'Go, lovely child, while I am still penitent.'

She looked at him then and perceived that his smile was more rueful than mischievous and his eyes were lacking that cool glitter that had so alarmed her previously. 'Why, I believe they are green!' she blurted out.

He laughed softly. 'Yes, it is all I ever had of her beauty from my mother.'

'She – she is no longer alive, sir?'

'Depend upon it, she is very much alive!' he assured her. 'And awaiting my immediate arrival in Oxfordshire.'

'You cannot possibly journey to Oxfordshire tomorrow,' declared Miss Devenish roundly, hoping that a practical, down-to-earth discussion of his situation would serve to depress his amorous pretensions. It did momentarily occur to her that all she had to do was to walk out of the room and leave him alone, but this she found herself strangely unable to do.

'I not only can, but I must,' he informed her. 'My mama does not at all care to be kept waiting, I can tell you.'

'But – ' she began doubtfully.

'My groom can drive and tonight's mêlée will surely provide sufficient excuse for my injury. No one need know of your part in all this.'

'No doubt I should thank you, sir,' she retorted, 'did I not suspect that such discretion is aimed as much at saving your face as my reputation.'

'Touché!' he admitted, then caught at the arm of a chair to steady himself. 'Goodnight, Miss Devenish. I will give you three minutes to get back to your room before I pull the bell-rope. And once there you will lock your door, if you please. I do not greatly care for the company belowstairs.'

'Goodnight, sir,' she said, momentarily diverted by this belated show of propriety on his lordship's part. Then, seeing his eyes close and his mouth twist involuntarily as if in pain, she added, 'Are you – can you manage?'

'Go, for God's sake, go!' The words were scarcely above a whisper, but she stayed no longer. As she closed the door she thought she heard him add: 'Sweet dreams, Cherry Ripe!' but then she was darting along the deserted passage in the direction of her room.

Once there and having turned the key in the lock, she took herself severely to task. To allow a gentleman, and a stranger at that, to kiss her was the outside of anything. But worse, far worse, was to have enjoyed the experience. Involuntarily, her fingers touched her lips as if to re-create the pressure of his upon them.

You are no better than a shameless hussy, Charity Annabelle Devenish! she informed herself. And the sooner you put tonight's doings out of your mind the better, for, depend upon it, he will. You are just a passing fancy to one of his sort – oh, pray that he is not too badly hurt! She then busied herself in putting her dis-

ordered room to rights, and was forced to smile when she came
upon the pistol, lying forgotten on a table. 'I'll send Bridie to his
room with it tomorrow morning. Then she can enquire after his
health.'

Despite her good intentions she was aroused at a late hour by
insistent knocking on her door, and climbed sleepily out of bed
to admit a woebegone Miss Hanrahan, whose recollections of the
previous evening's events were, mercifully, exceedingly hazy.
Cherryanne thought it best to take the offensive and assume a
displeasure she did not at all feel at her maid's having given way
to the influence of strong drink, but soon found that Bridie, who
tended to be somewhat lachrymose, held herself to be greatly to
blame for having deserted her young mistress in her hour of need,
and was quite prepared to accept any reasonable explanation for
the presence of a partially clothed and wounded gentleman in Miss
Devenish's bedchamber.

'Very Christian of you, I'm sure, miss, and if you shot him by
accident, no doubt it was no more than he deserved.'

'Yes, well, he has left his horrid pistol behind. Please to take it
to him, Bridie, and enquire after his well-being. I am persuaded
we ought to assure ourselves that he is quite comfortable before
we take our departure. That is the merest civility. His room is at
the end of the passage to the left.'

She caught her breath as Bridie, grumbling a little but otherwise acquiescent, took the pistol cautiously between finger and
thumb and went on her errand, for how was she to explain her
particular knowledge of the exact position of his bedchamber?
However, the usually needle-witted Miss Hanrahan was in very
bad skin that morning and more disposed to dwell upon her own
miseries than on any possible shortcomings in her mistress's conduct.

She returned within a few moments to report that the gentleman's room was empty and no trace of its recent occupant or his
possessions to be seen. Cherryanne promptly sent her downstairs
to see if he was, perhaps, taking breakfast, only to be informed that
the inn was practically deserted, only the landlord's wife to be
found and she so overset by the excitement of the previous even-

ing that she had no clear notion of whomsoever might have been staying at the inn.

The intelligence, conveyed by Kenyon, that Remus was much recovered and, given careful handling, should manage the journey to Amesbury, decided Miss Devenish to partake of breakfast without delay and proceed on her way. Further questioning would be both indiscreet and improper and his lordship was clearly in no very bad case else he could not have resumed his journey so readily.

'And that, Charity Annabelle,' she told herself severely, 'is the end of that adventure, and the sooner you put it from your mind the better!'

Despite this stricture she retrieved the pistol from where she had tossed it and, wrapping it carefully in a scarf, lodged it securely at the bottom of her valise, reminding herself that there was no knowing when the gentleman might not find he had a need for it and hold her responsible for its return.

CHAPTER
THREE

Her Grace of Evesham lay prone upon the sofa in her boudoir, vinaigrette clutched in one frail hand, while in the other a delicate lawn handkerchief was held pressed to her brow. From beneath its lace-edged border she peered anxiously at the tall figure of her son, silhouetted in the window embrasure against a vivid blue sky, and waited hopefully for him to comment upon the distressing tale she had been forced to impart to him, but no sound broke the serene silence of the golden October afternoon save the buzzing of a misguided late humblebee that had blundered in through the open lattice.

'I fear nothing else will answer, Damien,' she ventured at last. 'But I beg you will not be thinking that your father is to blame for any of it.'

'I am well aware, mama, of how His Grace has struggled unceasingly to relieve us of the burden of debt laid upon his shoulders by my grandfather.' The Marquis of·Shalford's normally pleasant voice was harsh with feeling. 'I would to God, though, that he had told me the whole. I had no notion we were so deeply in the suds, else I never would have indulged myself in needless extravagance.'

'Dear boy, he would not have it so.' The Duchess was moved to sit up to stress her point. 'He was of the opinion that to make you pay for the excesses of your grandfather was beyond anything cruel, and he had the highest hopes, you know, of winning free of debt until – until I – ' Remorse here quite overcame her and she sank back again on to the cushions, the tears streaming afresh down her softly flushed cheeks. At once he was beside her, allaying her distress, all trace of resentment gone from his manner.

'How could you know we were so close to Dun territory?' he

murmured, possessing himself of her handkerchief and gently drying her tears.

'I m-might have guessed,' she sobbed, 'w-when your father s-suggested I confine my gambling to – to loo and b-bassett! B-but to lose so much at piquet!'

'Who was your opponent?' he asked, watching her with a smile tinged with affectionate exasperation.

'Carlingford,' sniffed the Duchess.

'The devil!' exclaimed her startled son. 'Had you to pick so hardened a gamester?'

Her Grace's chin went up. 'I'd have you know, Damien, that I am no pigeon for the plucking!' she informed him loftily.

'At home to a peg in all the hells, I don't doubt,' he responded, a laugh in his voice. 'But Carlingford is something else – he did not suspect that you were all to pieces, I hope?'

'Certainly not,' replied his mama with dignity. 'I trust I know how to keep the line even if I'm beat to a standstill. It's only that – I cannot sell any more of my jewels because people will notice, and having paste imitations made is becoming so expensive. Besides,' she added naively, 'I have only two articles left that are of any value. Do – do they send duchesses to the Fleet, Damien?'

'I have never heard of it being done,' he assured her. 'But be certain that if such an unhappy situation should arise, I would see to it that you had the best possible attention.'

'Dear boy!' she murmured absently. 'Nonetheless, I am persuaded it would be most uncomfortable and I am sure your father would not like it above half.' The Marquis refrained from telling her that, as it was much more likely to be his father who would languish in prison for his wife's debts than she, he could quite conceive of His Grace not caring for it. 'Which puts me in mind to tell you,' she went on, 'he wishes to see you – on this very subject, I have no doubt, which is why I thought to speak to you first.' She regarded him pensively. 'You are such a handsome boy. I am sure there must be any number of heiresses who would be only too happy to –' She paused, arrested by the curious expression that came over his face. 'You are not – I mean, your affections are not engaged? Well, they can't be, can they, when you have been flaunting that brass-headed actress all over town any time this six months.'

'Really, mama!' Accustomed as he was to his mother's forth-right comments, the Marquis hardly knew whether to laugh or be indignant at her knowledge of his amorous activities.

'Yes, well, your *belles-amies* are always such high-flyers one cannot help but hear about them,' pointed out the Duchess with some truth.

'My aunt Stratton, I presume?' enquired the Marquis grimly, trying to coax the now frantic humblebee through the window to freedom.

'She – and others. Oh, Sukey, darling, do get down!' This last to her tiny sleeve-dog who took not the slightest notice but proceeded to establish herself comfortably on her mistress's feet. 'Is – your lady very expensive, Damien?'

He laughed shortly. 'The most rapacious female I have ever taken under my protection.'

'Will you object to giving her up? Not, of course, that it may be at all necessary if you are discreet. But then, you never are discreet, are you, Damien?'

He grinned at her wickedly. 'No more than you, my love!'

'Damien! Never did I play your father false!'

His green eyes narrowed in mockery. 'No, mama? I have often wondered about my chestnut locks!'

'My brother Edmond, the one who died young, had just that colour of hair, and you have my eyes. No question but that you are a Cavendish and owe very little to the Strattons.'

'That, mama, is what troubles me – no, don't fly into a pet! I am only quizzing you.'

She looked at him a trifle anxiously. 'You are quite sure you have not formed an attachment? This wound of yours,' she raised a hand to touch his empty sleeve, 'was it really an accident? I must confess it sounds the most unlikely story.'

The Marquis was only restrained from telling her the whole truth by the sure knowledge that whatever went in at her ears was poured out – in the strictest confidence, of course – to the first crony she met. 'No,' he assured her. 'The incident at the Winterslow Hut may sound improbable, but it was perfectly true.

I was not fighting a duel for a lady's honour or anything of that sort.' An involuntary chuckle escaped him. 'Quite the contrary, in fact.'

'Well, then,' said she briskly, 'all we have to do is to look about for an heiress for you. If she could be passably good-looking, it would be nice – for the sake of the children, I mean.'

'They never are,' he said with a sublime indifference for the physiognomy of his potential offspring. 'And, mama, not a word, if you please, of our pecuniary difficulties.'

'Our what?' The Duchess was lost in meditation. 'Oh, you mean the debts. But what about Carlingford?'

'He will be paid. How much, by the way?'

Her Grace took a deep breath. 'Close on five thousand,' she confessed.

Her son raised his eyes to Heaven. 'And that, I'll be bound, is not the whole sum of it. What of mantua-makers and milliners – to say nothing of that new barouche of yours?'

'They can wait,' said the Duchess with some asperity. 'If you contract to marry an heiress, my creditors will be only too happy to overlook my paltry debts in the hope that I shall recommend them to my daughter-in-law.'

'Just so long as this mythical lady does not get wind of it and hedge off,' said the Marquis, helping himself to a sugared almond from a dish of sweetmeats set on a table beside the sofa.

'Hedge off? And lose the chance of becoming a duchess for a few thousand pounds?'

'Add your few thousand pounds to my well-known profligate habits and the title may prove too expensive,' he warned her.

The Duchess looked suddenly concerned. 'One thing you must promise me, Damien. She need not be of exalted birth but, please, not the daughter of a tradesman. I could not abide a daughter-in-law that reeked of the shop.'

'You may rest easy on that head, mama. Nor could I.'

Her eyes filled again with easy tears. 'Do not think that I do not appreciate what you are doing, Damien, in offering yourself as a sacrifice. I, too, have made a Resolution. I shall retire to Bath to take the waters in the New Year.'

'To Bath? In God's name why, ma'am?'

B

'Rheumatism!' she said defiantly. 'At least that is what I shall say to explain my absence from town during the Season.'

'You've never had a twinge of it in your life!' he accused her.

'Of course not, but one must say something. And Bath is become so sadly provincial I am persuaded I cannot incur any debts when living there. I'll require to hire a house, of course, and perhaps you could – no, that is not to be thought on. You must bend all your energies to seeking for your heiress. I'll ask Quentin to find me a desirable residence. He is always most obliging.'

The Marquis allowed himself to wonder if his cousin, Sir Quentin Stratton, would be quite so obliging if he learned that the Eveshams had scarce a feather left to fly with, but he kept his thoughts to himself. The mention of Bath had put him in mind of a certain exquisite young lady who was, doubtless, well on her way to that dignified spa, though to be truthful, she had scarce been out of his thoughts since the previous night. An oddly tender little smile curved his lips and, unconsciously, he put his right hand up to touch his wounded shoulder. His parent eyed him with some apprehension. Frivolous and feather-witted though the Duchess might be, yet where her only child was concerned her affection for him was so powerful that he could never hope to deceive her, and when he remarked in his most casual drawl, 'I should not be too confiding with dear Quentin, mama,' she burst out:

'You cannot bring yourself to like him, can you?'

'Oh, I like him as well as one can a man who is waiting to step into one's shoes,' he returned shortly.

'He has been very useful to me upon occasion,' she demurred.

The Marquis's green eyes were sharp with suspicion. 'In what way?' he demanded.

'Oh, in raising the wind, I believe you'd call it.'

'I'd call it something else,' he retorted. 'Is he aware of your debt to Carlingford?'

'Well, he was there,' she admitted uncertainly. 'And it was no secret – how could it be? We had a crowd about us and bets were being taken freely on the outcome. He has sold some jewellery for me before, you know, when I have had a run of bad luck.'

'Why could you not have applied to me?'

'Because – because – ' The Duchess hesitated and made play with her handkerchief. 'I did not quite like your knowing how improvident your mama is, and you would be bound to insist upon paying up out of your own allowance, and that I could never permit.'

'Gammon!' responded her disrespectful son. 'I should think the whole world knows how improvident is my mama!'

'Oh, Damien, don't!' she implored, dabbing at her eyes prettily. 'You cannot conceive how mortifying it is for me to find myself in such a fix.'

The Marquis was unmoved by this *cri de coeur*. 'It would be as well if everyone believes your mortification to stem from an unwillingness to appeal to my father for funds rather than because you know the funds are not there to meet your obligations. You have told him about this?'

'Yes, but he seemed scarcely to comprehend what I said. He just sighed and said: "Don't you ever win, my dear?" Damien, I am so worried for him. His understanding seems to have become so clouded and he himself so frail.'

'He has had enough troubles on his shoulders to have driven a man twice as strong into his grave. He is worn to the bone while I have done nothing.' The Marquis's voice was bitter with self-condemnation.

'You know he would not allow you to do anything. He feels it to be his sacred duty to put the estate to rights.' The Duchess sighed. 'I have begged him to come up to London to see Sir Henry Halford or, if that journey is too great for him, to go to Bath where, I collect, there are several reputable physicians, but he declares he has complete faith in Dr Harvey.'

Damien gave a snort of disgust. 'Harvey was an old man when I was born, and that will be twenty-six years ago next Christmas Day.'

'Yes, and very inconvenient it was, too!' said the Duchess inconsequentially. 'With the house full of guests and the Prince of Wales promised to come down for the shooting in the New Year.'

'I doubt Prinny has quite forgiven me that. He has ever had a soft spot for you, hasn't he, mama?'

The Duchess, who still retained much of her former beauty and was generally held to be a remarkably handsome woman, permitted herself a small chuckle. 'I, at least, have worn better than he,' said she, preening herself with some satisfaction.

But the Marquis was thinking of more serious matters. 'I had best go to Studleigh and see my father,' he said decisively.

'Yes,' she nodded. 'But – be gentle with him, Damien. He has tried so hard.'

His eyes softened as he came to take her hand. 'I promise you my conduct will be unexceptional,' he said. 'What right have I to criticize when it has been for my sake and yours that he has borne so heavy a burden these ten years?'

'Oh, Damien, I have just remembered! Honoria Winton – you know, the Braidestones' daughter – has just broken off her engagement to that highly unsuitable young man. Now she would be the most famous match for you! And the Braidestones will be so relieved at having rid themselves of a penniless captain in a Rifle Regiment that they must welcome your suit with the utmost rapture! Not that he was not a charming boy – I quite see why Honoria was so taken with him – but the veriest fortune-hunter, I am assured.'

'*The* Rifle Regiment, mama,' he corrected her dryly. 'And I am in different case, I suppose?'

His mother looked quite shocked. 'You are a marquis, Damien, and a Stratton. The case is not at all the same. And you have known Honoria since nursery days.'

'Yes, a self-opinionated little chit with a will of iron. I remember her all too well,' replied her son resignedly. 'But I will place her on my list of possible brides. Now, since it is too late to set out for Studleigh today, I think I'll drive over to Blenheim. I collect that Sunderland is rusticating there, perhaps he might give me some advice on how to get out of the River Tick.'

She shook her head doubtfully. 'Sunderland, too, has to marry where money is,' she warned him.

'We'd best compare notes, then,' he said and then, in a kinder voice, 'don't fret yourself, mama, we'll come about – somehow. I'll be off.'

'You'll not handle the ribbons with that shoulder?'

'No, no, I'll take Lawson,' he promised her.

As he bent down to kiss her cheek, she raised a hand to touch his hair. He caught it and held it for a moment to his lips.

'Dearest little mama, were it only you and I, I'd whisk you over to Brussels or to Italy and there subsist very comfortably on a quarter of what we spend here.'

'Oh, how delightful that would be!' she breathed. 'And, you know, the Capels found it answered very well when they were all to pieces. But, alas, your father would never leave Studleigh and I cannot desert him. Damien, he has become so tired and ill, and yet he is but a few years past fifty. I often wonder if he has any pleasure left in living.'

'As bad as that?' The Marquis drew a sharp breath. 'Then I'll be away tomorrow. For, to be blunt, mama, if anything should happen to him the cat'll be out, and I must know how matters stand.'

'I'll close up this house and follow you to Studleigh next week,' said the Duchess with unwonted resolution. 'Not that it signifies whether I am there or not for your father hardly appears to notice and Studleigh quite casts me into the dismals, so huge and cold and uninhabitable as it is.' She heaved a deep sigh. 'You must know that to those of the staff who have been in our employ for some years, I have allowed it to be understood that some retrenchment is desirable. Foster came to me to enquire if that should include ceasing to provide the champagne blacking he makes for your Hessians.'

'To which you replied "Of course not! How could the odd bottle of champagne signify?"'

'Well, I do think it could not, and Foster quite agrees with me.'

'I am sure he does since I have no doubt the greater portion of each bottle goes down his throat!'

A frown creased the Duchess's fine brow. 'Damien, we don't want the servants to suspect anything of our difficulties, else we will find them slipping off to seek other positions and then the

trap will be down, because nothing advertises one's situation
more than to be deserted by one's servants.'

Her son, who knew that wild horses would not drag her devoted
staff from his mother's service, did not think this outcome to be
at all likely.

'They will merely conclude that you have been scorched a trifle
and are indulging in one of your periodical bursts of cheeseparing.
Don't, I beg of you, go to extremes as you did on the last such
occasion, and subject everyone to a diet of pea soup and toast
water!'

He then took his leave of her and went in search of his groom,
reflecting that if his father had been remiss in not keeping him
informed of his uncertain financial position, his mother had been
no less backward in not acquainting him with his sire's state of
health. But the blame rested squarely on his own shoulders for not
having seen how matters stood. The truth of it was that he and
his father had never been close. The Duke's greatest object in
life appeared to be to ensure that his son should not suffer any
financial distress and, grateful though Damien was for such kindness, yet he could wish that his parent had been more open with
him.

'The devil!' he mused as he stood, pulling on his gloves and
waiting for his curricle to be brought to the door. 'If an heiress it
must be, then the soonest done the better before our lack of the
ready becomes generally known. Honoria Winton, eh? I could do
worse, I suppose, though there's no saying she will have me.
Always was an independent little puss.'

Scowling heavily, he went out to his carriage while his mother's
footman watched him curiously. An odd mood his lordship was in,
to be sure, he that was always so ready with a bit of cheerful
banter or a quick curse if you were clumsy. Never one to harbour
a grudge, though, and no sooner said than over, like a summer
storm. Talking to himself, too, and not making much sense if
Thomas's ears had not played him false. That last remark had
sounded uncommon like 'Goodbye, Cherry Ripe, 'twas only a
foolish dream!'

Shaking his head at the odd ways of the quality, Thomas stole away to his room, there to ease off his new shoes which were pinching him intolerably and to wonder if he could prevail upon that new and very pretty housemaid to take a turn with him in the grounds after dinner in order to further their acquaintance.

CHAPTER
FOUR

November had been a succession of grey skies and heavy showers and December gave every promise of continuing in the same depressing strain. To Miss Devenish, standing at the window of her aunt's drawing-room, watching the raindrops coursing down the panes, it seemed as if the sun would never again shine upon Bath.

Lady Harpendene had not been quite in the right of it when she had foretold that Mrs Marsden would put herself out very little for the entertainment of her niece, for she had not allowed for the perspicacity of Mr Marsden, a gentleman known to his family and close friends as a 'downie' one, and fully awake upon every suit.

The Marsdens enjoyed a very tolerable degree of consequence in Bath, and their house in the Circus was furnished in the first stare of elegance. Having brought out and successfully married off a daughter in the previous year, Mrs Marsden had been fully alive to the necessity of bringing her niece to the notice of the Masters of Ceremonies of the Upper and Lower Assembly Rooms, and both Captain Wyke and Mr Heaviside had been most obliging in their attentions. Cherryanne's winsome face and pretty manners soon established her as one of the acknowledged Beauties but, having seen her niece set up so satisfactorily, Mrs Marsden gave all the appearance of having fulfilled her duties, declaring that nothing could be more tedious than to be for ever attending balls and routs, and quite forgetting that what might be of small interest to a matron in her late forties could well be regarded in a different light by a young lady of less than half her age.

Mr Marsden thought it prudent, however, to point out to his wife that, as it was to be expected that Miss Devenish would profit greatly from her grandmother's estate, care should be exercised in ensuring that she formed none but the most respectable of connections. He did not enlarge upon this theme. It was sufficient, he considered, for it to be understood that his niece had expectations.

He was not enough in Lady Harpendene's confidence to be more definite on this delicate point, but his mother-in-law had expressed herself forcefully on the occasion of their last meeting, declaring that, as she had made a very handsome settlement on Maria when he had married her and she had not the least intention of allowing any of her money to get into the hands of that Irish horse-dealer her other daughter had seen fit to espouse, her grandchildren would benefit the most after her demise. She further added that, as George's godfather had left him a handsome legacy which he seemed bent on dissipating in as short a space of time as possible, and Ariadne's husband was spoken of as being near as rich as Mr Ball Hughes, she proposed making Cherryanne the chief beneficiary of her will, as the poor child had no well-breeched parent to stand for her.

Mr Marsden accepted this dictum philosophically, merely remarking to his wife that he would be much surprised if the old lady did not cut up for a cool ten thousand a year and probably more, most of which might reasonably be supposed to come to Cherryanne, but this, after all, was pure speculation, the difficulty being that independent and spirited old ladies were apt to be unpredictable, and should Miss Devenish put a foot wrong she might well find herself without a penny piece. It was he who urged upon his wife the necessity of removing the girl from her grandmother's care before any such catastrophe should occur and, having seen and approved the young lady's person and character, a message was conveyed to his son and heir to the effect that his parents would be happy to have the pleasure of his company.

Mr Marsden, a fond but far from doting parent, recognized that his daughter had inherited the greater part of his astute nature while George had been cursed with much of his mother's easy-tempered complaisance, allied to a deplorable tendency to plunge into debt with no more concern for the consequences than if his father had been some latter-day Croesus. When he received a rambling and ill-spelt missive from his heir explaining how it was quite impossible for him to attend his parents at that particular moment, he was forced to repress the ignoble regret that his son's advanced years prohibited the use of a birch upon his person in such a manner as to bring his head out of the clouds and his thoughts to dwell upon more basic matters and replied that, as soon as George's social engagements should permit, his parents would be delighted to see him. Once under the parental roof, Cherryanne's sweet face should ensure his remaining there for a time, though his father was strongly of the opinion that George was likely to find himself with pockets to let before long and would be forced to retire from the London scene while he repaired his fortunes.

In this supposition, Mr Marsden proved to be right. His niece, who had no notion of the deep schemes revolving around her, was playing with the silken tassels of a cord holding back the window drapes and wishing she had, after all, gone with her aunt and uncle to attend a concert being held at the Kingston Rooms, when her attention was caught by the appearance of a cabriolet, which bowled briskly into the Circus from Gay Street and came to a halt in front of the house. The young gentleman who sprang down from it called out some brief instructions to his groom and hurried to the door. The clanging of the bell and the banging of the knocker proclaimed his eagerness to be in out of the rain and hinted at a considerable familiarity with the household by so imperious a demand for admittance.

Miss Devenish, who had glimpsed no more of him than a full-skirted, ankle-length driving coat, embellished with many capes, and a tall hat, set at a rakish angle upon his head, was not left long in doubt as to who this young spark might be. A cheerful confident voice was to be heard in the hall, greeting the Marsdens' elderly butler in the tones of one exercising the privilege of long acquaintance.

'And how are you, Bellamy, you old rascal? Still tippling m'father's brandy, I'll be bound!'

'Now, Master George,' admonished the butler in tones less out-raged than amused, which plainly indicated that this was an old joke shared between them, 'could you not have given us a hint of your coming? There's your room not prepared and – '

'Well, I might, of course, had I known – Bellamy, can you lend

me some of the ready? Got scorched t'other night, had to spout
my watch to pay my way down here.'

'So that's it! Come on a repairing lease, have you, sir? Your
father'll not be best pleased, Master George.'

'Not a word to him until I've spoken with mama. Where are
they?'

'Attending a concert.' There was a soft rustle as of paper. 'Will
five be sufficient, Master George?'

'Bless you – I swear you'll have it back tomorrow, but I cannot
be certain what may happen this evening and one can't have
pockets completely to let.'

Bellamy cleared his throat significantly. 'Miss Devenish is at
home, sir.'

"Miss Dev – d'you mean my little Irish cousin? Gad, I'd clean
forgot she was staying here. Now I come to think on't, m'father
wanted me down to squire her about. Couldn't be done, I was
engaged on too many fronts. What's she like? Is she a complete
antidote? Face like a horse?'

'Not like any horse I have ever seen, sir.'

Bellamy's voice then dropped to a conspiratorial whisper and
Miss Devenish, holding her giggles in check, picked up her tam-
bour frame and was seated, demurely stitching away, when the
door was flung wide to reveal her cousin George in all the glory
of cossack trousers, drawn tightly in at the ankle over his half-
boots, russet long-tailed coat, and a neckcloth fashioned into a very
creditable Horse and Collar, with shirt points reaching to his
cheek-bones. This vision of sartorial elegance stood staring at her
with an expression of the most comical disbelief upon his lively
countenance, while in the hall behind him, Bellamy permitted
himself a discreet smile as he bore away his young master's wet
driving coat.

Miss Devenish was the first to speak. Rising to her feet, she
advanced with outstretched hand.

'I imagine you must be my cousin George, though forgive me
if I say I have no clear recollection of you.'

'Nor I of you, coz, else I would have been here a month since!'
His admiration was so blatant that she was forced to drop her gaze
but could not help smiling. 'But what the – how comes it that you

are alone? Are the Bath beaux all stricken helpless? Not one devoted admirer to attend upon you?'.

She dimpled. 'To tell truth, sir, I was engaged to go driving this afternoon but, as you see, the weather was hardly propitious to venture forth with even so notable a whip as Sir Quentin Stratton.'

'Stratton, eh?' He whistled appreciatively. 'What's he doing in Bath? Should have thought he'd have found it devilish dull – I mean, to be set down amid the tabbies ain't at all his style.'

'I understand Sir Quentin came to Bath to see to the hiring of a house for his aunt, the Duchess of Evesham, who is coming to take the waters early next year,' said Miss Devenish with a nice assumption of detached calm, but her worldly-wise cousin was not deceived.

'Haven't seen him in Watier's this month past,' he declared. 'Now don't gammon me, Cherryanne, it don't take a month to find a house for Her Grace! No, no, there is something else to engage his interest in Bath. And if he takes you out driving, my girl, it means you are all the go!'

Miss Devenish resumed her seat and her embroidery. 'The Duchess is a wealthy lady, I collect?' she enquired in a tone calculated to discourage any further speculation on his part.

'Oh, the Evesham's aren't short of a penny. But why Stratton? Why could not her agent do the needful – or, come to that, why not Shalford?'

'Who is Shalford?' asked Miss Devenish innocently and was astonished at the effect of this simple question upon her cousin.

'Who is – ' He choked. 'My dear girl, you must not be saying things like that unless you wish to be put down as a complete flat! The Marquis of Shalford is the most noted Corinthian, the *ne plus ultra* – a trifle rakish, I daresay, but a sure hand! And, rake or not, there isn't a scheming mama of the beau monde who would not snatch him for a son-in-law did she get the chance!'

Thereupon Mr Marsden twisted a chair around and, seating himself astride it with elbows comfortably resting on its padded back, proceeded to fill in his cousin's astonishing lack of information on the subject of Lord Shalford. Clearly this nobleman was his ideal, and Miss Devenish listening, much amused, formed a picture in her mind of just such another worldly gentleman as Sir Quentin Stratton, polished, courtly, and all of thirty-five years of age.

To be the recipient of marked attentions from this confirmed bachelor was not at all to her taste, but so it had been since his arrival in Bath and, as he never overstepped the line and his manner to her was invariably more quizzical than amorous, she found herself at a stand in her dealings with him. For there was no doubt that it was a very considerable feather in her cap to be the object of his gallantry, while to be taken out driving by one of the best whips in the country gave rise to feelings of ignoble triumph over other less fortunate young ladies. Yet she could not be at her ease with Sir Quentin, despite the fact that he was vastly more entertaining than any of the younger bloods who worshipped at her shrine. Even her aunt had roused herself from her habitual lethargy to utter a delicately worded warning.

'It is a very great compliment, I allow, that Sir Quentin should have singled you out, but I must warn you not to entertain any hopes in that direction, my dear. He is of established bachelor habits and a most accomplished flirt. It would never do if you were to – well, read more into his attentions than was intended. To be sure, I cannot imagine what holds him here in Bath, for I am given to understand that he has taken the lease of a house in Royal Crescent for the Duchess.' She eyed her niece speculatively. 'It would indeed be beyond anything great if he had developed a tendre for you.' She shook her head and continued more briskly. 'But that must not be thought of and I beg that you will not do so.'

Miss Devenish promised her in all sincerity that she had no notion of thinking any such thing, and now, as she looked upon Mr George Marsden's pleasing open countenance and perceived the frank admiration in his regard, she felt that here was someone much more to her taste than a smooth man-of-the-world, turning his practised compliments. Rarely now did the recollection of mocking dark eyes set beneath sweeping brows, and the touch of a hard young mouth upon hers, obtrude itself upon her memory, though she had never ceased to wonder who he was, where he was, and if his wound had healed well. It was very plain that the gentleman had regarded the incident as the merest triviality, else he would surely have made some effort to follow up so promising a start, knowing, as he did, that her destination was Bath and that he had only to present himself at the Pump Room or the Assembly Rooms to be sure of meeting her or discovering her direction.

Miss Devenish and Mr Marsden found themselves to be in such good accord that half an hour had passed in easy conversation without their being conscious of it, and only the return of the master and mistress of the establishment restored them to an awareness of the passage of time.

Mrs Marsden, while expressing her delight at viewing her eldest-born again after so many months, also expressed her amazement that he should choose to visit Bath at the beginning of December. 'I marvel at your being here when the London season is still in force. Depend upon it, George, everyone will consider it the most odd circumstance.'

In this supposition she was quite mistaken for no one in Bath thought George's arrival to be in the least odd. Indeed his failure to put in an appearance at an earlier date had aroused much comment.

In deference to her husband's advice, Mrs Marsden had said no more than was necessary on the subject of Cherryanne's expectations, but there was resident in Bath a certain Mrs Fox-Mulliner, widow of an Admiral of the Red, who claimed to have been acquainted with Sir Giles and Lady Harpendene at one time. This lady gave it as her opinion that Sir Giles had been a very warm man indeed and, as his relict lived very retired, there was small doubt that her income must have increased considerably since he had been taken from her.

'Depend upon it, that young lady will come into a comfortable fortune when Alicia Harpendene goes,' she prophesied to her circle of cronies. 'George would be a fool not to make a push to secure the money to the family.'

When George's arrival in Bath became known – as it was within a few hours of his setting foot in the place, because Mrs Fox-Mulliner had had the good fortune to be stepping out of Mr Duffield's library in Milsom Street just as his carriage was brought to a stand in front of her by the leader of a tandem pair, drawing a phaeton ahead of him, having slipped on the wet surface of the road – the knowing ones wagged their heads wisely.

'Put it down to Sir Quentin's account,' they whispered, bonnet plumes nodding in unison. 'A high-flyer and a leader of the ton must marry where money is. George saw the danger and came at once.'

And they settled back in their chairs, eyes snapping in gleeful anticipation, to await the outcome. Though Sir Quentin might never succeed to the dukedom, his baronetcy was not altogether despicable and he was, after all, a Stratton. On the other hand, George had the advantage of living in the same house and he could do his courting in his slippers, as the saying went.

Mr Marsden senior was privately of the opinion that his son was likely to pass up any hope of future inheritance for a roll of soft to relieve his immediate embarrassments, so he resolved to lose no time in making the situation plain to him. Waiting only for his wife and niece to withdraw after dinner that evening, he turned his chair towards the fire and pushed the port decanter along the polished surface of the table towards his heir.

'Well, my boy, how much is it this time?'

George, who had hoped to lead up to the subject in a less abrupt fashion, was so startled by the geniality of his father's tone that he slopped port over the rim of his glass and was obliged to mop it up hastily with a shaking hand.

'I – I – it was Watier's, father,' he confessed with downcast eyes. 'The play is so confoundedly deep and my luck was out.'

Mr Marsden eyed him in some amusement. 'I expected no less to account for your unheralded descent upon us,' he remarked drily. 'How much?'

'Two – two thousand,' muttered George, taking a quick gulp of port to fortify himself.

Mr Marsden, doing a swift calculation, allowed his eye to rest upon his son's flushed countenance in so cold a manner as utterly to unnerve that young gentleman.

'Let me see,' he mused. 'When did I last settle your affairs? September, was it not?'

'Yes, sir,' admitted the culprit faintly.

'I am aware that when your godfather was so obliging as to

leave you a legacy which is invested so as to yield a tolerable
income, I was absolved of the necessity of providing for you out
of my own pocket. Yet you have overrun that income in the last
six months by close on four thousand pounds. While I am prepared to frank you to a reasonable degree, George, this is coming
it a bit too strong.' George squirmed miserably in his seat and was
understood to confess that his father had been everything that
was generous to him in the past, and he'd as lief take a beating as
lose his esteem. His father almost smiled. 'Personal discomfort
does not pay gaming losses, my boy, and my pockets – to coin a
phrase – are not bottomless. I will pay up this once, but on one
condition only.'

'And – and that is, sir?' George was staring at his father, half-
perplexed, half-relieved.

'That you mend your ways and resign yourself to marrying a
lady of fortune.'

'But, sir, what lady of fortune would marry me?'

'You price yourself too low, my boy,' drawled his father. 'You
are a well set up personable young man enough, fashionable in
your apparel, at home to a peg, or so I am informed, in the best
circles in town, nor am I so behindhand with the world that I
cannot set you up in some comfort until the sad day of my demise,
when you can expect to inherit rather more than a mere competence – something, of course, must go to Ariadne. No, not a
contemptible match for a young lady with reasonable expectations.'

George, who had never considered himself to be an eligible
parti for any young lady, much less an heiress, swallowed hard
and ventured to say that to be running headlong into matrimony
at the age of twenty-four was not altogether to his taste, however
tempting the lure.

'I can enter into your feelings on that head,' nodded Mr Marsden. 'But you must believe that I mean what I say in declaring
this to be the last time I intend to settle your debts. Also,' he
added, pouring himself more port, 'an unrivalled opportunity
presents itself for furthering my suggestion.'

'D-does it, sir?' George was still too bewildered by this unexpected development perfectly to take his father's meaning.

'Yes, she sat opposite to you at dinner tonight.'

Mr Marsden watched his son's expressive countenance for the expected reaction, nor was he disappointed.

'You mean – Cherryanne?' George gaped at him, open-mouthed. 'I'll allow she's a pretty piece enough, but she's no heiress – is she, sir?'

'I have reason to believe she is.' Mr Marsden rose and stood with his back to the fire, legs well spread apart, coat-tails tucked up so as to receive the full benefit of the heat. He was a fine figure of a man and his fifty years had treated him leniently. If there was a suggestion of a paunch to mar an otherwise shapely outline his height and breadth of shoulder rendered such an imperfection negligible. 'Your grandmother is of the opinion,' he went on, a faintly exceptious note creeping into his nicely phrased periods, 'that, between us, her husband and I can provide for Ariadne, while your tendency to part with your juice at the gaming tables does not prejudice her in your favour. Cherryanne will receive the greater part of her fortune.'

'But if grandmama don't care for me she won't like the match above half,' protested George, snatching at any likely straw.

'Which is why you must keep the line until the marriage settlements at least are agreed,' pointed out his father. 'If I propose to increase your income by two thousand a year, she can do no less for Cherryanne.'

George did some rapid mental arithmetic. 'Which will bring the tally up to above six thousand,' he said cheerfully.

'Just about the sum you have lost during a twelvemonth,' his father reminded him, and George's face fell. 'Firstly, you must control your love of gaming, and I know of no better curb than a pretty wife and several hopeful brats to your credit. Secondly, if all goes well and you do nothing to earn your grandmother's disapprobation, I am confident that a very much greater sum of money will come to you when she goes. I am thinking in terms of eight to ten thousand pounds a year.'

'Good God!' said George, stirred to something like enthusiasm.

'Worth containing yourself for a few years, don't you agree?' suggested Mr Marsden slyly.

George drew a deep breath. 'I'll do my possible, sir. But what if Cherryanne won't have me? After all, if she's that sort of heiress, she may consider me far beneath her touch.'

'But she don't know she *is* that sort of heiress. Her grandmother particularly wishes it to be thought that her expectations are not above the ordinary. Not but that people won't be trying to put two and two together, but they cannot know with any surety, so button your lip, George. We don't want the place beseiged by fortune-hunters.'

George agreed whole-heartedly. 'I hear that Quentin Stratton has been paying her some attention,' he remarked.

'Yes, but I don't think she cares for him above half. He can have no knowledge of her circumstances so it is to be presumed that he is merely indulging in a little light flirtation. At least, your mother will have it so. No bad thing, though, if you can direct her interest away from him.'

'He is too old for her, anyway,' said George with the cruelty of youth. 'Why he is ten years older than Shalford and Shal is near two years older than I am. I say, good thing it is not Shalford I have to compete against – I'd not have a chance in the world!'

Mr Marsden, whose acquaintance with the Marquis was limited to one chance meeting in London, yet had no doubt that his son's assessment of the situation was perfectly sound. His lordship, despite his easy manners, was no loose fish, nor was he a fool. Sir Quentin he knew little of, but had heard it said that he was generally known as one up to everything. If so, and his attentions to Miss Devenish proved serious, he might well queer the outcome.

'Come, let us set you on your romantic path,' he said affably, placing an arm around his son's shoulders. 'And, remember, treat her cousinly and in the most natural way.'

Together they strolled from the dining-room, chatting amicably, as if discussing nothing more important than the latest *on-dit* or whim of fashion, and went to join the ladies.

Presently, when George begged his cousin to favour them with a song, Mr Marsden sat back in his chair, gently tapping a foot in time to the lilting Irish air she had chosen, and approving the graceful picture presented by his son's fair head bent close to

Miss Devenish's dark one as he turned over her music for her. There was no doubt that the gentleman in residence held a vast advantage over other contenders and Mr Marsden had no intention of permitting George to forego any of that advantage.

CHAPTER
FIVE

'What perplexes me, Damien,' said Miss Honoria Winton in the tone of one anxious to be enlightened, 'is why you should feel obliged to offer for me at all. Not', she added hastily, 'that I am not fully sensible of the honour you do me by such a proposal, but I own that when my father told me you had asked his leave to address me, I was vastly surprised.' She subjected him to a long and searching regard, not entirely devoid of sympathy. 'Is it your mama, perhaps, being anxious about the succession?'

The Marquis amply repaid such regard. His exquisite coat of lavender-hued superfine proclaimed the master hand of Weston as surely as if his name had been writ upon the collar; his dove-grey nether integuments clung lovingly to his shapely limbs with scarce a wrinkle; his valencia waistcoat was in matching stripes of grey and lavender, while above it a crisp arrangement of white muslin, reaching almost to his ears, permitted no more than the merest hint of shirt points to be seen. A magnificent amethyst set in diamonds nestled amid the muslin, while on one slender hand a similar stone, square-cut into a handsome ring, provided his only other concession to adornment, if one discounted the single fob at his waist and the silver tassels swinging from his crystal-bright Hessians. In short, his lordship was the epitome of elegance as befitted one who had come a-courting Lord Braidestone's daughter, but the correctness of his address was thrown a little off balance by the lady's reception of his proposal.

'Lord, no! Mama ain't anxious on that head,' he replied scornfully. 'Why should she be?'

'Well, you know how they are – or perhaps you don't – but my mama has a longing to dandle her grandchildren on her knee and I'll warrant yours has, too. It is a great worry to me, I can tell you, because, being the eldest, I am expected to provide them the first, and you being the only son and heir to the title makes it imperative that you should be thinking of establishing your nursery.'

Damien, having been used to plain speaking from his mother all his life, took these remarks in the spirit in which they were offered.

'I cannot think that mama would enjoy being a grandmother above half, but you could be in the right of it,' he conceded, relieved at having such an adequate reason for his behaviour offered him. 'My father's not in very prime twig and if I could produce an imprint to gladden his heart – ' He stopped for she was nodding agreement.

'Just so, but why me, Damien? I'll allow we have known each other for ever, but you could have any diamond of the ton for a wife did you care to attach her. My sole claim to distinction has been in contracting an unfortunate connection and causing my parents to be out of all reason cross with me.'

She made a little grimace of half-amused remorse and settled herself on the sofa, motioning her visitor to be seated.

'Yes, what *were* you about to get yourself entangled with that fellow?' asked Damien curiously, disposing himself upon a chair with due regard for his coat-tails. 'I had never thought you to be lacking in good sense, Honoria.'

'Oh, Damien, you're a man and you don't know what it is to have every eligible gentleman of one's acquaintance paraded before one – not that my parents were unkind or tried in the least to *force* me – indeed, papa used to throw me into whoops by going over each one's points as if he was a horse being put up for sale! Which was true enough, I suppose.'

The Marquis felt himself going a trifle hot under his neckcloth. 'Do I take it that he did the same for me?' he enquired tentatively.

'Only to your credit, I assure you. In fact, he said it was the most capital thing that you should offer for me for he judged you to be sound at bottom in spite of your actresses and straw damsels. And, at least, you could not be accused of marrying me for my fortune. Oh, Damien, I do beg your pardon! I should not have mentioned your – your ladies, but my wretched tongue will run away with me and your dealings are such common knowledge that it just slipped out!'

But Damien's heightened colour was not occasioned by Miss Winton's reference to his mode of life, as his next remark showed. 'Do you – are you plagued by many fortune-hunters?' he enquired in a somewhat stifled voice.

'Oh, yes,' she said simply, 'that is why I got engaged, but it didn't answer because he – I – well, never mind, but at least it put a period to all that mortifying business of having gentlemen cast themselves at my feet and vow undying devotion when I knew very well that all their devotion was directed towards my twenty thousand pounds a year.'

'As much as that?' exclaimed the startled Marquis.

'Yes, my grandmother left it to me. Didn't you know?'

'Not precisely. Your father and I did not discuss anything of so – so mundane a nature,' explained Damien loftily. He did not add that Lord Braidestone, when he had recovered from the shock of learning that the most eligible catch in London wished to offer for his difficult daughter, had clapped him on the shoulder, wished him every sort of success, and proceeded to drink to it with such good will that Damien had been obliged to assist his prospective father-in-law to his carriage rather than have him spend what was left of the night sleeping it off at his club.

'Why should you discuss such a matter, indeed?' Miss Winton smiled upon the Marquis warmly. 'I must confess it will be very comfortable to marry a gentleman with as much money as myself. You know, I am beginning to believe we shall deal together famously – that is, if you are quite sure you wish to marry me.'

'I wouldn't have asked you if I wasn't, would I?' pointed out the Marquis reasonably.

'Oh, yes, you might, if your mama showed you where your duty lay and you felt no particular tendre for any other lady. I can lay no claim to beauty, Damien, and gentlemen only offer for me because of my fortune or – or, perhaps, because we are so long acquainted that my lack of countenance doesn't signify.'

This matter-of-fact expression of opinion caused his lordship to suffer acute embarrassment, but he forced himself to meet her steady gaze and replied, rather gruffly: 'You do yourself less than justice, Honoria.'

There was much truth in what he said for Miss Winton's

diminutive person, though decidedly on the plump side, was sufficiently dainty to allow of her being termed passably handsome. Her dark-brown hair fell in gleaming curls about her ears and she was the fortunate possessor of a pair of expressive grey eyes and a delightful, if rare, smile. Her habitual gravity of countenance was intensified by the firm set of her mouth and caused most people to suppose her to be much older than her twenty years.

Ignoring Damien's last remark, she went on thoughtfully, 'Selina, my nearest sister, is turned seventeen and must have her come-out in the spring. She is a very taking little thing and full of good sense. I am sure she will go on in a capital way with us to support her. She would really make a much better marchioness than I!' she added mischievously, glancing at him to judge how this suggestion would be received.

Damien rose and began to pace the floor. How was one to tell a lady tactfully that she was being married for her money?

'Selina may be all you say,' he got out at last, 'but she's no heiress.'

Miss Winton's eyes began to twinkle. 'And you've outrun your allowance and your papa says he won't stand the nonsense any longer? I thought that must be it!' Damien said nothing. Not for the world would he allow it to be known that it was his mother and not he who had brought him to such a pass. Miss Winton took his silence for assent and went on reflectively, 'I do understand but – come, sit down, Damien, and let us discuss this sensibly.'

'Nothing to discuss,' he said briefly. 'I've got to marry where money is and if you've a mind to be a marchioness and, in time, a duchess, that's it.'

'Would it not be sufficient for the present if you were just to be engaged where money is?' she suggested. 'I cannot believe your debts to be other than temporary and I am sure, knowing how the Duke dotes upon you, that he will loosen his purse-strings when he sees you conforming to his wishes. If you become engaged to me your creditors will hedge off until you can be on terms with yourself again.'

Damien thought over this proposition and could find much to recommend it. Admittedly, it would only stave off the evil day but, being of a naturally optimistic nature, he felt that time might well provide a solution and, if not, he had sufficient faith in his own ability and address to be reasonably confident of persuading Miss Winton to discharge her obligation to him and become his wife.

'How long a betrothal had you in mind?' he asked doubtfully.

'Oh, say, six months? Then, at the end of that time, we can declare that we do not suit.'

'But, Honoria,' he protested, 'you cannot be for ever terminating engagements. It's – well, it is not at all the thing, you know, and will earn you the reputation of being uncommon hard to please.'

'All to the good,' she nodded. 'That should scare off all but the most persistent suitors.'

Damien sat silent, leaning forward, elbow on knee, chin cupped in hand, turning her proposal over in his mind. His meeting with his father had proved abortive, he still had no clear idea to what extent the estates were encumbered, but when he had suggested seeking a wealthy lady for wife, the Duke's face had brightened and he had agreed in his courteous way that such a solution would make things much more comfortable for his heir.

With a start, the Marquis roused himself from his reverie to find Miss Winton watching him, head on one side, rather like a perky little wren.

'A penny for them, Damien,' she murmured. 'Or are they worth more than that?'

Of a sudden the Marquis knew that he could not do it. Had she been other than Honoria Winton, the honest, friendly child he had known all her life, whom he had picked up when she had fallen off her first pony and forced to go on riding in spite of being black and blue all over – in return for which kindness she had given him the measles – then he might have convinced himself that the cause justified the means, but to lure so trusting a creature into marriage with him on the pretence that the decline in his fortunes was of a transitory nature went against the pluck.

'Honoria,' he said, clasping his hands between his knees and staring at the floor. 'I must confess to you that our affairs are not in too good a state.' A soft chuckle brought his head up sharply. 'What the – I am gratified to learn that such intelligence affords you amusement!'

'Now, Damien, do not, I implore you, get upon your high horse!' she begged him. 'It has been so transparently clear from the moment you entered the room that this situation was not at all to your liking! I warn you, my lord, that if you wish to attach an heiress you must employ a great deal more address!'

He looked at her in dismay. 'The devil! I have not been too clever at it, have I? Forgive me, Honoria, but I could not deceive you.'

'Of course you could not,' she agreed comfortably. 'But it is only because I know you so well and – you are my friend, are you not, Damien?'

'Well, I hope so,' he said, wondering what was coming next and feeling annoyed with himself for having handled the business so clumsily.

'Then I may confide in you that, although I have broken off my engagement to Captain Ryder, I still have great hopes of marrying him.'

'What? Then why – ?' Words failed the Marquis.

'Because my dearest Jeremy is so foolishly proud a man that he cannot bear for it to be thought he is marrying me for my money and against my parents' wishes. He only offered for me because he feared he had compromised me, but it wasn't at all his fault, the dear fellow!' she concluded fondly.

'You, no doubt, arranged it!' said his lordship sagely.

Her infectious chuckle broke forth again. 'That's what I like about you, Damien, you don't need to have things explained to you.'

'Yes, I do!' he protested. 'How do you propose to make Captain Ryder marry you if he don't want to?'

'Oh, but he does want to. He loves me devotedly and it will, I am persuaded, quite break his heart when I get engaged to you.'

'We are getting engaged, then?'

'Yes, Damien,' she said in the kindly tone of one instructing a backward infant, 'because you must stave off your creditors and I my suitors, until I am twenty-one. That is in seven months' time.'

'And what then?' the unconvinced Marquis desired to be informed.

'I am not perfectly sure,' she confessed, 'but I hope you will have found some other wealthy young lady by that time and will go to Captain Ryder and tell him that, having discovered my devotion to him to be unfailingly constant, you are prepared to renounce me in his favour. After that, he can hardly refuse to marry me, can he? And, being of age, I shall not need my parents' approval. They only gave their consent the first time because I told them how indiscreet I had been, but mama soon guessed that was all a hum!'

The Marquis's eyes narrowed. 'Don't be a fool, Honoria!' he begged her. 'Of all the harebrained schemes – in any case, I cannot see that it helps my cause at all.'

'Damien, you will be the hero of the hour! Such exquisite sensibility! So noble a gesture! And any gentleman who sets aside twenty thousand pounds a year cannot be suspected of being short of the needful.'

'No, more likely astray in the attic,' objected his lordship. 'And that notion won't fadge for very long, either. Noble gestures won't pay my debts.'

'By then, every heiress in the country will be prepared to lay her fortune at your feet in order to help console your supposedly broken heart!'

The Marquis looked her straight in the eye. 'Honoria,' he said, 'no one is going to suspect me of having a broken heart.'

Miss Winton took this adverse reflection on her powers of attraction in good part. 'Well, you must *try*, Damien,' she adjured him. 'Pretend to conceal it bravely under an outward show of stoicism. In any case, by that time, we must have discovered an eligible lady to whom you can pay your addresses. Now, let us go and surprise mama. She is, I know, in a state of the highest fidgets.'

Lady Braidestone the Marquis found to be vastly more relieved than surprised. She had confessed to her spouse before he had left for his club that morning: 'Just pray the tiresome chit does not take it into her head to refuse him! She very likely could, you know.' But his lordship had been confident that Honoria would see where her duty lay.

'Mark you, I believe the boy's only offering for her because Evesham's not in very high fettle and is anxious for a grandson,' he said. 'But what of it? He's the biggest catch in the matrimonial market and they know each other well enough to rub along easily together.'

Lady Braidestone suppressed her doubts and received the news of her daughter's betrothal with commendable composure. 'I can only hope that your dear mother will be as content as I am with this delightful turn of events, Damien,' said she, extending a gracious hand to the Marquis.

'Make no doubt of that, ma'am,' he assured her, two imps of mischief dancing in his green eyes. 'When I disclosed to her my intention of offering for Honoria, she declared that nothing would give her greater satisfaction than to see me shackled to a daughter of yours!'

'Well,' allowed her ladyship. 'Your mama and I are old friends; such a connection can only afford us the utmost gratification.'

'Then what is distressing you, my lady?' said he, greatly daring.

'You, Damien!' Lady Braidestone, never one to mince matters, looked to where Honoria stood in her favourite posture, hands clasped in front of her, head on one side, watching them. 'It is like a peacock mating with a hedge-sparrow!'

'Dear ma'am, what an odd result that would produce, to be sure!' he mocked her, and she was forced to laugh. Really, the boy was a superb creature and she had ever had a soft spot for him, so she allowed him to kiss her cheek and called for wine to toast the newly betrothed couple.

*   *   *

Some half-hour later the Marquis took his leave and was walking in thoughtful mood along Park Place when he all but bumped into a gentleman who had placed himself squarely in his path.

'Well met, Damien!' said a rich, lazy voice. 'I had thought you to be still at Studleigh.'

'Going back there to stay over Christmas,' explained the Marquis briefly and without any great show of cordiality. 'Came up to town on a – on a matter of business. But you, Quentin, I had believed you to be in Bath.'

Sir Quentin Stratton glanced up at the house from whence his cousin had just emerged. 'Business successful, Damien?' he murmured provocatively.

'Yes, you may congratulate me!' The promptness of the reply sent Sir Quentin's eyebrows up into his hairline.

'Indeed, I do! My felicitations, Damien. A sudden decision?'

'An inevitable one. Or were you, perhaps, hoping that I would remain unwed in order to gratify your ambitions?' asked the Marquis, insultingly frank. Sir Quentin shook his head reprovingly at him.

'Dear boy! Even did you forgo matrimony the chances are that you would long outlive me. But it really is too bad for you to pick on Miss Winton. Why did you, I wonder? Not in Dun Territory, are you?'

'You must be thinking of my mama!' retorted Damien and could have bitten his tongue off for the indiscretion.

'What?' said his cousin in mock consternation. 'Do you tell me that Her Grace has been fleeced again?'

'I understand you stood by when she overstretched herself with Carlingford.'

'What would you have had me do? Come, Damien, you know you might as well talk to the bedpost as try to dissuade your mama when she is bent on squandering her blunt.'

'But Carlingford – he's little better than a gull-catcher! She's no match for him!' began the Marquis heatedly, then checked, closing his lips firmly together. Sir Quentin regarded him with detached interest.

'Now what has prompted this rare solicitude?' he wondered. 'Very touching, damme if it ain't! Surely this cannot be why – no, no, I'll not believe it!'

'Don't then!' advised his lordship lightly. 'But if you are thinking I am marrying Honoria for her money – why not?'

'Why not, indeed?' Sir Quentin was regarding him with something like respect. 'Don't tell me that Uncle Julius has at last put his foot down? A costly little piece, was she? You didn't – Damien! His Grace has never had to buy her off?'

Resisting a strong temptation to knock his cousin's fine white teeth down his throat, Damien permitted himself a rueful grimace. 'There were – difficulties,' he allowed, then, making an apparent effort to turn the subject, he went on casually, 'I am on my way to Jackson's for a little exercise. Do you care to join me?'

'Willingly. I have just been visiting our good Vernon who recommends that I employ regular physical exertion, as he so succinctly puts it.'

'Vernon, eh?' The Marquis looked curiously at his cousin. 'Nothing serious, I hope?'

The other waved aside his query. 'Nothing to signify – a shade overweight, no more. I went merely at the urging of my dear mother who is persuaded that Vernon must step into Halford's shoes before too long, and wishes to establish herself as one of his patients before the ton begin to crowd his waiting-rooms.'

Damien, who was fully cognisant of Lady Stratton's obsession with her health and eager pursuit of the newest names in medical science, nodded his understanding of the matter, and the two gentlemen fell into step together. As they turned out of Park Place into St James's Street, Sir Quentin remarked pensively: 'Poor Honoria!'

'Have no fear for her! I'll engage to be a conformable husband!' retorted Damien, albeit grimly.

'And that is the best she could hope for, to be sure!'

The Marquis visibly bristled.

'What do you mean by that?'

'Always thought she had a partiality for you. If so, it must be a matter of the utmost delight to her to have you drop into her lap like a ripe peach!'

'What?' Regardless of the stares of passers-by, Damien stood stock-still and stared at his companion. 'You're all about in your head, Quentin! She does not – she is – ' He then realized he could hardly explain that Honoria could not love him since she loved another.

'Yes?' Sir Quentin was observing his confusion in some amusement.

'She is not attached to me in that way,' said Damien flatly, and resumed walking at a brisk pace.

'Then why is she marrying you?'

'For the same reason that I asked her. Because, having been acquainted all our lives, we deal together very comfortably. Moreover, with younger sisters growing up, she wishes to be married and – and so do I!' he finished on a slightly defiant note.

'You astonish me!' Sir Quentin raised his quizzing-glass to inspect a particularly elegant equipage that was bowling past them. 'Devil take it if it ain't Medlicott! Now there's a man who did well for himself by marriage. Last time I saw him he was near out-at-elbows and now behold him – the finest Pink of the Ton.' He turned his glass upon Damien. 'Not, of course, that you were ever anything but a credit to your tailor but, to be frank, your previous mode of living has never given me the impression that, beneath it all, you yearned for nuptial bliss!'

'Hardly that,' admitted Damien, wondering how best to head his astute cousin off the scent, 'but my parents seem to think it my duty. I didn't see you at Brooks's last night,' he added, hopeful of giving the conversation a less dangerous slant.

'No,' confessed Sir Quentin, 'I thought that I was deserving of some relaxation after the strict propriety that obtains in Bath. When do you propose to – ah, tie the knot?'

'Oh, in six months or so.' Damien was being deliberately off-hand. 'What detained you so long in Bath?'

'This and that, you know. Like yourself, I – ah, I think it time to be married.'

'In the suds, Quentin?' enquired the Marquis with gentle malice.

'Shall we say I have a taste for the finer things in life and they are proving increasingly expensive,' sighed his cousin. Damien raised an interrogatory eyebrow.

'So she's well endowed?'

'I cannot be sure,' admitted Sir Quentin, 'but I intend to find out. Having played the field for so long I have no mind to rush into ill-considered matrimony at this late stage.'

'I take it, then, to be a matter of the head rather than the heart?'

'My dear Damien!' protested Sir Quentin in slightly pained amusement. They had crossed Piccadilly and were walking up Old Bond Street when he added casually, 'By-the-by, you were at the Winterslow Hut, were you not, when that damned unpleasant incident occurred involving a lioness and the Exeter mail?'

'Yes, I was. Why do you ask?'

'Oh, no reason save that my lady was there on that night also, though she claims to have slept throughout the entire affair. I should hardly have thought that possible, would you?'

There was a considerable silence, then Damien replied in a rather odd voice, 'Difficult, I allow, but not impossible.'

'Had you laid eyes upon her you'd not have forgotten. A most taking young Irish lady – Damien, have I said something? Are you quite well?'

'A slight digestive disorder, nothing more.' The Marquis managed a smile but it was hardly convincing. 'Perhaps I should have accompanied you to see Vernon.'

Sir Quentin's eyes narrowed speculatively but they had, at that moment, arrived at the portals of Mr Jackson's Academy where they were received by the ex-champion of England himself.

'You are quite a stranger, my lord. Been rusticating?'

John Jackson spoke with the ease of long acquaintance, his manner neither servile nor familiar, but when he turned to greet Sir Quentin a keen ear might have detected a shade of reserve in his mode of address.

'Been visiting m'father,' explained Damien briefly. 'You'll find me sadly out of training, John.'

'Then we'd better have a set-to with the mufflers. If you would care to strip, my lord, I will be with you in a very few moments. And you, Sir Quentin, what is your fancy today?'

'Nothing too strenuous,' drawled Stratton, watching the Marquis stroll away. 'A work-out on the punch-ball will do me very well. Don't be too hard on him, Jackson,' he added, nodding in Damien's direction. 'He has just got himself betrothed and, 'pon honour, I doubt he cares for it overmuch!'

Laughing softly as at some excellent jest, he sauntered into the crowded room, pulling off his gloves and nodding casually to several gentlemen of his acquaintance. Behind this genial exterior, his brain was busily recording the fact that two people known to him had been at the Winterslow Hut on that dramatic October night and neither seemed wishful of talking about it. Nor could the news of the Marquis's betrothal afford him any satisfaction. While Damien remained unwed it was reasonable to indulge in the hope that Nature or his lordship's adventurous spirit might put a period to his existence, but the prospect of his begetting a son was not, in his cousin's view, a pleasing one. Sir Quentin, for all his affectation of being one of the fashionables with few notions in his head beyond the set of his neckcloth or the choosing of his horses, had no intention of being ousted from the position of heir to the dukedom. Six months, he mused, was a long time. The lady might well change her mind – or be induced to change it.

CHAPTER
SIX

Being a young woman of considerable perspicacity and no little resolution, Miss Devenish had never before been confronted with any problem concerning her way of life which she had found herself unable to resolve but, upon reflection, it seemed to her that the only course open to her was to return to her grandmother and slip into the somewhat negative position of being a prop to that formidable old lady's declining years.

Christmas had been entertaining enough with its attendant revels, and the New Year might be thought to have produced a sufficiency of balls and rout-parties to delight any young lady willing to be pleased. Miss Devenish was quite prepared to allow that she was not willing to be pleased and, moreover, was of the opinion that, in so far as Bath was concerned, no more uninteresting and tedious town existed in all His Majesty's – or the Prince Regent's – realm.

Admittedly the situation had not been improved by Mrs Marsden's succumbing to a severe attack of influenza and George taking off for Grantham, there to stay with his paternal cousins for the hunting. This invitation had most kindly been extended to include Miss Devenish and, to be truthful, there was nothing she would have liked better for she was an ardent horsewoman, had not George's rather curious behaviour set her against the project. So, despite her aunt and uncle's protests to the contrary, she declared it to be her duty to stay at Mrs Marsden's side until she was fully recovered.

While not precisely making a push to attach her, George's attentions upon occasion were decidedly other than cousinly, and she was a little apprehensive of how he might conduct himself when away from his parents' restraining influence – if, indeed, such influence could be termed restraining, for she had a strong impression that Mr Marsden and, to a lesser degree, his spouse, regarded their son's efforts to ingratiate himself with their niece in a benevolent light. Why this should be so had Miss Devenish quite in a puzzle for George's artless confidences had soon informed her that he was perpetually short of the ready and, as he was clearly too indolent and easy-tempered to come to terms with his improvident way of life, surely the last thing his parents could envisage for him would be marriage to a penniless cousin? Lady Harpendene had said in a vague way that she would provide for her granddaughter, but her grandmother's somewhat pinchpurse mode of living had given Miss Devenish small hope of such provision being other than modest.

These melancholy considerations had her quite at a stand, and a letter received that morning from her mother had done little to soothe her agitated nerves.

Mrs FitzGerald Cunningham had been at pains to impress upon her daughter in what comfortable circumstances she now found herself, her husband the kindest and most thoughtful of men and everything just as it should be. They had recently moved into a house in one of Dublin's choicest squares 'upon which' – to quote her letter – 'Mr FitzGerald Cunningham has spared no expense to make pleasing and all done in the first style of fashion. I declare I am quite overcome with the attention he lavishes upon me and in deferring to my wishes in so good-natured a way that I am bound to consider myself one of the most fortunate of women. Nor is our old house at Lucan to be forgotten, for he has employed Mr John Sutherland to modernize and improve the gardens. Already the approaches are extremely well planned and the straight avenues of trees no longer offend the eye.'

At this disclosure Miss Devenish had shaken her head sadly for the noble avenues of oak and beech around her old home had never offended her eye. The concluding paragraph of the letter gave her even greater cause for dissatisfaction.

'I may have omitted to inform you,' her mother had written, 'that, a short time before Christmas, my husband was so fortunate as to come in for a considerable legacy from some aged relative whose very existence he had all but forgot.'

And that, reflected Miss Devenish, explained everything. The 'considerable legacy' was clearly sliding like sand through Mr FitzGerald Cunningham's eager fingers. He was a man to whom appearances were all; he had married a lady of infinitely better birth than himself and was resolved to show the world he could provide her with a setting worthy of her station. A laudable ambition, no doubt, but in Miss Devenish's considered opinion, her new papa would find himself with pockets to let before the year was out. Nor did it appear likely that he had changed his attitude towards his stepdaughter. On the contrary, her mother had ceased to lament Cherryanne's departure and no mention was made of any forthcoming visit in the summer as had been the case in previous letters. It was plain that Mrs FitzGerald Cunningham had arrived at the sensible, if selfish, conclusion that a present husband was worthy of greater consideration than an absent daughter, and was only too pleased to relinquish the care of the latter into the hands of her mother and sister.

'Oh, it is all too vexatious!' muttered Miss Devenish crossly. 'I'll go for a walk, that should shake the dismals out of me after being moped up here these last weeks.'

Knowing full well that her aunt, who was laid upon her bed according to her usual afternoon practice, would have insisted upon her being accompanied by a maid or footman, she let herself out of the house as unobtrusively as possible and was at once grateful for her warm, fur-trimmed pelisse and bonnet when she encountered the strong cold wind whistling about the Circus.

Unthinkingly, her feet led her along Brock Street towards Royal Crescent and, as she was about to turn into that noble sweep of buildings, a small dog came trotting briskly round the corner, trailing a leash which all but tripped her up. At once she was brought to the realization that here was no ordinary dog, but a Chinese aristocrat of the first stare, who gave her a cursory glance and continued on its way.

'That's all very well, oh Imperial One!' said Cherryanne who, though more familiar with the greyhounds and spaniels that ran wild about her home at Lucan, still had heard of the world-famed Oriental sleeve-dogs. 'But it seems to me that you are a vagrant, having run off from your keeper! I suggest you turn back and we proceed in the direction from whence you came!'

So saying, she possessed herself of the leash and gently urged the animal to accompany her. In this she was meeting with indifferent success for the little creature, having tasted freedom, was in no mood to forgo it without dispute, when a veritable whirlwind descended upon them in the persons of a small boy and an agitated young lady, the latter of whom cried out upon seeing the dog,

'Sukey, you naughty girl! How dared you skip away like that? Oh, thank you, ma'am, for having apprehended her! Pak, dear, you must never, ever allow your attention to be diverted when she is in your charge.'

The small boy was understood to say that he had never been desirous of taking the dog in his charge in the first place and there was no sort of use in blaming him for the occurrence. The lady, in the meantime, had picked up Sukey and was reading her a lecture on the impropriety of eluding her guardian.

'The Duchess is in a great taking over it,' she confided to Miss Devenish, 'for I made sure the little wretch would return to the house when she ran away from us, so, of course, I went back there to seek her and set the household by the ears. This mite was given to Her Grace by a dear friend, a famed traveller in the Orient, and not for the world would she have anything happen to her.'

'It is a rare species, is it not?' ventured Miss Devenish politely.

'Rare in this country to be sure, but in the East these sleeve-dogs are not uncommon. She is a Shih Tzu, but Her Grace says that makes her sneeze, so she calls her Sukey. My name is Honoria Winton,' she went on in the most friendly manner imaginable, 'and I accompanied the Duchess here yesterday and this is my brother Pakenham, who has had a tiresome bout of the chicken-pox so that my mother thought a few weeks of Bath air would be the very thing to set him up again. Are you a regular resident, ma'am, or like ourselves, do you visit here to take the waters?'

Miss Devenish, whose quick brain was putting two and two together, had concluded that the duchess referred to must be none other than Her Grace of Evesham, whose arrival in Bath was hourly expected, so she at once introduced herself and explained the circumstances which had brought her to Bath.

By the time she had come to the end of these they had arrived before a house in Royal Crescent which gave every sign of having been thrown into a state of considerable confusion. The front door stood open, and from a first-floor window an elderly butler was calling directions to a couple of bewildered footmen standing outside. As the two ladies approached, Miss Winton still carrying the runaway, he caught sight of them and heaved an immense sigh of relief. Then from the house there emerged the figure of a lady, looking perfectly distracted and wringing her hands to the accompaniment of a sort of wail of 'Sukey! Sukey!'

'Calm yourself, dear Duchess, we have her safe!' called out Miss Winton and at once, regardless of the bitter wind and the fact that she was wearing only the thinnest of shawls over her round gown of embroidered French cambric, the lady hurried down the steps to greet them. Upon hearing of the circumstances of Sukey's capture, nothing would please the Duchess other than that Miss Devenish should step inside and partake of a dish of tea, which invitation Cherryanne accepted with alacrity, thanking her good fortune that she had thought to change her morning robe for one of twilled florentine, worn with a velvet spenceret, and that her fur-trimmed pelisse and bonnet were perfectly *à la mode*.

Miss Winton, who seemed determined to be friendly, desired to be informed of all the social activities that obtained in the town.

'For it is the first time that ever I was in Bath,' she confessed. 'And you, I am persuaded, are well qualified to tell me how I should go on.'

'Do not, I beg of you, Honoria, expect me to escort you to countless routs and assemblies!' implored Her Grace, settling the reluctant Sukey into her satin-lined basket, while Cherryanne reflected that the Duchess and her aunt seemed to have much in common on the subject of chaperonage. 'There, my precious! You would never leave your mama, would you? It was just that, having been so newly come to this strange place, you could not find your way home, was that not so?' Miss Winton caught Miss Devenish's eye but they mutually refrained from comment while the Duchess went on reminiscently, 'She was the tiniest thing when I had her from dear Hester Stanhope, just before she left England to jaunter about the world.'

Miss Devenish, who had heard her grandmother speak of Lady Hester in rather more condemnatory accents, was about to enquire as to that incorrigible traveller's whereabouts when she heard her name being spoken in a tone of some surprise and turned to discover that Sir Quentin Stratton had entered the room. When the reason for her presence in his aunt's house had been made clear to him he seated himself by her side and paid her such marked attention that the Duchess was moved to comment *sotto voce* to Miss Winton that she now quite understood his readiness to attend her in Bath.

Sir Quentin had not been idle during the two months since he had last seen Miss Devenish. He had discovered who her grandmother was and, by the greatest of good fortune, had also found out that Lady Harpendene and his mother employed the same lawyer. From there it was a small step towards finding an employee of the worthy Mr Jonathan Thwaites who was not proof against bribery, and the likely extent of Miss Devenish's expectations was made known to him.

There was, Sir Quentin allowed, an element of risk about the whole thing which appealed to the gamester in him, but he could not believe he would be other than acceptable as a suitor for her granddaughter to Lady Harpendene. It but remained for him to win the young lady's approval and on that head he was not quite so confident since it seemed to him that she tolerated his attentions because nothing better offered rather than because she was flattered by them. This rare attitude in a young lady towards one who was accustomed to think of himself as something quite out of the common way piqued Sir Quentin more than he cared to admit, and it pleased him, therefore, to observe her charmingly deferential manner towards his aunt and the slight awe with which she regarded Miss Winton when she discovered her to be betrothed to the heir to the dukedom. A pretty little puss, he thought almost fondly, knocks Honoria into fits for looks and nigh-on as wealthy, if things fall out as they should.

The Duchess, complaining that she had been too long away from London, was requiring Sir Quentin to bring her up-to-date with all the latest crim. cons., when her butler entered to inform her that the last case had been unpacked, and where would Her Grace wish the two portraits to be hung?

'Oh, carry them in here, Drummond. I would like to assure myself that they have suffered no damage on the journey. You will think it quite idiotish of me, I have no doubt,' she said, turning to Cherryanne, 'but I can never be without these paintings, one of myself with my son as a child, and the other of him when he became twenty-one. I also cling to my pianoforte,' she added, motioning towards the handsome instrument fashioned by Rolfe in a mahogany and satinwood frame, which had already caught Miss Devenish's appreciative eye.

'And your glass and china and linen and silver – to say nothing of several other articles of furniture!' Sir Quentin reminded her. 'I don't doubt you would have a painting made of Shalford every year, could you persuade him to consent to it, and bring 'em all with you!'

'Oh, he thinks it a great waste of time,' she sighed. 'Nor can I fully comprehend his aversion to having his likeness taken, for, though I am his mama, I cannot but allow him to be a remarkably well-looking young man and most – most *paintable*! But you shall judge for yourself, Miss Devenish.' As she spoke two footmen came in, staggering slightly under the weight of a large frame which they propped up against the wall. 'This portrait was executed when Damien was but two years old,' further explained the Duchess. 'I think it to be the most delightful thing, though you, Quentin, are for ever condemning it as being untrue to life.'

When the wrappings were taken off and Miss Devenish was permitted to feast her eyes on the portrait, she had to confess there was much truth in Sir Quentin's criticism. Her Grace, rigged out as a shepherdess, sat poised against a background of woodland and storm-tossed sky, eyes gazing into infinity, one hand clasping a pomander while the other caressed the glowing curls of an unbelievably beautiful infant who stood at her knee.

'Very typical of Lawrence's earlier work,' pontificated Sir Quentin, getting up to study the painting in some detail through his glass. 'Too sentimental for my taste – and don't tell me that Damien ever looked so angelic, for that is pitching it a bit too strong!'

The Duchess pouted. 'I can always depend upon you to be captious about anything that touches Damien!' she snapped with rare asperity. 'But even your finicking taste cannot be offended by dear Sir Thomas's second portrait!'

This, a sizeable oval, was being set in an armed chair slightly out of Cherryanne's line of vision. As both the Duchess and Sir Quentin stood in front of it, she flushed and indignant and he looking mildly satirical, Miss Devenish discreetly positioned herself behind them, the better to view the painting.

At first, she could not believe what she saw. The dark, vivid face with its slight mocking smile, the brilliant eyes and the rich chestnut hair seemed like a dream from the past, and she hardly heard Sir Quentin saying: 'No, I allow that to be a very commendable likeness. There is less of the angel there and more of the devil!'

This comment brought an impassioned outburst from the Duchess in defence of her son and gave Miss Devenish a few moments in which to regain her composure and consign a cherished if faint hope to oblivion. He was the Marquis of Shalford and betrothed to Miss Winton – in any event, far too great a nobleman to interest himself in an unknown Irish damsel of little fortune. To her horror, she felt hot tears beginning to prick behind her eyelids but was saved from the ignominy of having this remarked upon by reason of a loud explosion sounding from somewhere inside the house, which so startled the company that their attention was quite distracted from any other thing. The door burst open to admit Master Pakenham Winton, his face a black mask, his frilled shirt-front begrimed, clutching a bottle in one hand and an iron spoon in the other.

'Please forgive me, ma'am,' he gasped, addressing himself to the Duchess. 'It was my thunder-powder, you see! I put too much in the spoon and the flames touched it.'

'Oh, Pak! Pak, dear, are you hurt?" Miss Winton, all sisterly solicitude, hurried forward but was brushed aside by Sir Quentin who advanced upon the small, bedraggled figure in a menacing manner.

'Hurt?' he rasped. 'He will be when I've had my way with him! Thunder-powder, indeed! Had you in mind to send the house up in smoke?'

Master Winton bravely stood his ground and denied any such intention, but Sir Quentin was not to be appeased and, taking the boy ungently by the ear, was proceeding to march him out of the room when the Duchess intervened.

'Don't be absurd, Quentin, of course he meant no such thing. If you had had any dealings with small boys you would know that they never *think*! Drummond, please take Master Pakenham in charge and see that he is cleaned up – and Pak! No more thunder-powder, if you please, Sir Quentin does not care for it!'

This last remark brought an involuntary smile to Miss Winton's anxious face and the suggestion of a scowl to Sir Quentin's as he relinquished his grip on the miscreant and allowed Drummond to lead him away. Miss Devenish, in the background, heaved a sigh of relief, for she could not but be grateful to Master Winton for creating such a diversion and had no wish to have him beaten for it. She broke the somewhat strained silence that had fallen upon the room by addressing herself to the Duchess.

'Will you please to excuse me, Your Grace? My aunt has no idea of where I may be, and if she should find me absent there will be another hue and cry set in motion throughout the neighbourhood.'

The Duchess quite understood and bade her a most gracious farewell, while Sir Quentin, his irritability smoothed over and his poise restored, insisted upon escorting her back to the Circus despite her protests that it was but a step away. So relieved was she to make her escape that she failed to take notice of Miss Winton's searching regard, but then she did not know that her moment of distress had been observed by that astute lady, who was pardonably intrigued to discover that her fiancé's portrait could arouse such emotion in the breast of a complete stranger.

'What a charming young lady Miss Devenish is, to be sure,' she remarked to the Duchess when they were alone.

'Yes, Quentin would agree with you there,' said Her Grace, who was glancing through some sheets of music that lay on top of the pianoforte.

'Is he, do you think, seriously attempting to attach her?' enquired Miss Winton in some surprise.

'I believe so,' nodded the Duchess. 'He had already asked my permission to bring her to call upon me, but your encountering her in this happy way is much more comfortable and less – ah – less – '

'Obvious?' supplied Miss Winton demurely.

'Just so.' The Duchess seated herself at the pianoforte and ran her fingers lightly over the keys. 'Depend upon it, Honoria, she's an heiress or he'd not be making a play for her. He likes to be well beforehand with the world, does dear Quentin. And I confess to finding her a most taking child with looks above the ordinary, and not at all forward in her manners. It will be nice for you, too, to have such an agreeable cousin. Oh, is not this air of Mr Thomas Moore's quite enchanting? Such a conversable young man as he is! " 'Tis the last rose of summer – " ' she trilled, relieving Miss Winton of the necessity of replying, which was as well, because that damsel's mind was quite obsessed with wondering just why Miss Devenish had turned deathly pale and had gazed upon the portrait of the Marquis with something like horror.

Miss Devenish, too, had much to occupy her mind. Sir Quentin was most assiduous in his attentions on their way to the Circus, and seemed bent on erasing any ill conception of his character that might have been formed during his bad-tempered outburst against Master Pakenham. So considerate was he that she almost sighed with relief when they arrived at their destination. That her absence had not been remarked upon was obvious from Bellamy's air of surprise as he opened the door in answer to Sir Quentin's peremptory knock.

'Has my aunt left her room yet?' she enquired, carrying matters off with a high hand.

'No, miss, but the master has just returned home.'

Miss Devenish hesitated, then, reluctantly, remembered her manners. 'You have not met my uncle, I believe, Sir Quentin. Would you care to step inside?'

Sir Quentin accepted the invitation with every appearance of gratification. On his previous visit to Bath he had heard much of Mr Marsden though, as the latter gentleman had no turn for dancing or cards, their paths had not crossed. It seemed a sensible thing to be on bowing terms with him and, if possible, to gain a measure of his approval before applying to him for permission to address his niece.

Mr Marsden was in his book-room, composing a letter to his son. He had been sadly disappointed in the way things had fallen out between George and Cherryanne, and blamed the young man for his inept handling of the business. When Bellamy entered to announce that Sir Quentin had called he felt an unwonted surge of irritation, then reminded himself that it was as well to know one's enemies. Nothing, therefore, could be more affable than was his greeting when he entered the drawing-room and Cherryanne presented her escort to him.

The enemy, he was bound to admit, came in a very personable guise and, listening to Sir Quentin's smoothly turned phrases and observing his elegant person, he realized that George had small hope of succeeding in his design against one so bang up to the mark. In short, he recognized his visitor as being as fully awake upon every suit as he was himself, and came to the swift conclusion that, if he was serious in his pursuit of Miss Devenish, then he must somehow have got wind of her expectations, for he was no Johnny Raw to be caught by a pretty face.

'Perhaps, my dear,' said Mr Marsden, turning to Cherryanne, 'you would be so good as to inform your aunt of Sir Quentin's presence?' Miss Devenish, grateful for the excuse to escape, at once left them and hurried away. Mr Marsden noted how his visitor's eyes followed her graceful figure and the curiously anticipatory gleam in them. 'I am assured, sir, that you will not be wishing to maudle your inside with tea at this hour of day,' he went on silkily. 'If you will step with me into my book-room I have a very tolerable sherry on which I would value your opinion.'

Sir Quentin expressed himself as being perfectly happy to oblige his host in such a way and presently Cherryanne, in her bedchamber above the book-room, heard the murmur of their voices and wondered what they could be finding to say to each other.

'Dear God!' she sighed, hands to burning cheeks. 'What to do?' For there was no doubt now that Sir Quentin was an aspirant for her hand – indeed, he had openly hinted at it during their short walk from Royal Crescent. Could he be asking her uncle's permission to address her? Such a possibility so alarmed her that, hurrying to her secretaire, she pulled out some paper and at once began to write a letter.

She got no further than 'Dear grandmama', then stopped, thoughtfully nibbling at the end of her pen. No, there was no time for it now and, in any case, she must think over carefully what she was going to tell Lady Harpendene. Slowly she put the letter away and went to survey her appearance in the mirror.

'Damien!' she whispered to her reflection. 'I never did know your name until today. Dear – Damien!'

As it chanced the circumstances belowstairs were not at all as she had feared nor as Sir Quentin had anticipated. After the customary formalities had been observed, that gentleman was speedily brought to understand that the way to Miss Devenish's hand and fortune was not going to be the rose-strewn path he had envisaged.

'Such a sweet child,' purred Mr Marsden. 'So devoted to her aunt that not even the prospect of a few weeks' hunting in the Melton country with my son could prise her from her side, and she is as fond of hunting as one would expect an Irish lass to be. Fond of George, too,' he added, filling up his guest's glass.

Sir Quentin took the point. 'Your son?' he queried mildly. 'Ah, yes, makes a good appearance in the first circles in town, as I recall.'

'He is young, of course,' allowed Mr Marsden, 'but time will remedy that and their union would be a felicitous binding together of the two branches of the family. However, I must not run on. It is the greatest bore in the world to be hearing of other people's hopes and aspirations.'

Confound the young puppy! thought Sir Quentin. It is a great deal too bad if I am to be outfaced by a fribble, quarter flash and three-parts foolish! Aloud he said agreeably: 'Such an outcome cannot but afford you the utmost gratification. Does your niece make a long stay with you, sir?'

'As to that I cannot say. Her grandmother has a certain claim upon her. Ah, I believe I hear my wife's voice. Shall we return to the drawing-room? I know she will be most eager to make your acquaintance.'

Sir Quentin bowed his acquiescence but, as his eyes met those of his host, he was made sharply aware that here was one house where his marital ambitions were unlikely to be received with any favour. This circumstance confirmed his suspicions that Miss Devenish's portion was likely to be a handsome one, else why was her uncle so set on securing it for his son? A swift decisive move was what was called for and, even as he was making his bow to Mrs Marsden, he was promising himself a visit to Lady Harpendene in the near future.

CHAPTER SEVEN

'The thing is, Bridie, that we can do nothing until we hear from grandmama. If she will but follow my suggestion and plead indifferent health then we can be away from here on the moment, for my aunt has small need of me now and the full season in Bath does not commence for some weeks.'

'Yes, miss.' Bridie made no attempt to conceal her satisfaction. Even less than her mistress did she relish Bath, a circumstance not unconnected with Mrs Marsden's dresser, one Miss Amabel Stone, a haughty madam, inclined to be hostile to anyone setting themselves up against her despotic rule which Bridie, being of a militant nature, was apt to do.

'You'll not be wedding Mr George, then?' she enquired as casually as if passing the time of day.

'No, Bridie, I think not,' replied Miss Devenish, equally composed.

'I'm glad of that, miss, for while he is a nice gentleman enough, he's a bit of a rattle and money burns a hole through his pockets. Sir Quentin Stratton, now,' she went on as she looped her mistress's hair skilfully into an arrangement of Apollo knots, 'he is very fine, to be sure.'

'Yes,' answered Miss Devenish repressively, for she was aware that to be discussing such things with even so old and trusted a retainer as Bridie was not at all *comme il faut*. Then her eyes met those of her maid in the mirror and the unhappiness apparent in her beloved mistress's regard so touched Bridie's kind heart that she threw her arms around Cherryanne and held her close.

'Ah, sure, don't I know what's eatin' your heart out, acushla!' she cried, lapsing as ever in moments of stress into her native idiom, 'Did you niver hear tell of him again, not his name nor anythin'?'

'He is the Marquis of Shalford,' Cherryanne's voice was expressionless, 'and he's betrothed to Miss Winton, the lady I met yesterday.'

'Glory be to God,' breathed the deeply impressed Miss Hanrahan. 'A marquis, no less! You'd best put him from your mind, miss.'

'Son to Her Grace of Evesham and cousin to Sir Quentin,' continued Cherryanne in a very damping sort of way, but Bridie was not to be so easily silenced.

'So that puts Sir Q. out of contention,' said she sagely. 'You'll not be marrying him when your heart's set on his cousin.' Carefully she placed a wide-brimmed velvet bonnet, trimmed with fur and ruched satin, upon Miss Devenish's neat head. 'Yes, back to your grandma is the best course, miss. She'll put you right.'

Miss Devenish entertained no such hope but allowed herself to be dressed in silence while Bridie, after one searching look at her face, prattled away busily on trivial subjects until the time came for her to leave for the Pump Room with her aunt.

No sooner was Mrs Marsden installed beside her cronies and Miss Devenish gone to fetch her a glass of the nauseous-tasting water than a slight commotion heralded the entrance of the Duchess, attended by Sir Quentin and Miss Winton. The latter, upon catching sight of Miss Devenish, raised a hand in salute, so that when Her Grace was comfortably settled, Cherryanne asked her aunt's permission to pay her respects to the newly arrived party.

'Indeed, I think it is just what you ought to do.' Mrs Marsden had been deeply impressed by her niece's encounter of the previous day and resolved to waste no time in furthering the acquaintance. 'I should be very happy to be presented to Her Grace – ah, here comes Sir Quentin to make his bow to us.'

In no time at all Mrs Marsden was seated in triumph by the Duchess, whose lively mind wished to be informed of all the latest *on-dits* circulating in Bath, while Sir Quentin, very well satisfied with the way things had fallen out, drew Miss Devenish a little way apart.

'I have it on good authority there is to be a Subscription Ball at the Assembly Rooms next Friday,' said he pleasantly. 'Can I prevail upon you to allow me to be your escort? Her Grace has expressed her willingness to be present.'

Cherryanne felt strongly tempted to inform him that she hoped to be gone from Bath before Friday, but contented herself with thanking him prettily and accepting his obliging offer.

'Miss Winton will be attending the ball?' she enquired.

'Oh, yes, to be sure. We have every hope that Shalford will be of the party as Her Grace is in daily expectation of his arrival.'

After that, all Miss Devenish wished for was to get out of the Pump Room and back to her aunt's house. Both Sir Quentin and Miss Winton, who joined them, found her to be somewhat distrait, which surprised the latter young lady who had put down her new acquaintance as being blessed with good sense beyond the common run. Sir Quentin, cherishing the hope that his marked attentions were the cause of Miss Devenish's discomposure, felt more than ever satisfied with his situation for, after all was said, no matter how capricious an old witch Lady Harpendene might be, she was the one whose approval counted for most, and his father's partiality for George would hardly outweigh the advantages of a union with the Stratton family in any sensible grandmother's judgement. Her Grace's condescension towards Mrs Marsden, too, could not fail to impress and, if he could persuade his aunt to take up that lady and her niece, Mr Marsden might well find himself having to change his tune.

So Sir Quentin preened himself and less fortunate maidens gazed enviously upon Miss Devenish, whose one prayer was to be permitted to escape from her distinguished company. By a happy chance, Mrs Marsden was committed to nuncheon with a friend, so they presently took their departure with mutual expressions of regard and the anticipation of meeting again in the near future.

Having deposited her aunt at her friend's house, Miss Devenish hurried home to be greeted by an exultant Bridie.

' 'Tis come, miss, from her ladyship!' she hissed as Cherryanne ascended the stairs and whipped quickly into her bedchamber. 'An' there's one for your auntie, too!'

Lady Harpendene had expressed herself at length over two closely written sheets. She had clearly been greatly shocked by the intelligence conveyed to her by her granddaughter. Not for a moment would she countenance her marriage to George, a loose fish if ever there was one, and she had a mind to ring a peal over John Marsden's head for daring to think up such a scheme.

'However, on second thoughts, I think it better to say nothing of what is in my mind.' Cherryanne could just hear her grandmother's crisp, precise tones as she read her letter. 'I have written to your aunt, informing her that I find myself troubled with a recurrence of the bronchitis I experienced last year, and would be glad of your company for a time. Do not, I beg of you, show her this letter.'

'Yes, but I must tell my aunt that I have received it, else she may learn of it through Bellamy and wonder at my withholding it,' protested Cherryanne.

'Give it to me, miss, and I'll make sure to mislay it,' promised the resourceful Bridie. 'When does her ladyship require us to set out?'

'On Thursday, she says. She will send Kenyon to Amesbury, there to await us. We are to rest at the George one night and hire a post-chaise, if needs be, to convey ourselves there, should my uncle be unable to despatch us in his own carriage.'

'Then there's no time to be wasted, miss,' said Bridie briskly. 'I'll have your trunks fetched down from the attics this very minute.'

Mr and Mrs Marsden were understandably distressed to learn of Lady Harpendene's indisposition and readily allowed that Cherryanne must join her grandmother without delay; Mrs Marsden lamenting that her own indifferent health prohibited her from accompanying her niece, while Mr Marsden, visualizing the old lady's acute illness or even demise without her granddaughter by her side, positively urged Cherryanne's immediate departure, offering his chaise, with groom and footman in attendance, to speed her journey to Amesbury.

A note despatched to Sir Quentin, explaining the reason for her being unable to attend the ball in his company on the following Friday, brought him hot-foot to offer his sympathies and any assistance that she might require. His manner was such that she could not but be gratified by his concern while, at the same time, wishing him a thousand miles away.

'I cannot flatter myself that my absence will do anything to diminish your enjoyment of the occasion,' she protested.

'Oh, I shan't bother to attend unless Honoria wishes for it,' he said. 'The Duchess received a letter from Shalford today, informing her that my uncle is in none too good case which may hold him at Studleigh some days longer, so she is in a state of considerable anxiety.'

This intelligence, as may be imagined, did no good at all for Miss Devenish's already harassed nerves. Studleigh, as she had come to realize, was no very great distance from her grandmother's house and, though on her previous sojourn at Chilcomb she had encountered none of the ducal household, the possibility that she might meet his lordship while out riding or at some local function could not be entirely discounted.

Sir Quentin at last took himself off, vowing that she had but to raise her finger and he was her servant to command, which extravagant promise caused Mr Marsden, who was a witness to it, to look very pensive indeed.

They arrived at Amesbury on the Thursday afternoon to find Kenyon already installed there in the highest comfort, and their start was delayed by several hours on the following morning by his having to execute various commissions for her ladyship.

'May the divil fly away with him!' raged Bridie. 'He could well have done all that before ever we arrived and now – see! We are only past Stockbridge and 'tis nearly dark and – what's that?'

'That' was clearly and unmistakably a call to 'stand and deliver' and Kenyon, no hero in anyone's service save his own, immediately pulled the carriage in to the side of the road.

The door was wrenched open to reveal a masked figure, bearing levelled pistols. 'Forgive me, ladies,' said a harsh voice, 'but if you will part with your money and baubles without question, then the sooner all of us will be on our way.'

'You'll have nothing from me!' blazed Cherryanne. 'How dare you threaten us!'

'Oh, miss, don't be vexing him now!' pleaded the shivering Bridie. 'Give him what he wants and let us be off.'

'That's good advice, little lady,' sneered the highwayman, thrusting his masked face close to hers. 'Don't force me to lay hands on you for I promise you'll rue it. 'Tis mortal cold weather to be leaving a gentry-mort like yourself stripped of her clothes by the roadside!'

Miss Devenish, on whom this threat had no other effect than further to stir her temper, blessed the curious fancy that had possessed her to take the Marquis's pistol from its hiding-place, prime it as she had watched her father do his weapons in happier days, and leave it ready to her hand in the carriage holster.

'You are but one against three of us, sir,' she retorted boldly. 'And – yes, Bridie, quickly now!'

Momentarily, as she had hoped, the man's attention was diverted to Miss Hanrahan, cowering back against the squabs in her corner. In one swift movement, she possessed herself of the pistol and fired it. Nothing appeared to happen for an interminable length of time, the reek and smoke of the powder hung in the air, and when it cleared the menacing figure was no longer to be seen.

'Holy Saints, miss, have you killed him dead?' Bridie, surprisingly, came to her senses the quicker and was out of the carriage before Miss Devenish had laid down her smoking weapon. Kenyon was fully occupied in soothing Romulus and Remus who, being unused to gunfire, failed to see why they should have to support such barbarity.

'Is – is he still alive?' ventured Miss Devenish, peering down at the recumbent figure on the ground.

'I think so, miss, though you've near blown his ear off,' reported Bridie, making cautious inspection.

'Th-then h-hand me his pistols, if you please,' commanded Miss Devenish, attempting to still the tremor in her voice. 'There may be others of his kidney lurking near.'

As Bridie thrust the weapons at her the sound of horses approaching at the gallop caused her to clutch nervously at them and aim vaguely in the direction from which the riders were approaching.

'Careful now, miss, don't be loosing off at shadows!' implored her anxious henchwoman. 'Who – who goes there?'

At once the galloping hoofs slowed to a trot and a voice crisp with authority replied: 'What's to do here? Can I be of help?'

As the speaker rode up to the chaise Miss Devenish cried out in relief at sight of his dress which proclaimed him to be a military gentleman. 'Oh, thank Heaven, sir, I believe you may be of great assistance to us!'

He sprang from his horse, giving the reins into the hand of his companion and, on being favoured with a brief summary of events by Miss Devenish, knelt to inspect the fallen highwayman.

'No, he's not dead,' he proclaimed, 'nor, indeed, very gravely injured. A glancing shot, which has stunned him. I think it best, Mason,' he went on, turning to his groom, 'that you ride on to Winchester for assistance, while I remain with these ladies lest our friend here should prove mischievous.'

'Forgive me, sir, but would it not be the quicker course if he could be laid on a seat in the carriage?' suggested Cherryanne. 'If you and your man will ride with us, I have his pistols to ensure his good behaviour.'

The officer rose to his feet, brushing the dust from the knees of his trousers, and eyed her with respect. 'Indeed, ma'am, it would be the very thing, could you bear with having so rude a fellow for a travelling companion. Once in Winchester it will be the simplest matter to hand him into safe-keeping.'

He had stepped up to the door of the chaise as he spoke and Miss Devenish had the opportunity of studying his appearance more closely. This she found to be much in his favour, for he had a fine open countenance and a most pleasing address. His figure and bearing were uniformly good and handsomely set off by his dark-green regimentals. Miss Devenish liked what she saw and, to judge by the glow of admiration in his eyes, her sentiments were entirely reciprocated.

'If I may present myself, ma'am,' said he, making a very creditable leg in spite of the inert body sprawling at his feet. 'My name is Ryder, Captain Jeremy Ryder. I arrived at Plymouth yesterday on leave from the Army of Occupation and was obliged to make a call in Salisbury on my way, hence the happy chance of my taking this road. I would esteem it an honour to escort so intrepid a lady wherever she shall wish to go. Do you journey beyond Winchester tonight?'

'To Chilcomb only,' she explained. 'To my grandmother, Lady Harpendene.'

He laughed. 'Then we travel the same road, ma'am. My parents live at no great distance from her ladyship's home.'

'Ryder? Why, of course!' she exclaimed. 'Your sister, Caroline – I remember well! She has often spoken to me of you, and in the kindliest manner imaginable!'

'Then am I doubly fortunate!' he declared, his blue eyes dancing mischief at her. 'For now the whole matter resolves itself without difficulty. But first we must tie this troublesome fellow up securely.'

This was done with the aid of some stout cord produced by Kenyon, and the unlucky highwayman, trussed like a chicken, was bundled into the chaise. Captain Ryder, giving his horse into his groom's charge, seated himself beside the man – not, he protested, because he doubted Miss Devenish's ability to hold him in check, but rather to keep an eye upon his wound which, though roughly bound up, was still bleeding copiously.

The short journey was greatly enlivened by the Captain's cheerful conversation and, as good fortune would have it, on entering Winchester they encountered a small group of officers emerging from The Fighting Cocks, one of whom was known to him.

These gentlemen all expressed the most lively admiration for Miss Devenish's resolute behaviour and, clearly envying Captain Ryder his unassailable position as her escort, offered to relieve them of their unwelcome burden and convey him to the County Gaol. This courtesy Miss Devenish accepted with a pretty show of gratitude while Bridie, whose nerves had been sorely lacerated by the preceding events, gave voluble thanks for so fortunate an outcome to the affair.

Their reception at Chilcomb Manor was gratifyingly cordial, Lady Harpendene declaring that the place had been as dull as the tomb since her granddaughter's departure, and when she had been told of their recent adventure and the reason for their military escort, nothing would please her but that Captain Ryder must stay to dine with them.

'As you say your parents are not expecting you, it will be no hardship on them to forego your company for a few more hours,' she said firmly, giving him no choice but to submit with a good grace.

To Cherryanne's relief the dinner set before them was vastly superior to the general run of such meals in her grandmother's house. She almost suspected it of being, in a sort, the fatted calf set before the returning prodigal. Spitchcocked eels and scalloped oysters were supported by a pair of Cornish hens and a French raised pie, while the second course offered a handsome saddle of mutton, stewed rump-steaks with onion gravy, potato pudding, a Chantilly basket and a florendine of oranges and apples. Discovering herself to be very hungry, she set to with a will, and decided that a spice of danger undoubtedly gave an edge to the appetite.

Throughout the meal Captain Ryder maintained an easy flow of conversation and had many interesting anecdotes to recount of the life led by the Army of Occupation, though he admitted he would be happy enough to return to more warlike duties. Cherryanne guessed that he was a serious-minded young man, for all his light-hearted exterior, and that the trivialities of a peacetime headquarters held little attraction for him. Then he spoke briefly of his experiences in the Peninsula with the green-jacketed Rifles of the Light Division, and she felt that he had known no happier times and, to him, they had been their own reward.

His pleasing manners and nice deference to her ladyship were most gentlemanlike, and nothing could have been more agreeable than his interest in Cherryanne's impressions of Bath until she mentioned her meeting with the Duchess of Evesham and Miss Winton. To her surprise, Lady Harpendene dismissed the subject in a few words and began talking of the excellent shooting to be had locally. Captain Ryder ably followed her lead, but Cherryanne could not but observe that he had become very pale and there was a pinched look about his nostrils as if he was under some severe stress of emotion, and it was with a distinct sense of relief that she rose to follow her grandmother into the drawing-room, leaving him to enjoy his port in solitude.

'Had I had the opportunity I would have warned you not to mention *that* connection,' Lady Harpendene said disposing herself comfortably by the fire and allowed Cherryanne to place a footstool for her. 'I don't know the full story, but there was something very havey-cavey about the whole affair. It was said by many that he is a fortune-hunter – and that I'll not believe of Athene Ryder's son! – and that he compromised the Winton girl in order to get her parents' consent to wed her. Then another story would have it that 'twas he who terminated the engagement because he could not stomach being franked by his wife – nearer the truth, I'd say. He seems a pretty enough behaved young man to me.' Cherry-anne, who had listened to these revelations in some astonishment, confessed that Captain Ryder had impressed her in much the same way and that, having met Miss Winton, she could not quite picture her being compromised by one who was plainly a gentleman unless she had a mind to it.

Lady Harpendene darted her a shrewd glance. 'Well, who knows but you may be in the right of it there. But let us turn to your case. Your letter said so much and yet not enough. If George was away from home, why this urgent need to leave Bath?' Miss Devenish enlightened her as much as she thought fit, and was relieved to learn that her grandmother was vastly interested in Sir Quentin's part in the business. 'Can't say I know anything to his discredit,' she admitted. 'But Her Grace of Evesham I knew as a girl, for your grandfather was at one time a close friend of her father, Lucilla Cavendish she was then, a pretty featherwit, but with charm in plenty. It came as no surprise when she snared Evesham's heir – rather a dull stick and with little but his title to commend him. I hear tell,' went on her ladyship, displaying a social knowledge not to be looked for in a dowager of advanced years, long out of society and allegedly enjoying indifferent health, 'that her son is as hey-go-mad as she.'

Miss Devenish sternly repressed the desire to inform her grandmama that the Marquis had also inherited his mother's looks and charm, but contented herself with saying that she had found the Duchess not to have the least height in her manner and that she was thought to be generally amiable.

'No doubt,' snapped her ladyship. 'When all's said, she's a Cavendish. The breeding is there. Sir Quentin Stratton, now,' she continued in a more reflective tone, 'from all accounts he is something of an out-and-outer, though not such a high-flyer as his cousin. What do you dislike in him?'

Miss Devenish, marvelling yet again at her grandmother's knowledge of a world in which she took no part, was at a loss to answer sensibly.

'I hardly know,' she said at last. 'Unless it is that he thinks so highly of himself that the importance of others is of no account to him.'

'Depend upon it, his wife's importance would be of great account to such a man. So why should he favour you?' Her ladyship's eyes sparkled with curiosity. 'For your aunt hinted at it – oh, well before Christmas, and in such matters she is no fool. She thought it but a passing flirtation, however, and has not mentioned it of late. What you say puts a rather different complexion upon the matter.' She stared thoughtfully into the fire, her thin, beringed fingers playing with the fringes of her shawl. 'I wonder if – '

Miss Devenish was not privileged to hear what had captured her grandmother's imagination for Captain Ryder had joined them and presently took his leave, protesting that Cherryanne must be fatigued after the hazards of her journey, and his parents surely gone to their beds before ever he set foot in their house.

He expressed his thanks so adroitly to Lady Harpendene for her hospitality, at the same time disclaiming any credit in disposing of the highwayman, that she was quite in charity with him, and graciously gave him leave to call at Chilcomb Manor whenever he pleased. She also extended a firm invitation to him to bring his parents to dine on whichever day in the week following would be convenient to them.

Miss Devenish, wondering a little at her ladyship's extreme amiability, accompanied him to the door and watched him secure his sabre while his helmet and gloves were being fetched. To her surprise, he spoke quickly in a low, constrained voice.

'Had you – did you meet Lord Shalford while you were in Bath, ma'am?'

'No,' replied Cherryanne with perfect truth. 'I had not that pleasure, sir.'

'Pleasure?' He almost spat out the word. 'Well, perhaps I wrong him.'

'What can you mean?' Instinctively, she bristled in defence of the Marquis.

'Nothing you could know about, ma'am,' he replied levelly. 'But his reputation is none too nice.'

'His mother seems devoted to his interest,' Cherryanne felt obliged to point out. 'And surely, Miss Winton –'

'Miss Winton has ever been tolerant of his – failings!' He stopped abruptly as if regretful of having said so much. Then he was bidding her good-night in the most natural manner, and promising himself the pleasure of calling again in the very near future. Miss Devenish made suitable reply and returned to the drawing-room, her mind a whirl of conflicting ideas.

'A well-set-up young fellow,' commented Lady Harpendene, who was leafing through the latest issue of the *Ladies Magazine*. 'Though, of course, regimentals always favour a good figure. Is Shalford as good-looking?'

'He's beautiful!' replied Cherryanne, the unexpectedness of the question throwing her quite off-balance. 'I – I mean his portrait depicts him as being very – very personable.'

'Like his mother no doubt,' nodded Lady Harpendene calmly, but she had missed nothing of her granddaughter's confusion and, as her maid prepared her for bed that night, she continued to speculate on what exactly had driven the girl to leave Bath in so precipitate a fashion.

Despite her constant complaints, the worst illness that afflicted her ladyship was boredom, and she had missed the company of her lively granddaughter more than she cared to admit, but she had no intention of allowing Cherryanne to abjure the fashionable world and bury herself in Chilcomb. The more immediate and important problem, however, was the question of Mr Marsden's behaviour. Clearly, he had put two and two together, and he was in a better position than any to judge of her circumstances. A better position, yes, but only she and her legal adviser knew the full extent of her fortune, nor could he know anything of the recent will she had made, however shrewdly he might guess, for she had employed a new young lawyer to draw it up for her as old Thwaites was muttering about retirement, and she had no use for his partner, a sly rogue if ever she saw one.

Then there was Sir Quentin to be thought on, a high stickler, so she had heard, and too confirmed a bachelor to lose his head over anything less than a fortune. Was it possible that the Marsdens had allowed some whisper of Cherryanne's expectations to drift abroad? Hardly likely, she concluded, if they wished their son to marry the girl. Nor did Cherryanne appear to relish his attentions, but no one was going to force her into marrying him and that she must well know. Why then so urgent a demand to be rescued from Bath?

It was not until she was drifting into sleep that she recalled her granddaughter's almost violent outburst at mention of Lord Shalford. Whatever had called that forth it was not just the sight of a portrait, her ladyship was in no two minds on that score. Somewhere she had met the Marquis and the meeting had been a memorable one. Nor had it taken place in Bath for then it would have been the most natural thing in the world to have spoken of it instead of twittering away about portraits. If one thought the matter out to its proper conclusion, there was but one person who had been in constant attendance upon Miss Devenish since her arrival in England and that was her loyal maid, Miss Bridget Hanrahan. If a meeting had taken place between her mistress and Lord Shalford, then Miss Hanrahan must certainly have been cognisant of it.

A slight smile touched her ladyship's thin lips. It would be unwise to speculate, she thought drowsily, but events would certainly bear watching.

CHAPTER
EIGHT

My lord of Shalford was in a thundering bad temper nor could he
account for it save by the fact of his having received a letter from
his mother that morning, telling him among other things that
Quentin appeared to have set his sights upon marriage to a charming young Irish lady, one Miss Charity Annabelle Devenish.

'Presumably', Her Grace had added, 'her expectations are
adequate, since I cannot conceive of Quentin's succumbing to the
tender passion.'

The Marquis's dark brows drew into a heavy scowl as he
crushed his mother's letter almost viciously in his long fingers.

'Adequate for Quentin, yes,' he muttered, 'but scarce in the style
of twenty thousand pounds a year, and I can hardly settle for less.'
His father had at last made known to him the extremely delicate
state of their finances and Damien, shocked beyond measure at
thought of the thin ice on which he and his mother had been
skating, had resolved to remain at Studleigh to take some of the
burden from the Duke's bowed shoulders. 'At all events, I cannot
go to Bath,' he pondered. 'It would sicken me to my soul to see
Quentin paying court to her. God! What a fool I am! What is she
to me or I to her that I should fear a meeting? Depend upon it,
it would be the very thing to set me right! I'd discover her to be
just another pretty pampered miss, and could wish Quentin success with hearty goodwill!'

But in his heart he was not so certain of the outcome of a second
encounter with Miss Devenish, so he remained at Studleigh.

That young lady was discovering that life could still provide
something of enjoyment for her, for the weather held clear and
springlike and with Captain Ryder and his sister to escort her
when riding or walking, and everyone in the neighbourhood
apparently bent on giving entertainment to enliven the captain's

stay, the days passed pleasantly enough. If ever she allowed her secret thoughts to dwell on Studleigh and the Marquis, she could reassure herself with the reflection that the one was all of ten miles distant, and the other, no doubt, in Bath attending on his lady.

It was one morning, some two weeks after her arrival at Chilcomb, when she was preparing to ride over to Cobblers, the Ryders' pleasant old house, to join her friends for their daily exercise, that a small boy came running with a message to say that Miss Caroline was confined to her room with a feverish cold and Captain Ryder had been summoned to London for a meeting with his Colonel-in-Chief, General Sir David Dundas. The day was so enticing Miss Devenish formed the opinion that it would be a great shame did she forego so pleasing a prospect, so she decided to say nothing to anyone but to continue on her way alone. Her grandmother, she had no doubt, would insist upon Kenyon accompanying her, which was not at all to her taste for he scarcely ever ventured above a canter and she loved to urge Betsy, the lively little mare that Lady Harpendene had given her, into showing off her paces whenever opportunity offered.

Quietly she trotted the mare out of the yard, nodding casually to Kenyon as if she was just riding over to Cobblers in her customary way, but no sooner was she out of sight of the house than she turned off the road and, jumping a low hedge, was away across country, pursuing a course which she had done on a previous occasion with the Ryders. Then Caroline, who was not as enthusiastic a horsewoman as she, had protested that she had no mind to be galloping for ever, so after going no more than three or four miles, they had turned back. Today, however, Miss Devenish was in no mood to turn back. It was a brilliant late February morning and Cherryanne could not help but respond to the beauty all around her. Lost in her thoughts, she allowed Betsy to make her own pace and so they went on, mile after mile, until, quite suddenly, she realized she was totally and irrevocably lost. Betsy, too, was blowing a trifle, as was not to be wondered at since she had covered a considerable distance at a steady pace since leaving Chilcomb.

Hearing the sound of water, Cherryanne dismounted and perceived a little stream disappearing between deep banks into what appeared to be an enclosed and wooded demesne. As there was no way for Betsy to get at the water outside the confines of the wood, Miss Devenish did not hesitate to explore until she found a gate through which she led the mare back to the stream.

The demesne was a neat and well-ordered place, with several tempting grassy rides radiating out from a small clearing through which the stream gurgled, its banks now sufficiently low for Betsy to be able to ease her thirst. As they stood by the water the sun became quite obscured, a few heavy drops of rain began to fall, and from the overcast skies there sounded an ominous rumble of thunder.

'Oh, no!' sighed Miss Devenish, looking about her for shelter and finding none under the leafless trees. 'Betsy, my love, we had best make a move from here. There must be a woodcutter's shed in which we can hide until this blows over.'

Betsy was in full agreement with her for the rain had intensified sharply and a flash of lightning, followed immediately by another clap of thunder gave clear warning that the storm was upon them.

Hastily re-mounting, Miss Devenish galloped down the widest of the rides but was forced to continue, getting wetter by the moment, for close on a mile, before she saw in front of her the dark immensity of a yew hedge, stretching as far as the eye could see in a deep curve in either direction. This afforded only slight protection as the rain was coming straight down with pitiless ferocity and Miss Devenish, mindful of the long ride home in a soaking wet habit, turned Betsy's head to the right where the ride followed the line of the hedge.

Just as she was despairing of ever finding shelter, she came upon an archway cut in the thickness of the yew and an iron gate set deep in its shadow. With a sigh of relief she dismounted and, pulling the now thoroughly nervous mare under the arch, looked about her.

Beyond the gate was laid out with exquisite precision an Italian garden, neat with box-trimmed walks and entirely shut in by the hedge save for the archway in which she was sheltering and a similar one on the far side, directly opposite to her. Through that farther opening she could glimpse the chimneys of a considerable mansion and promptly decided to seek assistance for, by this time, she was very wet indeed and the storm showed no sign of abating.

Leading the agitated Betsy, she crossed the garden and, on passing through the other gate, discovered that it, in its turn, gave on to a pleasing stretch of lawn, skilfully planted with groups of trees and shrubs, while to her left the stream, flowing away from the house, was spanned by a rustic bridge.

This aspect of the building, though clearly not the main frontage, was a most impressive one, having a large central terrace, protected by projecting bays, and paved in differing shades of grey and rose-coloured stone. Stone benches commanded a fine view across the wide lawns to where a suggestion of a further series of enclosed gardens was hinted at by other hedges of yew. No ordinary gentleman's residence this, reflected Miss Devenish as she mounted Betsy again and urged her towards a line of buildings, which promised to house the stable block, just visible past the long stone façade of the house. Had the circumstances been other than they were and her need of succour less desperate she must have suspected the identity of this imposing property, but all she could feel was relief when, on entering the stable yard, she encountered an elderly groom, crossing at the run with a sack over his head, who at once took Betsy's bridle and led her under cover.

'God's sakes, miss, ye're like a drowned rat!' he exclaimed in reproving tones as he helped her to dismount. Flicking back a sodden ostrich feather that had flopped over her left eye, Miss Devenish stood in a pool of her own making while he handed Betsy over to a lad with instructions to rub her down and give her a hot mash. 'That way she'll take no harm,' he promised. 'Now for you, miss, if ye'll follow me.'

Half-expecting to be treated in like manner, Miss Devenish, squelching at every step, meekly followed him by a covered way into the main house. Here they encountered a serving maid who was despatched with all speed to fetch the housekeeper so that, at the end of what seemed to Cherryanne to be endless miles of passages, she was greeted by a large, motherly female with innumerable keys depending from her girdle, who took one look at her and cried out in consternation.

'You poor young lady! Come with me, if you please, and allow me to make you more comfortable.'

Miss Devenish was only too willing to be made more comfortable and, in no time at all it seemed, she was being stripped of her outer garments and wrapped up warmly in a blanket. 'A hot mustard-bath, miss, is what I have ordered to be prepared for you. There's nothing better to stave off a chill, so you must sit in it until the damp has been soaked right out of you.'

'And very likely until I am as red as a lobster!' thought Miss Devenish ruefully but, submitting with a good grace, she followed her benefactress to an apartment wherein stood a vast hip-bath, placed before a blazing fire and with tall screens set discreetly about it. The room, which was long and narrow, with doors placed at either end, was stone-flagged and ill-lit by a few high, deep-set windows. Steaming buckets of water were being conveyed by footmen into the room, taken from them by two serving maids who then bore them round the screens and emptied the contents into the bath until it was so full that she feared to move lest the water should spill over the thick rug on which the bath was set, and so hot she could scarce breathe.

'There, miss, I'll leave you for a time now and see to your clothing.' The housekeeper, whose name Cherryanne had found to be Mrs Pritchard, gave an approving nod and set a pile of large, soft towels on a stool near to hand. 'No one will disturb you until I come back.'

After the good woman's departure the room became perfectly quiet save for the crackling of the logs in the wide fireplace and, insensibly, the stillness and the warmth contrasting so powerfully as they did with the noisy elements prevailing outside, worked upon Miss Devenish's weariness and her eyelids began to droop. Drawing up her feet, she let herself slide further down into the bath until only her head, covered by a mob-cap provided by Mrs Pritchard, and her knees remained visible.

Presently, as from afar off, she heard a door open and, with an effort, aroused herself, expecting to see the housekeeper's kindly countenance peering round the screens to enquire how she did. But the footsteps approaching her sanctuary were not those of Mrs Pritchard nor one of the maids, for it was a man's firm tread that sounded on the stone-flagged floor. Hastily she reached out for a towel and sat up again, clutching it to her nervously.

'Who-who is that?' she quavered.

'I beg your pardon if I intrude – good God!'

He had stepped round the side of the protecting screens and was staring at her in comical dismay. Cherryanne's heart gave a sickening lurch as she recognized the tall figure, dressed with careless elegance in riding-coat and buckskins, that she had last seen, half-clothed and more than half-cut, at the Winterslow Hut. Pulling the towel up even higher about her face so that only her eyes were visible between it and the over-large mob-cap, she thanked Heaven for the indifferent lighting and the impossibility of his recognizing her in such a guise – if, indeed, he remembered her at all.

'I g-got wet, you see, and Mrs Pritchard th-thought th-this the best thing for me!' she stammered in a very small voice.

'My poor child, forgive me!' The Marquis bowed himself out of sight behind the screens, but there was a laugh in his voice as he went on in a manner calculated to soothe her fears, 'You have all my sympathy, I know Pritchie's mustard baths of old! I am persuaded they saved my life on at least two occasions!'

Just then the door opened again and Mrs Pritchard's voice was heard, uttering in shocked accents, 'Master Damien! My lord! What can you be about?'

'Devil take it, Pritchie, could you not have warned me that you had an elf in a tub there? I've scared the life out of the poor child!'

'Poor child – ' Mrs Pritchard cast one look around the screens upon Cherryanne's shrinking and towel-enveloped form, then, nodding as if fully comprehending the situation, she took his lordship by the sleeve and led him out of the room, while Miss Devenish, heaving a profound sigh of relief, skipped nimbly out of the bath and set to drying herself vigorously and in great haste. Her relief would have been less complete had she been priviledged to overhear the conversation taking place outside the door.

'My lord, she's no child! 'Tis a young lady who was caught out in the storm, poor thing, and that habit of hers will not be dry in a se'ennight, so wet as it is. From near Winchester she comes, lives with her grandmama, I collect, and when I discover the old lady's direction I'll bid Watkins call there with a message for he's away to Winchester on business for His Grace within the hour.'

'A young lady, is she?' queried Damien with scant interest. 'But how is she to be got home if her clothes are as wet as you say?'

'I thought – there are some clothes of Her Grace's hanging up in her closet, old things she don't have much use for save when she is down here. She's taller, maybe, but a cloak and a round gown would suffice and, seated in a chaise, who's to see?'

'Who, indeed?' The Marquis sounded faintly bored. 'But it would be a sight quicker if I drove her in my curricle.'

'And got her soaked to the skin again? No, thank you, my lord, I'll not have her death on my hands!'

He laughed. 'Have it your own way, Pritchie. But she'll not be fit to venture out for several hours after your mustard infusion! Best offer her a meal.'

'I had in mind to do that, my lord,' said the housekeeper with quelling dignity. 'Will you be partaking of one today?'

'Cannot be certain but it is very unlikely, for all that I am so sharp-set I could eat an ox.'

Mrs Pritchard permitted herself to sniff. 'That is what comes of riding out before seven o'clock with nobbut an apple and a morsel of cheese in your belly!' she declared roundly, but the Marquis only laughed again and slapped her affectionately on her well-rounded haunch.

'Bless you, Pritchie, I love you! Now had it been you in that bath nothing would have held me back from tearing down the screens and flinging myself upon you!'

'Get along with you, Master Damien – my lord!' she expostulated, bridling. 'What nonsense you do talk, to be sure!' Then, as a thought struck her, she added: 'You didn't – she wasn't – ?'

'I did not and she was not!' he assured her solemnly. 'Never, alas, was bath-towel so decorously, if damply, draped around the female form!' He pulled out his gold repeating watch from his pocket. 'The devil! I must be away. Don't look for me before the dinner hour. Have a care for your little elf and send her home by whatever means you choose.'

With a wave of his hand he strode off, leaving Mrs Pritchard looking after him with an expression of resigned disapproval, then, shaking her head in affectionate exasperation, she returned to see how Miss Devenish was faring.

D

She found that young lady sitting by the fire, closely wrapped in every towel she could find and looking somewhat apprehensive. In order to soothe her presumably lacerated sensibilities, Mrs Pritchard assured her that his lordship had taken her to be a child and, in any case, no shadow of impropriety could attach to the incident since she herself had entered the room upon his heels. Miss Devenish appeared not to be greatly placated by these assurances and begged to be told if she had taken sanctuary in the Duke of Evesham's residence. When informed that this was the case and that there was no question of her setting out for home for several hours and then in borrowed clothes and in one of His Grace's carriages, she became almost distraught. The mere mention of lunch had her in a quake until the housekeeper promised her that His Grace was keeping to his room, not being in the best of health, and his lordship was gone out, Heaven knew where, and not likely to be seen before dinner-time.

When, at last, the heat of the mustard bath had subsided, her hair was dried and brushed until it shone, and she was arrayed in a most becoming loose robe of striped tabbinet over a flounced cambric petticoat, with a discreet tucker filling in the low-cut décolletage, and a handsome Norwich shawl draped over her shoulders.

Satisfied that her charge looked as fresh as could reasonably be hoped for, Mrs Pritchard led her to a delightful chamber on the first floor of the house, which commanded a fine view of the gardens and park. Here a dignified butler was putting the final touches to an appetising repast set out upon a circular rosewood table in the centre of the room and begged to be allowed to serve miss with whatever she fancied.

Miss had no hesitation in choosing mulligatawney soup, followed by a slice of cold turkey and a salad, and looked about her with the liveliest interest. She was surprised to discover that the room, though well proportioned and handsomely furnished enough, yet bore a slightly shabby and out-moded appearance. The Persian carpet was worn dangerously threadbare in places, while the faded brocade drapes were in need of new trimmings, as were several of the chairs. On the other hand, the mahogany and satinwood furniture, which mostly derived from the workshops of the great cabinet-makers of the last century, shone with a richness of colour that spoke of loving care and, unless Miss Devenish was greatly mistaken, she was eating off a service fashioned by Spode in their new Italian pattern which had greatly taken Lady Harpendene's fancy when it had first appeared the previous year, but which she had turned down as a needless extravagance for an elderly lady not given to entertaining.

The butler, having satisfied himself that her needs were attended to, withdrew discreetly and Cherryanne, her appetite whetted by her long ride and the happenings of the day, promptly got up from her chair by the fire and went to inspect the delicacies laid out on the table. She was considering the relative merits of cheesecake or anchovy toast, which was keeping hot on a plate-warmer, when the door opened behind her.

A trifle put out at being discovered in the act of helping herself, she picked up a plate and placed a piece of toast upon it in as composed a manner as she could contrive, when an amused voice said lazily: 'Ah, our waif of the storm, I presume? Forgive my joining you thus unexpectedly, but my morning's duties were quite washed out by the heavy rain. I trust my people are looking after you, ma'am?'

With a startled gasp she spun round to face him, the toast shot off the plate to land, anchovy side downwards on the carpet, while the plate slid from her nerveless fingers and, catching the edge of the table, broke clean in two before falling to the floor.

For a full ten seconds they stood, staring at each other, his face almost ludicrous in its expression of astonishment, hers flushed and horrified at the sight of him whom she had thought to be well away from the house.

'Cherry Ripe!' he breathed. 'It can't be – it *is*!'

'I – I've broken the plate!' she whispered in what she knew to be the most foolish manner and swiftly bent down to collect the pieces. At once the spaniel, which had entered at his master's heels, rushed forward to devour the tasty morsel and was promptly cuffed by the Marquis, who dropped to one knee to retrieve the toast and help collect the broken china. Wordlessly, they rose, he still staring disbelievingly at her, and placed the debris on the table while the spaniel, seizing his chance, crept between them to lick the carpet enthusiastically where the anchovy had rested upon it.

As if wishing to be assured that she was real and no phantom of his imagination, the Marquis grasped both her hands in so fierce a grip that, involuntarily, she winced.

'What are you doing here? Are you – were you the child in Pritchie's bath?' Still speechless, she nodded, her cheeks suffused with colour, and with a short laugh he released her. When he spoke again, his voice held that hard mocking note she so well remembered. 'Oh, my dear, what an opportunity was lost – or did your courage fail you at the last?'

That stirred her temper and loosed her tongue. 'I am not here of intent, that I promise you! I was quite lost and had no notion of what this house was. I had been told it was t-ten miles distant from Chilcomb.'

'Quite lost and ten miles from home? Oh, if you came across the fields no more than six or seven, I should suppose. But – un-attended, Miss Devenish?' He had picked up a bowl and was helping himself to soup with an air of unconcern. Miss Devenish, a little shaken to realize how odd her situation must appear, assumed an air of composure and reseated herself by the fire to eat a fresh slice of anchovy toast, while the spaniel, tail gently thumping, placed himself in front of her and watched every mouthful with pleading eyes. 'Or had you thought to look over what well might be your future residence?' went on that hatefully cold voice.

'I do not understand you, my lord.'

'I think you do, my dear.' Pulling up a chair, he sat beside her, smiling in the most amicable way though the smile did not reach his smouldering eyes. 'I learn from my mother that you are in daily expectation of receiving an offer from my cousin, Quentin. He is, after all, my heir.'

'But you, my lord, are betrothed to Miss Winton,' she protested, quite bewildered by his blatant hostility.

'True,' he agreed, savouring his soup as if he had no thought for anything else in the world. 'But that is, shall we say, a circumstance open to the caprices of nature. May I ask does Quentin know of our – ah, previous encounter?'

'Not through any word of mine!' she flashed back at him.

'Very wise,' he pronounced. 'Something of a high stickler, is dear Quentin. Could well hedge off if he got wind of our tripping in and out of each other's bedchambers.'

Miss Devenish choked slightly. 'If he – how can you – '

He looked at her with raised eyebrows. 'All most indiscreet, ma'am, I do assure you. I am persuaded he would not consider it at all proper conduct in his future wife.'

'It requires two to make such a contract, sir!' she retorted furiously.

'What? Do you tell me you would turn him down? Oh, Miss Devenish, how green do you suppose me to be?'

She sprang to her feet, thereby nearly putting a period to the life of yet another plate, eyes bright with anger. 'I don't suppose you to be anything, my lord, other than insufferably rude! Is such behaviour natural to you or is it merely assumed to – to humiliate me?'

'Rudeness, Miss Devenish,' said he coolly, setting down his soup-bowl, 'should always be intentional, otherwise it merely smacks of insensitivity. Pray be seated and allow me to give you some wine.'

'Thank you, no. I'll not inflict myself further upon your hospitality,' she retorted, trying for a self-possession to match his own. 'If you would be so kind as to summon Mrs Pritchard I will leave this house at once.'

'You cannot do that,' he reminded her as he hesitated over the choice of potted lobster or oyster patties, 'until I give permission for a carriage to be brought round for you.'

'I'll ride Betsy! I'll walk, if need be!'

Her desperation was so plain that it penetrated his angry resentment and, momentarily, his face softened.

'No, no, sit down. Forgive me.' He stood, looking at her in a sort of helpless fury. 'It's just that – that I had put the very thought of you from me – that I – ' He stopped, too late aware that he should say no more, that his incivility stemmed from the knowledge that she was not for him and he must do everything in his power to discourage such a connection, even to the point of making her take him in dislike. Which object, be it said, he was succeeding in admirably, for Miss Devenish was so incensed with him that she could not conceive how she could ever have thought him to have any sort of charm or address.

'You think I designed this meeting, do you not?' she blazed at him. 'That I arranged for a storm to burst over me so that I had to run for shelter here! Let me tell you, my lord, that had I wished to visit Studleigh I could have done so in a very different manner for not only am I acquainted with your mama, but my grandfather was well known to Her Grace's father. If Sir Quentin has in mind to offer for me he is not precisely scraping a wife from out of the gutter! Now, if you please, I will go home to my grandmother and tell her how I have been received by the grandson of her husband's friend. I doubt she will a find a tale a diverting one!'

That shaft went home, bringing the colour to his cheeks. 'Who is your grandmother?' he asked sharply.

'Lady Harpendene, and her husband – '

'Sir Giles, of course!' He snapped a finger and thumb. 'I remember him when, as a child, I used to stay with my Cavendish grandparents.'

'I am profoundly touched, my lord, that you should recall so humble an association!'

This biting sarcasm had the surprising effect of yet further soothing Damien's ill-humour. Believing it to be his duty to wed Honoria or some other wealthy young woman, he had endeavoured to put all thought of Cherryanne from his mind, but the sight of her in his own home, wearing his mother's clothes, had so shaken him off-balance that he had lashed out at her in a kind of frenzy, wanting to hurt her, to accuse her of trying to trap Quentin for the consequence and position he could bestow upon her, longing to hear her deny it and yet refusing to believe her when she did so. In short, his lordship was experiencing acute pangs of jealousy and had Sir Quentin walked into the room at that moment he would have met with a reception to surprise him, but as he did not and Miss Devenish was conveniently to hand, she was fated to be the recipient of the Marquis's bottled-up spleen.

But his fury had spent itself and, seeing her standing there, hurling defiance at him, while the tears sparkled in her eyes, brought him to a realization of how ill he had behaved.

'I beg of you, ma'am, to accept my most humble apology,' he said, sketching her a slight bow. 'Pray, be seated again and take a glass of wine with me to signify your forgiveness of my atrocious lack of conduct.'

Miss Devenish, however, was not so easily mollified. 'I have no wish to take wine with you, sir,' she returned. 'And do not touch me, if you please!' she added, backing away as he put out a hand to lead her to her chair.

He paused, half-smiling. 'Would you shoot me for it yet again?'

That put her in mind of the fact that she ought to be enquiring after his wound, but she was much too angry even to consider such a civility.

'I will have your pistol sent to you without delay, my lord. I have used it but once in repelling an attack from an – an assailant.'

'What?' He began to laugh. 'Another over-amorous admirer?'

'A footpad for whose churlishness some excuse might be made since he had not the advantage of a gentleman's upbringing. In any event, his designs were rather upon my possessions than my person.'

The Marquis's eyes flashed. 'You hit shrewdly, ma'am,' he drawled, then, pouring out two glasses of wine, he handed one to her.

For a moment she hesitated before, accepting the glass from him, she very deliberately tossed the contents full in his face. Quite taken aback by the swiftness of her action, he stood unmoving, and the sight of him with wine dripping down his cheeks put her so in mind of the first time she had seen him, standing in the rain, looking up at her outside the Winterslow Hut that, despite everything, she could not refrain from laughing.

As on that previous occasion, he erupted into sudden anger and took a step forward, his hands reaching out as if to seize her. Instinctively, she recoiled in alarm and there is no saying what might have happened next had not the butler chosen that moment to re-enter the room. Taking his handkerchief from his pocket, the

Marquis carefully dried his cheeks, his eyes never leaving her face.

''Fore God, ma'am,' he said softly, 'I wish Quentin well of you!'

Then he turned on his heel and was gone, leaving her standing with the empty wine-glass in her hand, looking remarkably foolish, and the butler staring after him in open-mouthed astonishment.

CHAPTER
NINE

Lady Harpendene welcomed her granddaughter home by giving her a tremendous scold, which was occasioned more by the anxiety she had experienced on Cherryanne's behalf than by any serious condemnation of her behaviour. She was all eagerness to learn what had passed at Studleigh but as she was engaged with the rector, Mr Gordon, who had called to solicit a subscription for the maintenance of the church, she had to contain her curiosity until his departure.

Beyond saying that she had received the most considerate treatment and that the Duchess's gown and cloak must be returned without delay, Miss Devenish seemed disinclined to dwell upon the incident.

'Did you encounter His Grace or any other member of the family?' Lady Harpendene demanded to be told.

'His Grace, so the housekeeper informed me, is keeping to his room on account of some indisposition. Lord – Lord Shalford did me the honour of joining me for a brief time at lunch.'

Oh-ho! thought her ladyship, so here we have the reason for those pale cheeks and refusal to discuss what, after all, must be a notable experience for a modest young lady. Aloud she said mildly : 'And did you find him to be as handsome as his portrait?'

'Oh, yes,' said Cherryanne tonelessly. 'He is excessively good-looking, as like to his mother as he can stare.'

'And of an obliging disposition?' Lady Harpendene, who had been engaged on a game of patience until disturbed by the rector's visit, gathered up her cards with a small sigh of exasperation .'I cannot conceive why I attempt this wretched game. It never comes out.'

'No, not in the least obliging!' Cherryanne could not conceal her resentment at the cavalier treatment the Marquis had accorded her. Her grandmother glanced at her sharply but was prevented from questioning her further by the sight of a phaeton turning in at the main gate and bowling smartly down the drive.

'Great Heaven, whoever else is calling at this hour of day?' she complained. 'You must receive 'em, I am going upstairs to change my dress for dinner.'

With that she swept out of the room, leaving Cherryanne to tidy the cards and fold away the table. She had hardly completed this task and was hastily smoothing the folds of her lavender blue crape gown when Lady Harpendene's butler announced:

'Mr George Marsden to see you, miss.'

'George! But I had thought you to be still in Grantham? It is not – oh, do not say that my aunt is in poor health?'

'No, no, nothing of that sort,' he assured her, kissing her hand with a nice assumption of gallantry. 'All in good fettle when I left 'em in Bath.'

'Bath? So you have been home?'

'Yes.' He looked around him anxiously. 'How is the old lady? Is she about?'

'She is perfectly well, I believe, and has this moment gone to her bedchamber to change her dress,' replied Miss Devenish, who had not failed to observe her cousin's somewhat secretive manner and wondered at it.

'Then we have a few moments. Cherryanne – oh, damme, I'm no fellow for pretty speeches and this ain't going to be a pretty speech anyway?'

'Well, come and sit down while you make it,' said his cousin sensibly. 'Shall I ring for wine?'

'No, I thank you. Waste of time. Not but that it wouldn't help me to say what I've got to say.' He tugged at his neckcloth which seemed to be restricting his utterance, while Miss Devenish eyed him with some concern. 'Thing is, m'father sent me.'

She nodded comprehendingly. 'No doubt to enquire after grandmama?' she suggested.

'Yes, that as well, of course, but – Cherryanne, will you do me – I mean – oh, the devil! Will you marry me?'

'George,' said Miss Devenish when she had recovered from

the initial shock of this bluntly worded proposal. 'You don't really want to marry me, do you?'

'No,' he confessed, then, realizing that so forthright a denial was hardly courteous, he hastily endeavoured to redeem himself. 'I daresay I'd best make a clean breast of it. You – you don't wish for me as a husband, do you, Cherryanne?'

'No,' agreed Miss Devenish, equally frank. 'But I want to know what all this signifies. You'd best tell me the whole, George, and quickly before grandmama comes down.'

'Yes, by Jupiter!' He eased himself on to the sofa beside her as smoothly as his modishly tight breeches would allow and mopped his gently perspiring brow. 'Depend upon it, she'll be as mad as fire when she learns about this.'

'When she learns about what?' asked the mystified Miss Devenish. 'Oh, George, do stop being so provoking! And why are you not still at Grantham? Aunt Maria had no expectation of your early return.'

'Yes, well, that's part of it, y'see.' Young Mr Marsden struggled on manfully, his face growing ever more crimson. 'She's – well, she's a world above me, of course, and odds on it, she won't have me.'

'Who? Aunt Maria?' Then, seeing the look of scorn he directed at her, light began to dawn on Miss Devenish. 'You've met a lady for whom you have conceived a profound admiration?' she suggested, endeavouring with difficulty to conceal her amusement.

'That's it!' assented George in huge relief at having his predicament so readily understood.

'Then why,' puzzled Miss Devenish, 'do you feel obliged to offer for me?'

'Because when I got home and told m'father, he'd have none of it. Said I had paid you very marked attention, sufficient to have led you to believe that I – in short, he said the only gentlemanly thing to do was to make you a proposal.'

'Fiddlesticks!' said Miss Devenish forcefully. 'You did not lead me into believing anything of the sort.' George ran a hand distractedly through his carefully arranged locks.

'I had to ask you to please m'father, otherwise there'll be no getting him to consent to my offering for Serena.'

'And if you offer for her without his consent he is not likely to make you a further allowance when you marry her?'

'There you have it!' said he, delighted at her ready understanding of the case. 'But if I go back and tell him you've turned me down – well, he's at a stand, ain't he?'

'But,' said Miss Devenish sweetly, 'I have not turned you down, George. Not yet, anyway.'

He stared at her, bewildered. 'B-but you don't wish to marry me! You said so.'

'That,' said his unpredictable cousin calmly, 'is a horse of another colour. I think there would be no harm in our having an understanding, quite a private one, of course, until we can accustom grandmama to the idea.'

George gulped. 'You – you'd best be careful what you're about, Cherryanne,' he warned her. 'Papa thinks you might well be receiving an offer from Quentin Stratton. It wouldn't do to be having an arrangement with me if he's dangling after you.'

'That's just what I have in mind,' said she crisply. 'George, if we keep our engagement quite private no word of it need reach your Serena's ears, need it?'

'Her father, Sir Geoffrey Wharton, is taking up a diplomatic appointment in Paris,' said George doubtfully. 'The family leave for France at the end of the week.'

Miss Devenish beamed upon him triumphantly. 'So they are most unlikely to hear of our – arrangement. I, of course, shall regard it as being of a sufficiently binding nature to oblige me to turn down any other offer I may receive. This surely must appease your father and, when later we find that we do not deal together, you will have performed your part and he cannot then reasonably withhold his approval from your paying your addresses to Miss Wharton.'

George was of the opinion that there was something deuced smoky about the whole business, but could not quite put his finger on it.

'If you don't care to marry Stratton, you've only to say so,' he pointed out. 'Though, mind me, Cherryanne, he's a famous catch. You would be quite totty-headed not to take him.'

But Miss Devenish was lost in her devious plans and scarcely heard this sapient piece of advice. 'You need not be bound to me for long, you know, just for a sufficient length of time to show that I do not choose to marry Sir Quentin. You see,' she elaborated, 'if he offers for me and I refuse him, who's to know of it? He certainly will not tell and I cannot.'

'No one would believe you if you did!' remarked George with some truth.

'Just so. So you see – '

'No, I do not! Why must everyone know that you won't have him? Stratton's no favour:te of mine, but I call that behaving a bit shabby.'

Miss Devenish bit her lip. She could hardly tell her cousin that she had but one person in mind when planning this deception, and why it should be so imperative to ensure that the Marquis knew she had decided against marrying Sir Quentin she could not, as yet, be perfectly certain. Of one thing only was she assured, that Lord Shalford was the most odious, disagreeable, ill-mannered creature it had ever been her misfortune to meet and it was her intention to bring home to him very clearly that she had no wish to be allied to him or to any member of his family. As for poor Miss Winton, she could only sympathize with her in her misfortune at being betrothed to such a Monster and wonder how she found the fortitude to support it. Furthermore, it was not to be supposed that Mrs Marsden would keep silent when she was informed of her son's engagement to her niece. The news must eventually filter through to the Pump Room and so to Her Grace's ears, and how much kinder it would be for Sir Quentin to hear of it in such fashion and be saved the humiliation of a rebuff. And, unless her appreciation of his character was far and wide, that would be the end of the matter. She had shown a preference for George and, even if she did not carry through her intention, the Stratton pride would never accept the position of second-best.

She became aware that George was regarding her in a very suspicious way and hastened to account for her conduct.

'It's grandmama, you understand,' she explained, marvelling at her own duplicity. 'She thinks so highly of all the Stratton family she – well, if I did not accept Sir Quentin, I am persuaded she would be vastly displeased. But I cannot accept him if he don't offer, can I?'

George shook his head. 'It won't answer, Cherryanne. It will displease her a sight more if you get engaged to me.'

'So, of course, we must win her over.'

'Small hope of that,' he assured her.

'Then, in time, we will have to yield in the most affecting way. Oh, George, do please oblige me in this!'

In her anxiety she had clasped his arm and was gazing up into his troubled countenance when Lady Harpendene's voice startled them both to their feet.

'What is all this? George, what brings you here?'

'To – to enquire after your health, ma'am,' gasped her flustered grandson. 'If – if I may say so, you look to be in prime twig!'

'You may not say so!' she retorted irascibly. 'Prime twig, indeed! Such misuse of the English language is enough to make Dr Johnson turn in his grave!'

'Indeed, ma'am? Er – friend of yours, was he?'

At this juncture, Miss Devenish, seeing that George was doing his cause no good at all, tactfully intervened. 'George also came to see me, grandmama,' she said demurely.

'Why, may I ask?'

'To make me an offer of marriage,' said Miss Devenish, and waited for the explosion. To her amazement, none came. Lady Harpendene seated herself in her accustomed chair and surveyed her two grandchildren with an almost benign air.

'And what did you answer him, miss?' she enquired mildly.

'I – I gave him to understand that, if the proposal had your approval, I – I would be happy to oblige him,' stammered the vastly taken aback Miss Devenish.

Lady Harpendene pursed her lips thoughtfully as if considering the idea from every angle. 'Not the best match in the world for you,' she said at last. 'But George has a reasonable competence and, no doubt, his father, in gratitude at seeing him safely shackled, will improve upon it.'

'He – he spoke of allowing me two thousand a year, ma'am.' George's large blue eyes were fixed upon his grandmother as a rabbit's might when fascinated by a stoat.

'Then I make no doubt you will do very well,' said Lady Harpendene, as if that settled the matter, 'and, if you have a mind for it, I shall do over the old Dower House and give it you for a wedding present.'

Miss Devenish wondered if her brain had not been a trifle addled by the emotional strains to which she had been subjected during the past twenty-four hours. Somehow she found words to thank her grandmother, but she could not help but compare Lady Harpendene's acceptance of her betrothal to George with her expressed opinion when her granddaughter had hinted earlier at the possibility of such a happy outcome. Then her ladyship had declared that nothing would persuade her to lend countenance to the match, now it seemed she was all complaisance. Catching George's agonized expression, Cherryanne took his hand and, pressing it significantly, said that at present they had no intention of making their engagement public.

'Why ever not?' asked Lady Harpendene blandly.

Miss Devenish found herself at Point-Non-Plus. There was, indeed, no reason in the world why the announcement should not be made since her grandmother had no objection to it. She was about to advance some feeble argument about obtaining her mother's approval when she perceived, through the gathering dusk, the lights of a carriage coming towards the house.

'We – we appear to have another caller,' she ventured nervously. 'Whoever can this be, I wonder?'

'Some neat article in search of a meal!' snapped Lady Harpendene, tugging the bell-pull vigorously. 'We will dine at seven o'clock – and don't tell me that ain't time and enough for you to change your dress,' she added to her dumbfounded grandson who had no intention of telling her anything of the sort, 'for tonight it must suffice. Metchett,' she said to her butler when he appeared in answer to her ring, 'see that Mr George has everything he requires and you will please deny me to any other callers.'

'Yes, m'lady.'

As the butler led the unhappy Mr Marsden away, an imperative knocking sounded on the front door. Lady Harpendene raised her eyebrows slightly but, beyond remarking that some people had no notion of time, paid little attention. For her part, Miss Devenish hardly knew what to say and was almost grateful when her grand-mother commented in her forthright way.

'A pity George affects such singularity in dress. It makes him look a perfect ninny since to be attracting attention in such a manner requires neither sense nor taste but, doubtless, he would rather be taken for a fool than not be noticed at all.'

'Grandmama,' said Cherryanne desperately, 'if you hold so poor an opinion of George why are you willing for me to marry him?'

'Come to that, miss,' said Lady Harpendene grimly, 'why have you now decided he will make you a proper husband when but two weeks ago you expressed yourself forcibly to the contrary?'

Miss Devenish was saved the trouble of accounting for this reversal of her opinions by the entry of her ladyship's footman, who begged pardon if he had done wrong but the gentleman, when informed that Lady Harpendene was not receiving, had requested that his card be carried to Miss Devenish in the hope that she might spare him five minutes of her time.

'He is on his way to Studleigh, m'lady, and wishful to be there for dinner,' went on Roger, anxious to justify so late and munifi-cent a caller. All very well for old Metchett to hiss at him to admit no one, but a guinea was a guinea, look at it how you would, and such generous vails did not often come Roger's way.

At mention of Studleigh all vestige of colour had left Miss Devenish's cheeks but, fortunately, Lady Harpendene was too exasperated to notice and snatched up the card from the salver proffered by the footman.

'Sir Quentin Stratton,' she read out and turned an enquiring eye towards her trembling granddaughter. 'Hmm. Well, since he is here I suppose it only civil to receive him.'

Roger heaved a sigh of relief and slid from the room, thanking the saints that he had escaped a trimming, while Miss Devenish, wondering what further surprises Fate had in store for her, thought it advisable to seat herself hurriedly lest her knees should cease to support her, and directed an expectant gaze upon the door.

Sir Quentin, ushered into the long drawing-room by an obsequious Roger, was a shade taken aback to be confronted by an imperious-looking dowager, wearing an old-style stomacher front gown of black bombazine, with long sleeves of embroidered book muslin; her silver head crowned by an intimidating turban, ornamented with jet and black velvet.

'Forgive my denying myself to you at first asking, Sir Quentin,' said this regal personage, extending him her hand on which flashed a profusion of rings, 'but I had not understood you to be an acquaintance of my granddaughter's.'

'The apologies must be all on my side, ma'am,' said he, not to be outdone in courtesy. 'My only excuse must be my anxiety to waste no time in learning how you and Miss Devenish go on and to request if I may have the honour to present myself again at a more acceptable hour.'

Lady Harpendene positively beamed upon him. 'You will take a glass of wine with us, sir,' said she in a tone which brooked no argument. 'Roger, the best sherry, if you please, and the Sercial Madeira.'

'Yes, m'lady,' muttered Roger and removed himself with all speed to be confronted by Metchett who demanded to be told by what right he had admitted the gentleman against her ladyship's strict command.

' 'Twas Miss Devenish he asked to see, and her ladyship is not displeased at all, I'd say,' retorted Roger smugly. 'I'm to fetch wine.'

'Then I'll take it in, my lad, and you can get about your duties in the dining-room! Is the gentleman likely to stay for dinner, d'you know? There's naught but alamode beef and a tansy pudding and Mr George to be reckoned on.'

'Said he was on his way to Studleigh to dine,' Roger threw back over his shoulder as he went in search of the wine. Metchett sighed in relief. Mr George, being family, was not of great moment; provided he got enough to eat he scarce noticed what went down his throat, but this other gentleman was a different kettle of fish. Real quality and of some consequence from the glimpse Metchett had of him as Roger had ushered him in and, as like as not, come a-courting Miss Cherryanne. At thought of that the old man hurried after Roger for, beyond doubt, the young fribble would not think to set out the best glass nor rub up the tray and the bottle-tickets before he brought them up.

Meanwhile, Sir Quentin was greeting Miss Devenish and making her a mighty pretty speech on her appearance.

'The country air, I have no doubt, is responsible for those glowing cheeks,' he complimented her, appreciating the charming picture she presented in her blue gown with its crisp white frilled collar outlining her lovely face.

Lady Harpendene was privately of the opinion that her grand-daughter's high colour could be attributed to other causes than the salubrious Hampshire air, and her sharp eyes took in every detail of her visitor's person. Elegant of form, fashionable in his apparel and with a smooth tongue, she understood very well why Cherry-anne had taken him in dislike. He was too much the finished article to please her, so sure of himself it made one positively itch to give him a good set-down. But why had she felt driven to attach herself to George?

An illuminating discussion with Miss Bridget Hanrahan, during the course of which certain suspicions had been confirmed and Bridie left in no doubt that Miss Devenish had already confided to her grandmother the relevant details of the affair at the Winters-low Hut, had given Lady Harpendene the notion that her grand-daughter might be playing a deep game, though whether it was being undertaken out of spite or from some more commendable emotion she could not be perfectly certain.

'I had hoped to persuade Miss Devenish to visit my racing stables which are situate not many miles from here,' Sir Quentin was saying. 'I have one or two likely beasts in training for the Newmarket Meetings and, I confess, despite my friend Osbaldes-ton's disapproval, a few steeplechasers.'

'While racing on the flat can only afford delight to the onlooker, the whole conception of a steeplechase is repugnant to me,' stated Lady Harpendene firmly, 'though it surprises me that such a valiant rider to hounds as Mr Osbaldeston is against it.'

'Can I prevail upon you, ma'am, to join us in looking over my animals?'

'Thank you, no.' Her ladyship had no intention of being carried over the ground too fast. 'But my grandson, George Marsden, is staying with me and, I am sure, would be happy to be of your company.'

Sir Quentin was well aware of George's presence at Chilcomb. A chance encounter with Mrs Marsden the previous day had elicited the information that her first-born was paying his grand-mama a long overdue visit.

'It will be comfortable for my niece to have George to attend upon her,' she had prosed on in her languid way. 'Though from what my mother tells me, she does not lack for company. Captain Jeremy Ryder, the son of near neighbours, is, it would seem, devoting much time to her entertainment, as are other young gentlemen in the district.'

Sir Quentin had murmured that such a circumstance was only to be expected when the lure was so tempting, but the mention of Jeremy Ryder had alerted him to the dangers of the situation. Captain Ryder had failed in his attempt to secure Honoria Winton's fortune, what could be more likely than that he would now try his luck with Miss Devenish? The possibility of being beaten to the post by a short head by either George or Captain Ryder did not commend itself to Sir Quentin, and he immediately formed the intention of going to look over his stables and judge of the position for himself.

'Mr George Marsden will be most welcome should he care to join us,' said he, at his most urbane, and Miss Devenish found herself with nothing to say other than to thank him for his civility and determine upon a day agreeable to both parties.

When Sir Quentin took his leave a little later, it was in the comfortable conviction that, if George had come to Chilcomb to declare himself, he either had not screwed his courage up to the necessary pitch, or his cousin had given him an unfavourable reply. In any event, Sir Quentin thought himself to be very neatly placed and resumed his journey to Studleigh well pleased with his situation.

CHAPTER
TEN

'No, George, I think it only right that you should at least hint of our – our arrangement to Sir Quentin. I cannot feel it to be at all the thing to be accepting his hospitality under false colours.'

'Damme, I hardly know the fellow!' exploded young Mr Marsden with understandable irritation. 'To be confiding in him what is supposed to be a private family matter is doing it a bit too brown!' Two days had elapsed since George's descent upon his grandmother's household and the cousins were riding over on the prearranged date to view Sir Quentin's stables. 'I have a better notion,' said George suddenly. 'Odds on't Shalford will be there today. I know Shal well enough to drop a word in his ear and he'll warn Stratton off.'

Miss Devenish thought this to be a capital notion, though the very possibility of being again confronted by the Marquis set her heart racing in the most disturbing way.

'You promise to stay close to me!' she implored.

George grinned. 'As close as a lover!' he vowed.

'That is what you are supposed to be!' she reminded him tartly, and his smile faded.

'How long do we have to keep up this charade?' he grumbled. 'Grandmama don't seem to care a fig for our attachment, and she ain't handing over any of her blunt. Unless your mother raises some objection – and you've owned that to be most unlikely – there'll be nothing against our making the announcement, and then we'll be in the suds. At least, I shall be because Serena cannot fail to hear of it.'

Miss Devenish mentally apostrophised the unknown Miss Wharton. 'The sooner you can get Shalford's ear, the sooner we can terminate our engagement,' she said encouragingly. 'If not today, could you not ride over to Studleigh tomorrow on some pretext? Then we can quarrel over some trivial thing and I can ring such a peal over you that will send you back to Bath or London, vowing never to return. Well, perhaps not quite like that, but I shall think of something!' Mr Marsden was understood to mutter that that was precisely what he was afraid of, but their conversation was cut short by the sight of two riders approaching them across the fields and Miss Devenish's joyful exclamation of surprise. 'Why, it is Captain Ryder and his sister, Miss Caroline! You are to meet them tonight at dinner, you know.'

'And that's another thing,' said George darkly. 'Why, if you please, was grandmama so insistent upon Stratton returning to dine with us? It's my opinion that she wants to show me up in his company and prove to you what a poor choice you have made.'

Miss Devenish thought this to be more than likely but there was no time to be pondering on Lady Harpendene's curious behaviour for the next few minutes were taken up with presenting George to her friends and enquiring after Miss Ryder's health.

'Why, Caroline, I declare I have never seen you in such good looks!' she cried, clasping her friend's hand with warm affection.

'Indeed, to look at you, ma'am, no one could suppose you to be recovering from an indisposition,' confirmed George, who clearly was greatly taken with the young lady's appearance. This was not to be wondered at, for Caroline Ryder, if not regularly handsome, possessed a sweetness of expression and a delicacy of complexion beyond what was usual.

To Cherryanne, cosing in the most friendly way with Captain Ryder as they rode behind the other two, it was plain that George could find no fault with his companion, and she was moved to hope that his passion for his Serena was not destined to be of a lasting nature. The chill wind had prompted her to wear a short cloak of the same russet cloth as her habit, and into the pocket of this she had slipped the Marquis's pistol, for she was resolved to lose no opportunity of returning it to him and she could hardly despatch someone to Studleigh with it without some explanation of how she had come by it.

As she rode, she could feel it bumping gently against her thigh, a constant reminder of his lordship and of a passage in her life which held for her none but the most unhappy memories. Never would she allow her thoughts to dwell more on such an odious creature! So disorderly was her state of mind on this subject that it did not occur to her that to be handing over a pistol to a gentleman with whom she was presumed to have had but one chance encounter might well occasion comment, and how else to dispose of the weapon was difficult to imagine.

After a short time the quartet's paths diverged, the Ryders turning back to Cobblers and the cousins continuing on their way to Otterbourne. They parted with mutual expressions of delight at the prospect of improving their acquaintance later in the day – George, indeed, could not keep his tongue off Miss Ryder for the rest of their journey, and Cherryanne noted with secret satisfaction that no mention was made of leaving Chilcomb in the near future.

Sir Quentin, all gratifying attention, was awaiting their arrival, and George's breezy enquiry about the Marquis elicited the reply that his lordship was engaged on a tour of the estates since it was his intention to remove to Bath within the next day or so. Miss Devenish hardly knew whether to be pleased or not by this information but, as they sat down to a nuncheon, the excellence of which led her to suspect it had come straight from the Studleigh kitchens, she fancied she caught a speculative look in her host's eye as it rested upon her, but put it down to George rather overplaying his part and assuming a markedly possessive manner.

Did she but know, Sir Quentin's doubts sprang from a very different source. It was not until after dinner on the previous evening, when the Duke had retired to his room and the two younger gentlemen were alone, that he had mentioned calling in at Chilcomb on his way to Studleigh. For an instant, he had glimpsed an expression on the Marquis's face that had caused him to feel a trifle uneasy.

'I have made the acquaintance of your lady,' Damien had drawled, stretching out his long legs to the fire. 'A taking little piece, I'll give you that.' As he related how Cherryanne had been forced to take shelter at Studleigh, Sir Quentin's sense of unease intensified. Why had not Miss Devenish spoken of this? Did she hope the episode would pass unnoticed? Damien's next words supported this last theory. 'Pure chance, would you say? Or a natural curiosity to view the house she might well be mistress of one day? If I had not been at home, none of us need have known of her visit. She did not tell you of it?'

'There was scarce time, my call was so brief.' Sir Quentin was treating of the matter very lightly. 'And, perhaps, she did not wish for her grandmother to know of her peregrinations for, I'll warrant, the old lady would give her a rousing set-down for venturing so far unattended.'

'As I understand Pritchie sent a message to Lady Harpendene to apprise her of Miss Devenish's whereabouts, that cock won't fight,' pointed out Damien sweetly. Sir Quentin, however, refused to be drawn.

'I protest you make too much of what was no more than an unfortunate mishap,' said he, dismissing the incident as of little importance. But later that night, on returning to his room, he had spoken long and quietly to his valet.

The following day produced some interesting results of these deliberations. Lord Shalford had suffered a wounded shoulder during his stay at the Winterslow Hut, no one knew quite how it had occurred, and one of a pair of fine pistols had disappeared. Foster, his lordship's valet, had been shut up very sharply when he had remarked on the loss. The wound had been explained away as an accident which had taken place during the confusion caused by the lioness's attack, but Foster still harboured a degree of resentment at not having been taken into the Marquis's confidence. More than that, being a loyal servant, he was not prepared to divulge, and certainly not to Sir Quentin's man who, though he contrived to turn his master out in a very creditable fashion in spite of some glaring shortcomings, was a frippery fellow when all was said, and hardly an adornment to his calling.

Sir Quentin, less censorious than Foster, was prepared to suffer Harding's occasional lapses in sartorial matters in order to enjoy the benefit of his sharp ears and sharper tongue, and his interest had been vastly stimulated by Foster's admissions. It was to be even further titillated when he gallantly offered to take Miss Devenish's cloak and stepped out of the room where their meal had been set for them to lay it on a bench. The weight of the pistol aroused his curiosity and, putting his hand in the pocket, he drew it out.

'Oh-ho!' he murmured. 'Now why does the lady require to carry a weapon? Does she fear her cousin – or me? A mighty handsome affair it is, too, one of Manton's, I'll wager.' He held the pistol in his hand, his fingers caressing the walnut stock, inlaid with silver, then an exclamation escaped him as he felt, just above the brass gilt mount, the entwined letters DS. ' 'Fore God, Shalford!' he breathed, knowing it to be the Marquis's invariable practice to set his initials on his weapons, and at once recalled the tale of a missing pistol. He stood for a moment, lost in thought, and the expression on his face was not a pleasant one. When he returned to the room a moment later however, he was once more the solicitous host, and Miss Devenish was forced to admit that she had never liked him half so well.

The stable buildings were most agreeably set in the midst of well-timbered parkland. They were flanked on the one side by a big, old-fashioned house which served as lodgings for the grooms and stable-boys, and on the other by several amply stocked fish-ponds. The property, Sir Quentin was obliging enough to explain, he leased from his uncle, though it was not part of the main Studleigh estate.

'Shalford's interest lies in the Hunt rather than in the Turf, and in his driving cattle, so I thought it best to be away from all that, for he often houses as many as twelve couple of hounds at Studleigh for his own pleasure, though he mostly hunts with Beaufort's pack.'

'I'd hoped that Shal might be here today,' remarked George, who was enjoying himself hugely. 'Haven't set eyes on him in an age.'

Sir Quentin consulted his watch. 'In fact he should not be very far distant at this moment,' he said, 'for I know he has a meeting with his agent at five o'clock, and his last call was to have been at a farm not three miles from here. Should you care to seek him out, I can take Miss Devenish up in my phaeton, while my groom could ride her mare and guide you to the farm and from thence on to Chilcomb.'

'Oh, capital!' George was full of enthusiasm for the scheme,

Miss Devenish understandably less so. While on the one hand she was eager for George to speak to the Marquis, on the other she could not relish a tête à tête with Sir Quentin. That gentleman was quick to reassure her.

'My groom can carry your saddle for so short a distance,' he told her kindly. 'Don't be thinking we will have that obstruction placed between us for all of the way.'

Miss Devenish would have been very glad of any obstruction placed between them but found herself unable to raise objection to the arrangement. Presently the party moved off, George quite oblivious to her appealing glances and believing himself to have contrived the matter very neatly.

It was not until he had turned off to the farm, accompanied by the groom riding Betsy, that Cherryanne was put in mind of the pistol and the impossibility of now disposing of it. Then it was that she found it no longer reposed in the pocket of her cloak. So alarmed was she by this discovery that she was quite unable to pay attention to what Sir Quentin was saying and replied so little to the point that he rallied her lightly upon it.

'Twice have I made the most unexceptionable observations,' he remonstrated, 'to which, I fear, you have paid scant attention. What is it, Miss Devenish? What troubles you?'

'N-nothing!' stammered Cherryanne. 'It – I – it will pass.'

'You are not concerning your pretty head over the slight impropriety of our situation, alone together unattended?' he enquired. 'Lady Harpendene will not care for it, I daresay, but I flatter myself I can persuade her to accept me as a proper escort for her granddaughter in any circumstances.' Then as she shook her head, nervously dreading what might be coming next, he went on softly, 'Is it, perhaps, some displeasing recollection that is causing you unease? Have no fear! I assure you that it is not in the least likely that we shall be set upon by a lioness!'

She turned a startled face towards him. 'I had no such notion in my head, sir, I do assure you!'

'Had you not, Miss Devenish? Then why the need for this?' He drew out the pistol from his pocket and laid it between them.

'Oh, th-that!' said she, essaying a little laugh to prove her indifference to questions concerning pistols or lionesses, 'I have got into the way of carrying a weapon ever since I was accosted by a footpad – did you not know of that affair? No, indeed, how should you.'

'It seems,' he remarked, pleasantly enough, 'that you have had many adventures of which I know nothing.' Hastily, she recounted the details of her first meeting with Captain Ryder, and he nodded as if satisfied. 'As intrepid as you are beautiful, it would appear, but – maybe a shade unwise on occasion?'

'W-what can you mean, sir?' she got out, clasping her hands tightly together to stay their trembling.

'How does it come about, Miss Devenish, that you are defending yourself with one of my cousin's pistols?'

Cherryanne prayed that the ground would be obliging enough to open up and swallow her, Sir Quentin, the carriage and all, but quite understood that nothing so unlikely could be hoped for. 'He – he left it behind him at the Winterslow Hut,' she said at last in a very low voice.

'So you did chance upon each other there? How strange that neither should have spoken of it. How very strange!'

'I did not know who he was then,' she whispered.

'And you found out – of course! When you saw his portrait in Her Grace's house in Bath. I had thought you to be somewhat discomposed that afternoon but put it down to another source. How very imperceptive of me.'

She could not care for the note of sarcasm in his voice, quite unlike his usual softly modulated tones. 'I – I do not understand you, sir.'

'I think you do, Miss Devenish.' He drew the bays to a stand and turned to face her, the reins lightly clasped in one hand, clearly enjoying himself. 'What a famous game you have been playing with me, my dear! And being overtaken by a storm so as to be forced to seek shelter at Studleigh – as neat a way of arranging an assignation as ever I've known! Or is his lordship proving fickle in his attentions so that you had to – ah, jog his memory?'

'No, no!' she burst out. 'It was not so, I assure you! How could I have foreseen the storm or that Lord Shalford would be there or – or – '

'Or that he would come upon you in your bath – a pretty touch, 'pon my word!'

'He told you that?' she half-sobbed, hands pressed to burning cheeks.

'No, give my rakehell cousin his due, he'd not betray a lady. But servants are not always so dainty in their ideas. It would surprise you to learn the memories a shilling can recall. Answer me one thing, Miss Devenish. Why did you feel obliged to shoot him at Winterslow?' Her face gave him the confirmation he needed. 'So you did, eh? My felicitations, my dear, 'tis no wonder he does not care to speak of it! Too forward, was he? But you must know his reputation – had you in mind to pique him, to excite his interest, by a show of resistance? Young blades such as Shalford rarely meet with opposition.'

'Sir Quentin,' she broke in desperately, 'you wrong me, you wrong us both. Nothing passed between Lord Shalford and I that – that outraged the proprieties.'

'Don't gammon me!' His voice was suddenly harsh. 'D'you think I don't know Shalford? Oh, I allow you may have been more sinned against than sinning, but if you put a bullet through him it was for a good reason, I'll be bound! I am sure Miss Winton will understand that, too. And your grandmother.'

'Oh, please!' she exclaimed involuntarily. 'Don't tell them! It all sounds so much worse than it was.'

He sighed sympathetically. 'These things do, I always find, and never redound to the lady's credit however innocent she may be. An unpleasant business, is it not?'

Miss Devenish had to admit that it was. And Shalford, the cause of all her misery, would merely shrug and look inexpressibly bored, for he would not suffer, of that she was certain. It was the accepted thing for gentlemen to have irregular connections and Miss Winton must have been well aware of the Marquis's rakish reputation when she became engaged to him. She was roused from her gloomy cogitations by Sir Quentin's quiet laugh.

'You have the solution to hand, my dear. I want you for my wife. What fairer can I say? Shall you make me a truly happy man?'

'And still your tongue?' she flashed back, edging away from him as he stretched out a hand to her.

'Would I set up a scandal-broth about my wife? What a fool you think me! Nor can I believe you have been more than indiscreet – but to choose Shalford as your partner in such impropriety is enough to black your name. If you marry me you will be as Caesar's wife, above reproach. Come, my pretty kitten,' he went on coaxingly, 'let us have no more holding off.'

Before she was aware of his intention, he had relinquished the reins and had seized her in a close embrace. She felt the warmth of his body pressed against her and smelled the slightly musky odour of the scent he wore.

'Sir, I beg of you!' She struggled to free herself. 'This is no way to treat a gentlewoman! It – it is not seemly!'

'No?' he murmured, bending his head to hers. 'Is not a lover permitted some little familiarity?' She opened her mouth to cry out but any sound was effectively stifled by his lips. Her right hand, groping desperately to obtain some leverage against him, closed over the barrel of the pistol, lying forgotten between them. She knew it to be unprimed but retained her hold on it until he had left off kissing her and sat up to straighten his neckcloth. 'Shall we continue on to Chilcomb, ma'am?' he asked coolly. 'And acquaint Lady Harpendene with our intention of being wed? Will she take to the notion kindly, d'you think?'

Miss Devenish thought that her ladyship would most likely consider her granddaughter to have taken leave of her senses in getting herself betrothed to two gentlemen in as many days. In any case, she was quite resolved that, cost her what it might in loss of reputation and future content, she would never marry Sir Quentin, so, as he turned away to gather up the reins, she lifted the pistol and brought the butt down upon his temple with all the force of which she was capable.

Taken unawares, he gave no more than a startled grunt before toppling over into the road. The bays, sensitive to the lack of control and fretting at their bits, needed no further incentive to move off. Before she could take them in control they had broken into a gallop and it was all she could do to save herself from being thrown out after Sir Quentin. They were spirited but beautifully light-mouthed beasts and Miss Devenish, who was a very fair whip, was getting them nicely in hand and beginning to debate whether she ought, in all charity, to turn back to see how her late escort did, when she was confronted by a flock of sheep, accompanied by many newly-born lambs, straying all over the road in the care of a country fellow who could do no more than remove the straw from his mouth and gaze at the approaching vehicle in fascinated horror. His dog, however, had other ideas and very properly came rushing forward to ward off any attack upon his charges.

This put Miss Devenish in something of a quandary for it was plain that the bays disliked having their heels snapped at and were so hot at hand that she doubted her ability to hold them much longer. To her immense relief, a track opened up upon the left and, aided by the persistent dog, the phaeton lurched about and the equipage shot up the narrow defile at breakneck speed. She was dimly aware of a voice calling out behind her but was far too concerned with trying to hold the now thoroughly agitated horses to pay any attention. As the track widened and there appeared to be no likelihood of being faced with another vehicle in so desolate a spot, she decided to give her pair their heads and let them run themselves out.

Three minutes later she perceived her mistake in so doing for the track led direct to a disused quarry and they were almost on the brink of it before the horses responded to her frantic efforts to restrain them. But this time the turn was too sharp, the track too rough, and the carriage swung over on its side on the very lip of the quarry. The last coherent recollection Cherryanne had for a long time was of herself spinning through the air while the terrified horses fled on as best they could, hampered as they were by the overturned vehicle.

From a distance away, a solitary horseman riding across a high ridge saw the phaeton burst out from behind a patch of brushwood and wondered at its curious behaviour. Then, with a muttered expletive, he swung his horse's head in that direction and galloped at full stretch down the sweep of hillside. The bays were at a stand when he got to them; sweat-lathered and trembling, they had not gone above a hundred yards with the carriage acting as a brake upon their progress. The Marquis spoke to them soothingly and they responded to his familiar voice, but setting the vehicle upon its wheels was too heavy a task for him to attempt unaided.

'God's teeth, what's befallen Quentin?' he muttered, and turned his horse to ride back along the track. The first thing that caught his eye was the pistol, lying where it had fallen in a tuft of grass. Dismounting, he picked it up and when he recognized it for what it was the full implication of what might have occurred came home to him. 'Cherry Ripe!'

Swinging himself into the saddle again, he urged his horse forward and only the sight of something fluttering in the light breeze caused him to pull up within feet of the quarry's edge. It was a black ostrich feather, still clinging bravely to a lady's riding-hat, and it rested upon the very lip of the chasm.

Dropping to his knees, he peered down into the depths, but nothing stirred in the gloom below. 'Quentin! Miss Devenish!' he called, his voice harsh with anxiety. Answer came there none but, as his eyes accustomed themselves to the poor light, he perceived a figure which he had no doubt was the lady's, resting on the floor of the quarry by the sullen-looking pool of steel-grey water that filled much of the area. Realizing that she had but to make the least movement and she would be plunged into its depths, he sought frantically for a way to get down to her. On one side of the quarry only was there a possible descent, but so loose was the shale and rock that he feared he might precipitate a minor avalanche if he attempted it. But something had to be done and that at once to bring her into a position of greater safety. He felt hurriedly in his pockets for a scrap of paper on which to write a message but found nothing. 'The devil!' he growled. 'None can know where I am. It's home for you, Crusader old fellow! At least your arrival without me will give 'em thought.'

Tying back the reins, he gave the horse a smart blow on the flank and saw him, after a hesitant start, head off in the general direction of Studleigh. The patient bays, standing by the overturned phaeton, watched his progress enviously but the Marquis shook his head. 'No, poor fellows, you're safe enough there, and you'll attract the attention of any passer-by – if such there be in so God-forsaken a spot!' Then, cautiously, he lowered himself over the edge of the quarry and began to feel his way downwards.

At first all went well, his feet and hands retained their grip and he was becoming increasingly hopeful of completing the descent without incident when, about half-way down, he felt the movement of the shale and his progress took on an involuntary speed, ending up by his crashing into a heap of boulders at the bottom, with pieces of rock flying about him like giant hailstones. One of these struck him so shrewd a blow on the back of the head as to render him partially insensible, and it was not until the noise of further rock movement above him warned him of possible danger that he staggered to his feet and began to make his way towards the inert body of Miss Devenish. The left sleeve of his riding-coat had been ripped from elbow to wrist and he became aware of a warm stickiness welling out from under the torn cloth. This he discovered to be issuing from a deep gash in his forearm and already there was an ominous swelling about his left hand and wrist which seemed to presage further injury.

'A fine rescuer of distressed damsels you are!' he chided himself grimly and stepped into the pool, keeping close to the side and testing every step with caution. To his relief, the water in no place came over the mahogany tops of his riding boots, but the thought of what Foster would have to say of their condition brought a wry smile to his mouth.

Then he was beside her and lifting her gently away from the pool's edge to a patch of nearby grass. She stirred as he touched her and moaned faintly, as if in pain. Reassured at least of her being alive, he propped her against one knee and loosed the lace cravat at her neck. She opened her eyes and looked up at him in a wondering sort of way as if not perfectly certain of who he might be.

'Miss Devenish,' he implored her. 'Tell me how you are hurt, so that I may help you.'

'It's – oh, my shoulder!' she gasped and lapsed again into insensibility. Swiftly, he unbuttoned her jacket and eased it off.

'Dislocated,' he decided. 'And I'll wager that collar-bone is broke. And how am I to put back a shoulder without causing further injury to the broken bone – even supposing I could undertake the task with one hand.' For his left wrist was becoming increasingly painful, while the amount of blood he was losing from the tear in his forearm led him to tie a handkerchief around it as best he could and secure the knot with the aid of his teeth.

During this operation Miss Devenish again regained consciousness and lay quietly, watching him. Her head was so addled from the bumps it had received in her fall that the only emotion she experienced was a profound thankfulness at being alive. It did occur to her to wonder at the Marquis being there beside her. Surely it should have been someone else – George? Sir Quentin?

He raised his head from his completed task to meet her speculative regard. 'Does it hurt a lot?' he asked softly. The expression on his face contrasted so strongly with how he had looked at their last meeting that her eyes filled with tears. 'Oh, my dear!' he said in quick distress. 'I – fool that I am! Brandy is what you need.' Plunging a hand into the capacious pocket of his riding-coat, he produced first the pistol, which he laid on the ground, and then a silver flask. 'Please God it is still intact,' said he, unscrewing the stopper one-handed with some difficulty.

The sight of the pistol brought immediate recollection to Cherryanne's bemused brain. 'Sir Quentin!' she cried out.

'Yes, what *has* happened to Quentin? He's not down here, too, is he? There, if you can take this in your good hand, I'll support your head with my arm.'

She took a gulp of the brandy and choked. 'I – I hit him with the pistol,' she spluttered.

'What the devil for? Don't say he had gone beyond the line of what was pleasing – Quentin? I'll not believe it!' he teased her, fearing that she was all about in her head and not knowing what she was saying.

'He was trying to blackmail me,' she persisted.

'Now that I could believe,' he nodded, still humouring her. 'My dear cousin ain't too nice in his notions when he sets his sights on something.'

'He had found out about us at Winterslow,' she informed him.

'What? Damnation!' exploded his lordship. 'Have some more brandy.'

'I don't want it, thank you, it makes me cough and that hurts my shoulder.'

'Drink it,' he repeated inexorably. 'That shoulder is going to hurt a deal more before the night is out, and you'd best be a trifle bosky to sustain it. For, with darkness coming on, there is small hope of rescue before morning. Good girl! Now, have you a handkerchief? Your face is covered in dust and scratches.' Gently, he wiped her cheeks and dried her tears. 'Courage, Cherry Ripe!' he whispered, smiling at her so tenderly she hardly recognized him. 'Now, continue your tale about Quentin. I collect he fancies he has discovered something to your discredit and hopes to black-mail you. What form does this – er, blackmail, take?'

'Marriage,' she said flatly. 'If I do not wed him he will tell all the world of my scandalous behaviour – including the bath at Studleigh!'

'Does he know you are betrothed to George?'

'He would not regard it if he did!' she retorted. 'So George did – speak to you?'

'You sent him, of course!' His eyes were alight with amuse-ment. 'Poor George! How could you use him so? And you have cause to be grateful to him for he held me so long in conversation that I was forced to take this short cut to be back at Studleigh in time to meet my agent. Had I not done so, I would not have seen the phaeton and found you. Much use I am likely to be to you,' he added caustically, 'with an injured arm and –' But she had checked him with a cry of dismay at sight of the blood still oozing from the cut. 'Oh, that is nothing, but I fear a broken bone in my wrist.' He raised his head to look upwards. 'And it is a mighty long haul to the top! By Jupiter! There is someone peering down at us, I'll swear! Hey, there!' He rose to his feet and waved vigorously. A thin, piping voice answered him. 'It's only a child, but he can fetch help.'

The next few minutes were spent in instructing the infant in what he should do. This was not as simple of achievement as might be supposed, for the boy, who appeared to be of tender years, seemed not to have any great understanding of the matter. At last, however, he was persuaded to call his parents or some adult person and Damien sat down with a sigh of relief.

'I can only hope his tale will be accepted,' he said doubtfully. 'Now, if you please, tell me more about Quentin.'

E

Miss Devenish, on whom the brandy was having the inevitable effect, found herself to be remarkably sleepy, but did her best.

'He – he was resh – resolved not only to inform grandmama, but also to tell Mish – Miss Winton,' she got out with difficulty.

The Marquis laughed shortly. 'Honoria would not care a snap of her fingers for anything he might say. She's got no more love for him than I.' Miss Devenish hardly heard him for her head was drooping and her eyes closing. 'My poor hurt girl!' Carefully, he drew her into his arms, resting her head on his shoulder, and pulled her jacket around her shoulders. 'Go to sleep, sweetheart.'

There was nothing Miss Devenish would have liked better than to go to sleep but she felt that a declaration of intent was required. 'I don't wish to marry your cousin,' she said firmly.

'Then you shall not,' he promised her. 'Leave the handling of Quentin to me.'

'Thank you, my lord,' she murmured and her last waking thought was a vague but strong impression of being kissed which, of course, was merely a fancy brought about by her weakened and drowsy state, and a most improper one at that.

*   *   *

About the same time, Sir Quentin, hobbling along the road, was overtaken by George and the groom.

'Stratton! What the devil's to do? Where's Cherryanne?'

'Bolted!' snapped Sir Quentin, then, very conscious of the groom's pricked ears, he ordered him off Betsy and bade him continue his journey on foot. 'Sprained my ankle,' he explained as he hoisted himself with difficulty into the saddle.

'Yes, but – where is she?' reiterated the mystified George.

'Back at Chilcomb, I've no doubt. Girl's taken leave of her senses!'

'But why?' As they moved off at a smart trot, Sir Quentin wincing at every movement, George eyed him doubtfully. 'Have you – did you come to cuffs?'

'You could describe it as such,' replied the other with some asperity. 'I offered the lady matrimony and, upon her not immediately declining my suit, I ventured to plant a chaste salute upon her cheek. Whereupon she repulsed me in a very violent manner. I at once released her and turned to my horses. While my attention was thus engaged, she struck me a heavy blow on the head with the butt of a pistol.'

'The butt of a pistol?' repeated George in blank astonishment.

'A pistol belonging to my cousin Shalford, I may add, and ask her, if you please, how she came by that!'

'Shalford?' George's eyes opened still wider.

'Yes, he who has been carrying on a clandestine connection with Miss Devenish these last months,' rasped Sir Quentin, his malice giving stimulus to his imagination.

But that was too much for George. 'You'll not speak so of my cousin!' he roared. 'You'll answer to me for that, Stratton!'

Sir Quentin, realizing he had gone too far and having no mind to be fighting a duel over so humiliating an affair, drew in his horns. 'If I wrong the lady, put it down to my natural disappointment and confusion,' he sighed. 'But to be deceived by so fair a face is well-nigh unbelievable.'

'What d'you mean "deceived"? Did she confess to an affair with Shal?' George's hostility was still unabated and Sir Quentin made haste to pour further oil on these very troubled waters.

'She could not deny it, dear boy.' He then proceeded to give a carefully balanced account of Miss Devenish's behaviour, true in essence if not in implication, which lasted until they got back to Chilcomb, by which time he had talked himself into a good humour again and almost believed every word he had said.

Poor George was quite cast down, wondering how Cherryanne was going to contrive a way out of this scrape, and why neither of his friends had seen fit to take him into their confidence.

CHAPTER
ELEVEN

Sir Quentin flattered himself that he had vastly improved upon his story when he recounted it to Lady Harpendene. Displaying all the reluctance proper to a gentleman breaking the news of her granddaughter's improprieties to a lady of breeding, he touched upon the Marquis's well-known dissolute habits and how the suggestion of an irregular connection with him could permanently blight Miss Devenish's prospects with all the delicate hesitancy of a butterfly alighting upon a flower.

Her ladyship heard him out in silence and then said: 'That's all very well, but where is she now?'

'That, I confess, has me in a puzzle,' admitted Sir Quentin, who felt that Lady Harpendene was not playing her part just as she ought. The least she might do, he considered, was to deplore her granddaughter's want of conduct. 'No doubt she feels a natural aversion to meeting me again so soon after what has passed between us, and has sought the company of a friend or neighbour.'

'The Ryders!' broke in George, who had been listening to the conversation with increasing discomfort. 'Shall I go over, ma'am, and enquire if she is there?'

Lady Harpendene drew a meditative finger around the gilt rim of the small mahogany table beside her. 'No,' she said after a moment's consideration. 'If she is at Cobblers and does not intend to return here tonight, Mrs Ryder will certainly apprise me of the fact. Nor do I think it likely that Charity would do such a thing. She may lack discretion but she does not want for courage. Am I to infer, sir, that your obliging offer for her has been withdrawn?'

Sir Quentin found himself resenting the lady's tone of voice. For a gentleman of the first respectability such as he to be involved in so equivocal an affair was the outside of enough, and had he not been uncommonly pressed for the ready he would have been much inclined to drop the whole thing. Last settling day at Tattersalls, however, had been rather more than his pocket could comfortably afford, and if events did not turn out as he had planned, he feared he would have to sell up his stables, so he smiled wistfully and adopted the rôle of injured lover.

'Dear lady, whatever the world may say, I am assured Miss Devenish was guilty of no more than youthful imprudence. I will, of course, stand by my offer for her.'

George opened his mouth to protest but was shocked into silence by a fierce glare from his grandmother.

'Very magnanimous of you, to be sure, Sir Quentin. Your sentiments do you credit. But I got the impression that Charity was disinclined to favour your suit?'

Sir Quentin cleared his throat gently. 'That is so, ma'am. But perhaps, upon reflection – if I might prevail upon you to support my pretensions?'

'Then no word of scandal need get about,' mused her ladyship.

'Just so!' He was almost purring with satisfaction at her ready acceptance of the solution. 'And now, if I might presume to request some attention for this ankle of mine which, I fear, is proving a little tiresome?'

'And here have I been prosing away for ever while you have been suffering the greatest discomfort,' said she, all sympathy. 'George, assist Sir Quentin to your room and summon Metchett, if you please, to attend upon him.'

Left alone, she sat staring into the fire, brooding over her granddaughter's behaviour. If the child had not returned within the hour a search must be mounted. She glanced at the darkening sky and wondered if she ought not, after all, have allowed George to ride over to Cobblers. Though she knew Cherryanne to be a sound whip she was handling an unfamiliar pair, and there was no knowing what might have happened. And why had she not come home and given her version of the story before Sir Quentin had had the chance to arrange the facts to his liking? Lady Harpendene's face took on a very grim expression. So he was going to have the girl, was he, and by whatsoever means he could?

That told its own story, nor had Lady Harpendene missed the threat behind the softly spoken words.

'Coxcomb!' she muttered fiercely. 'Takes me for a ninny-hammer, does he? Must have high expectations of my ability to make a handsome settlement upon her, for he's no ardent young lover. Oh, drat the child! If she would but come home!'

That, however, was not in Miss Devenish's power to do. The Marquis had been in the right of it when he suspected that the small boy's story might not be accepted by his elders. He was the son of a nearby farmer, a good sort of man enough but not over-tolerant of childish pranks. It was only when he heard mention of a carriage being overturned and a pair of horses standing by that his attention was held.

'We'd best go see, I suppose,' he grumbled. 'Though, mark me, boy, if I find you've been romancing again, you'll not sit easy for a week. What were you about, up by th'old quarry? You know you've been bidden to stay away from it.'

The urchin, feeling that chastisement was going to be his lot in any event, admitted to having chosen that path in order to get back to the farm before dark.

'And that it will be before long,' interposed his mother. 'Jem Cockayne, if there are poor souls trapped in that quarry, you cannot reconcile it with your conscience to do naught about it.'

'There's little to be done now save give them some comfort for the night,' said her spouse, shrugging on his coat. 'And a bitter cold one it promises to be, too.'

'Take blankets with you,' she urged.

'Aye, and ropes and a bite of food. No, boy, you'll stay here with your mother. I'll not run risk of you falling over th'edge in the dark. The men'll not be over-pleased at having to go out again after a day in the fields. Not at all the sort of place to be at night, th'old quarry.'

The Marquis could vouch for the truth of that last remark. The dank mist that hung over the water still further increased the gloom of the place and, as the light faded, so did the cold become more biting. He had slipped one arm out of his coat so as to enfold Miss Devenish more closely, and had wrapped her cloak tightly about her lower limbs, but, even in her half-insensible state, she shivered fitfully, and the prospect of the night ahead of them was not a pleasing one.

At last, when he had almost given up hope of any assistance being forthcoming before morning, he was roused by a certain commotion up above and the glad sight of lanterns twinkling along the quarry's edge against the evening sky. Then a stentorian bellow had him on his feet, shouting back and waving, though there was small hope he could be seen against the blackness of his surroundings.

'God bless us, 'tis Lord Shalford and Lady Harpendene's granddaughter trapped down there!' marvelled Mr Cockayne, after a deal of conversation, conducted at the full pitch of their voices. 'Get that carriage righted and you, Hal, drive as if the devil was at your heels to Chilcomb. Th'old lady will be in a rare taking, not knowing where the lass may be.'

'What about the Duke, master? Should I ride over to Studleigh?' volunteered another voice.

Mr Cockayne chuckled. 'What His Grace don't know won't hurt him, and I warrant his lordship has spent a night or two from home before without asking his papa's permission! No, I need you here. Now, let us have a lantern down first. 'Twill test the length required of rope.'

After several attempts, a place was discovered where the rope hung free of obstruction, and the Marquis untied the lantern and set it beside the now fully awake Miss Devenish. Then the blankets were lowered and he tucked them round her as best he could.

'It is something to be thankful for, to be sure, that between us we have one pair of hands,' he jested gaily, seeking to alleviate the strain apparent on her wan little face. 'They have sent off to fetch a doctor, though what good he may do I cannot say, for it would be altogether too dangerous a thing to attempt to lower him down here in the dark. Come, a little more brandy.'

'No, no,' she protested. 'It makes me so sleepy. I want to help you if I can.'

'Don't be a fool, child!' This reply was so much in his usual autocratic style that she almost laughed. 'How do you expect to survive with only me to care for you unless you are three parts cut?' He was smiling at her in the most unnerving way, so she gave in and took a reluctant sip. 'I'll join you, if I may,' said he, draining the flask. 'I have asked for more to be sent down to us.' He chuckled suddenly. 'What would I give to see our rescuers' faces if they discover us in the morning to be completely foxed!'

'M-most improper,' said Miss Devenish primly, stifling a strong desire to giggle.

'My dear, it's going to be most improper, however one looks at it.' He was all at once grave. 'It might be said – it *will* be said by some – that our injuries are not so severe as to – well, never mind. But you'll possibly have to marry me.'

'You're to marry Miss Winton,' she pointed out.

'Oh, Honoria'll understand.'

Miss Devenish felt that this remark required some elucidation but could not allow herself to be sufficiently clear in the head to attempt such a thing.

'The D-duke and Her Grace,' she managed, clutching at her fast-receding sobriety. 'Th-they could not p-possibly ap-approve of so – so unsuitable a connection for you.'

'It would break my father's heart, I think,' said the Marquis, half to himself. Miss Devenish, not unnaturally, took the wrong view of this remark, and reminded herself that such an attitude on His Grace's part was only to be expected, and that it was as well that she did not care for the Marquis above half, though allowing she was better pleased with him now than before she had fallen into the quarry, so that even if he should feel obliged to offer for her she would have no hesitation in refusing to take advantage of his gentlemanlike behaviour. After which considerable mental exertion, she snuggled up to him and dozed off again, which did nothing to help his deliberations at all. 'Oh, my Cherry Ripe!' he groaned, leaning his cheek against her hair. 'Marry you and see my poor father ruined, or marry Honoria and live out a mockery for all my days? And what of you, I wonder? Would the thought of becoming my wife quite disgust you?'

But Miss Devenish, under the combined influences of the brandy and a slight fever brought about by the pain of her injuries, had drifted into a gentle stupor and could offer no advice on this troubled question.

The next thing to disturb the Marquis's ruminations was the

sound of George's voice re-echoing around the sides of the quarry.

'Shal! Hey, Shal, old fellow! How in thunder did you get down there?'

'Climbed down to help Miss Devenish,' explained his lordship briefly. 'But she is in no case to be moved. Have you got a doctor?'

'Yes, here with me. Dr Arbuthnot, Lady Harpendene's man. She's in a great state, I can tell you.'

It then transpired that the doctor was a gentleman well stricken in years and afflicted by the rheumatics so that any faint hope of having him lowered to the quarry floor was soon dispelled.

'Not going to help things, m'lord, if I join you down there with a broken limb,' he declared and Damien, concerned though he was for Cherryanne, had to admit the sense of this reasoning. 'But I can send down whatever is needed to ease the lady's discomfort, and by first light tomorrow I shall have a young colleague out from Winchester who will make small beer of the descent.'

Within a very few minutes the beleaguered pair were provided with a basketful of medical necessities and food. Miss Devenish, once more roused from her feverish slumber, was persuaded to take a little sustenance, finishing up with a glass of wine generously laced with laudanum. Not surprisingly, she fell asleep again almost at once and the Marquis, whose throat was beginning to feel the strain of conducting conversation at the full pitch of his vocal chords, was about to settle down as best he could for the night when George called out again to acquaint him of his intention of remaining by the quarry's edge during the hours of darkness.

'Do try for a little sense, old fellow!' recommended the Marquis. 'First thing we know we'll have you crashing down on top of us when you turn over in your sleep! No point to it in any case – what further harm can come to us here? You'd best be off to your bed and conserve your strength for the morrow. How is Quentin, by the way?'

'Sir Quentin,' said George so tersely it was clear that, but for the presence of many pairs of interested ears, he would have expressed himself more forcibly, 'has returned to Studleigh in his phaeton, driven by his groom. He felt it to be his duty to acquaint the Duke with your predicament. I say, Shal, did you and – oh, I cannot ask you that now!'

'No, don't!' advised the Marquis kindly. 'But don't be believing every word my dear cousin says either.'

'That I'll not,' promised George. 'But as for leaving you and Cherryanne alone here all night – well, I don't like it above half, I can tell you. Suppose it should come on to rain, you'll be near drowned!'

'And what d'you think you'd be able to do about that?' enquired the Marquis reasonably, wishing very much that George would go home, for the loss of blood, the throbbing of his wrist and the effort of constant shouting, had begun to make him feel a shade fagged. Mr Cockayne mercifully intervened.

'His lordship's in the right of it, sir. There's naught you can do and it bain't goin' to rain, I give you m'word on't.'

The still protesting George was led away, promising to have all the neighbourhood about the quarry's edge by cockcrow. Damien, sighing with relief, settled his back against a rock and, pulling over both of them the fur carriage rug that Lady Harpendene had had the good sense to provide, resigned himself to a long and uncomfortable night.

*   *   *

True to his word, George was back at dawn with a host of willing helpers. The doctors arrived a few minutes afterwards and a lengthy consultation ensued on the most felicitous method to be employed in rescuing the unfortunate pair. Then a Captain Dangerfield gave them the benefit of his naval experience and suggested the making of a form of cradle or frame of timber, such as was employed by shipwrights in lowering persons down the side of a vessel. This notion was at once agreed upon and, after much disputation and hammering by the unskilled carpenters, the young doctor made the first hazardous descent amid fervent shouting of advice, and arrived safely on the quarry floor to the general relief of all.

A quick examination of Miss Devenish's shoulder caused him to shake his head and lament the fact that he had not been able to attend to it the previous night. 'For I will not attempt to conceal from you, ma'am, that it will be a difficult and painful thing to put it back in place after so long a time.'

'Then the soonest done the better, sir,' said she, managing a little smile. 'Must I bite on the bullet?'

Over her head, the two gentlemen exchanged a quick glance. 'If you are to make the ascent to the top, ma'am, you must be fully sensible,' explained the doctor carefully, 'so I may not offer you any palliative to fortify you.'

'Indeed, sir, my lord here has poured so much brandy down my throat that I have taken it in strong dislike,' she informed him. 'So please to be about your task as speedily as you may.'

Brave though were her words, she could not refrain from a gasp of pain as the doctor grasped her shoulder and, at once, Damien caught her free hand in his. 'That's it, my gallant girl, hold on fast!' he entreated her. 'Get it over with, man!' he added under his breath.

The doctor, looking from his face to Cherryanne's, raised his eyebrows slightly but said nothing, concentrating upon his work; the Marquis meanwhile keeping up a flow of conversation in order to divert the patient. But it all proved too much for even Miss Devenish's resolution and, on a half-suppressed sob, she fainted away.

'Good!' proclaimed the doctor. 'Now I can finish the business at my leisure.' This he did before turning his attention to the Marquis's injuries. 'She will have to be strapped into that contraption,' he went on. 'The smallest jolt and she could likely lose consciousness and tip out. Hmm. Yes, there is a bone broken there, my lord, and that gash will need several sutures. You'll not find the journey upwards an easy one either.'

As the doctor was bent upon setting the bone without delay, Damien did not feel it incumbent upon him to answer until the painful business was over. After a brief respite, he helped set Miss Devenish in the cradle, wrapped closely about with blankets and roped securely to the wooden frame. As he watched her being drawn up slowly above his head, he experienced such acute pangs of anxiety on her behalf as made him want to turn away lest he should witness the disaster of a rope breaking and her falling from her roughly fashioned conveyance.

No such catastrophe, however, occurred and the swaying figure was received by willing hands and pulled into safety. By the time he himself had arrived at the top, Miss Devenish had already been whisked away in Lady Harpendene's carriage with her doctor in attendance. George had stayed to receive him and another young gentleman with him, whose face was unfamiliar to the Marquis but who offered, civilly enough, to drive him back to Studleigh.

'Neighbour of mine, Captain Jeremy Ryder,' explained George. 'How is it with you, Shal? How d'you come to make such a cake of yourself as to break your wrist?'

Damien, returning the cool regard of a pair of very steady grey eyes, admitted to having behaved in a perfectly cock-brained fashion, but his mind was more occupied in assessing Captain Ryder's scarce concealed hostility than in paying heed to George's artless prattle. So this is Honoria's dearest Jeremy, he thought, and from all the signs, he don't love me overmuch!

A groom, pressing forward through the quite considerable throng that had gathered to view these uncommon proceedings, came quickly to his side, touching his hat. 'I have your carriage waiting, my lord.'

'You here, Lawson? Does my father know?'

'Yes, my lord. Sir Quentin thought it best to acquaint His Grace with the details of your unhappy plight.' He paused significantly. 'Sir Quentin, my lord, is leaving for Bath this morning.'

Damien nodded as if satisfied, then, thanking Captain Ryder for his kind offer, he turned to the doctor who had just been hauled up and, commending him for his good offices, suggested that he called at Studleigh the following day to satisfy himself of his patient's continued good progress. The young man, now as flustered as he had been cool before, could not but be aware that to be summoned to attend at Studleigh must do a great deal for his consequence in the district, and readily accepted.

Captain Ryder, listening to this exchange and hearing the Marquis thank his deliverers without the least height or condescension in his manner, looked exceedingly thoughtful. Having seen his lordship safely bestowed in his carriage and accepted a cordial invitation to accompany George to dine at Studleigh as soon as could be arranged, he set off in his gig to drive back with that voluble young gentleman to Chilcomb.

'Dashed noble of Shal to fling himself down there to aid Cherryanne. Shouldn't wonder if there wasn't a mite of truth in Stratton's story, after all.'

'What story?' enquired the captain, immersed in his own thoughts and listening with only half an ear.

'Oh, some rodomontade about Shal and Cherryanne being better acquainted than any of us had an idea of.' Seeing the astonished expression on his companion's face, George hastily added: 'I daresay Stratton was cutting a sham – sort of thing he'd do if it suited his purpose.'

Captain Ryder negotiated a difficult bend in the track before turning to regard his companion very steadfastly. 'What precisely does Stratton hope to achieve by setting about such a rumour?'

George sighed. 'Nothing for it but to tell you the whole – but, mark me, not a word to a soul, on your honour!'

The required assurance having been given, Captain Ryder listened with mounting amazement to what Mr Marsden had to say. 'I can well understand your desire to call Sir Quentin to account,' he said warmly when the tale was told, 'and if he persists in his despicable intention, I'd be happy to stand second to you.'

'My thanks, but grandmother says nothing can be done until we hear Cherryanne's side of the story.'

'Oh, so Lady Harpendene knows it all?'

'Yes, and to judge from the steel in her eye, she ain't going to knuckle down to Stratton's threats.'

'I think,' said Captain Ryder after a moment's reflection, 'that one other ought to be informed of this circumstance – Shalford himself.'

'Shal can hardly call his cousin out,' objected George, 'and then – well, Miss Winton might not care for it – another lady and all that. No, best hear what Cherryanne has to say. I ain't such a gudgeon as to call Stratton a bouncer, but it seems to me he's gone a bit beyond the line.'

'Being hit on the head with the butt of a pistol might, of course, have influenced his judgement adversely!' suggested the captain with a twinkle.

'Yes, and I'd like to know just what he had been about to make her act so!' declared George heatedly. 'Planting a chaste salute on her cheek – that's all a hum if ever I heard one! Cherryanne's no missish young lady – why she even lets me kiss her cheek sometimes!'

Captain Ryder agreed gravely that there was no accounting for it and the two gentlemen continued on their way to Chilcomb, reasonably well satisfied with each other's understanding of the matter.

CHAPTER
TWELVE

'Will you have the goodness to inform me, Honoria,' burst out
Her Grace when the door had closed behind Sir Quentin's com-
placently limping form, 'what maggot has got into that creature
that he should so wish to discredit Miss Devenish and Damien?
Oh, Damien he was ever jealous of, but the lady he hopes to
marry – it is out of all reason nonsensical!'

Miss Winton carefully folded away her fine stitchery before
making reply. 'Ma'am, I only understand that he means mischief,'
she said, the sparkle in her eye belying her quiet manner. 'Depend
upon it, if Miss Devenish does not agree to become his wife, then
the whole story will be made known – with suitable embellish-
ments, I have no doubt. He knows we will not speak of it – we
won't, will we?' she added in a warning tone.

The Duchess sighed dramatically. 'How could you think I
would utter a word? Oh, I have no right to be discussing such a
thing with you, for you are to marry Damien but – but Miss
Devenish – he would never –' Her voice broken by sobs, Her
Grace found herself quite unable to continue.

'Dear Duchess!' Miss Winton, all ready sympathy, went to
sit beside her and proffer a handkerchief. 'Of course, he would
never but, you see, his reputation is such that others will not
believe that. And I am not going to marry him.'

'W-what?' The Duchess was so arrested by this statement that
her tears ceased to flow.

'Oh, no,' explained Miss Winton calmly. 'It is only an arrangement to stave off his creditors and my unwelcome suitors for a
time.'

Her Grace's dismay was almost ludicrous to behold. 'But,
Honoria, Damien's debts are the least of our troubles! It – it's
his grandfather and – and me!'

Miss Winton, who had long had her suspicions as to the real state of affairs, repossessed herself of her handkerchief which the Duchess seemed bent on tearing to shreds. 'Tell me all about it, ma'am,' she invited and this Her Grace, first vowing her to secrecy, did with admirable lack of sentiment.

After the tale was told Miss Winton sat, lost in thought, for a few moments. 'I shall set out for Chilcomb first thing tomorrow,' she said at last, 'and offer to render any assistance possible in helping to care for Miss Devenish. That way, at least some of Quentin's wicked gossip may be discounted.'

The Duchess eyed her with mounting respect. 'But, according to him, they spent last night together in the quarry,' she said doubtfully.

'What choice had they?' Miss Winton rose and shook out her skirts with an air of decision. 'What interests me is why Quentin is so set on having her for his wife. She must be a considerable heiress – her grandmother, perhaps, Lady Harpendene?'

'Harpendene?' echoed Her Grace, whose agitation and concern for Damien had been so great that the name of Miss Devenish's grandparent had quite escaped her notice. 'Can it be Sir Giles's relict? I remember her well – a Tartar, if ever there was one! She was a Douglas, but held old "Q" – Queensberry, you know – in such poor regard – as who would not, horrid old man! – she quite severed her connection with the family. Depend upon it, she will insist upon Damien doing the proper thing!'

'All the more reason I should see her at once,' said Miss Winton, 'and hear Miss Devenish's story for myself.' She paused, half-smiling. 'So Damien was really wishful of marrying my twenty thousand pounds a year?'

The Duchess's eyes filled again. 'Yes, the dear boy! He was resolved on making himself a sacrifice on – on – '

'The family altar?' supplied Miss Winton. 'I confess I cannot quite conceive of Damien's maintaining such a rôle! What an atrocious husband he would have made me!'

'Oh, no, my dear!' protested Damien's mama. 'He would have been everything that was conformable, and would have treated you at all times with the utmost delicacy and consideration.'

'Hmm!' was all Miss Winton vouchsafed in reply. 'Well, if I am to set off first thing in the morning I had best go and instruct my maid to pack a few clothes for me. May I borrow your travelling chaise, ma'am?'

'But of course you may!' In her distress, the Duchess rose also and clasped Miss Winton to her bosom. 'Bless you, dear Honoria! By standing friend to Miss Devenish you will show that you, for one, put no credence in these spiteful reports.'

But as she went upstairs, Miss Winton was turning over the various very odd circumstances of the affair and, to her active mind, the most noteworthy point was that Sir Quentin was unlikely to have set about such rumours without foundation. Malicious he might be, but a fool he certainly was not.

* * *

This fact had not escaped Lady Harpendene's notice either, but, wishful though she might be to have a long cose with Miss Devenish, that young lady's state of health prohibited any such inquisition. The shock and injuries of her fall had thrown her into a high fever and, though Dr Arbuthnot declared that such a condition was only to be expected and would soon be shaken off by one with as strong a constitution as her granddaughter, Lady Harpendene could not be perfectly easy in her mind. Cherryanne's fever, she considered, did not stem entirely from her bodily weakness and she saw to it that only Bridie and herself were constantly in attendance upon her granddaughter so that any light-headed murmurings were unheard by other ears.

On the day following the rescue from the quarry, a magnificent basket of fruit arrived from Studleigh, together with a formal letter from the Marquis, saying all that was proper and begging to be informed of Miss Devenish's condition. He also explained that the Duke was in very indifferent health which prevented his son from leaving his side for any reason whatsoever at that moment but, immediately it was possible, he would do himself the honour of calling upon her ladyship to make his enquiries in person.

'Gentlemanly thing to do, of course,' pronounced George. 'Say that for Shal – never backward in any attention.'

'But no word from Sir Quentin,' mused her ladyship.

'Grassed!' proclaimed her grandson. 'Whole county ringing with the story now – Shal's the local hero.'

'Maybe,' said his grandmother drily, 'but that does not help your cousin's case – quite the contrary, in fact. If Shalford was so ready to risk his life to save her, it might be argued that he held her in some esteem.'

George was forced to allow that could be so. 'But, confound it! He would have done the same for any female, so that can't signify. Devilish fearless sort of fellow.'

Lady Harpendene paid little heed to her grandson's conjectures but seated herself at her Davenport desk of Irish bog yew, given her years before by Captain Devenish when the dibs were in tune, and drew out the secretary slide to pen a reply to the Marquis.

'There,' she said, signing her name with a flourish, 'now there is nothing more to do other than to wait upon events.'

The next event worthy of mention was so unexpected as to throw Lady Harpendene's calculations quite out of joint. Roger had just set a lamp at her elbow and made up the fire when the sound of a carriage approaching the house caused her to look at him in question.

'Not Mr George, m'lady,' he volunteered. 'I am instructed to inform you that a message has been received from Cobblers to say that they are holding him there for dinner.'

Lady Harpendene folded her *Hampshire Chronicle* very precisely and laid it down. 'We will have more lights, if you please, Roger, and tell Metchett I am receiving callers.'

'Yes, m'lady.'

Roger's hopes that the visitor might prove to be that same well-breeched gentleman who had called a few nights previously were dashed at sight of the young lady who descended from the carriage and, bidding her abigail await her in the hall, required Metchett to announce her to Lady Harpendene.

'Miss Honoria Winton to see you, m'lady.'

Miss Winton walked briskly into the drawing-room, unloosing the fastenings of her velvet mantle as she did so.

'It is excessively good-natured of your ladyship to receive me,' said she in her direct manner. 'I am greatly concerned to know how Miss Devenish goes on. I trust she has taken no lasting hurt because of her unhappy accident?'

Lady Harpendene, whose amiability stemmed from curiosity rather than good nature, reassured her visitor on that point and begged her to be seated.

'Bad news travels fast, they say,' she remarked, a faintly sardonic edge to her voice. 'May I ask, Miss Winton, who was your informant?'

'Why, Sir Quentin, to be sure,' replied Honoria, drawing off her long, stone-coloured Limerick gloves and laying them on the sofa beside her. 'The alarming story he had to tell when he arrived back in Bath last night so wrought upon my sensibilities that I felt obliged to come at once to discover for myself just how things were.'

Her level gaze met Lady Harpendene's and the elder lady was left in no doubt as to the meaning behind her words. 'I have been unable to discuss the unfortunate affair with my granddaughter,' she said, resolving to play her cards with care until perfectly assured of her visitor's intent, 'because of her recurring fever. This evening, however, she seems to be in a good way to improving and I am persuaded that tomorrow she will be in better case and able to give me her account of what took place.'

Miss Winton pensively pleated a fold of her sensible Angora wool gown between finger and thumb. 'If I can be of assistance, ma'am, I would be happy to remain for as long as suits your convenience,' she offered.

Lady Harpendene thought furiously and decided that Miss Winton's suggestion did suit her convenience. 'I am very much obliged to you,' she said. 'Your presence here will do more than anything to suppress any breath of scandal that should attach to – to – ' She paused, at a loss for words to express herself without giving offence, but Miss Winton's composure was unruffled.

'To the association between Miss Devenish and Lord Shalford, you would say, ma'am?' she suggested. 'Sir Quentin seems bent on enlarging upon the concoction but, for myself, I cannot believe his story.'

'There is never smoke without fire,' said her ladyship bluntly. 'And it is true that they met at the Winterslow Hut.'

'And she shot him,' agreed Miss Winton.

'They also met at Studleigh t'other day,' pointed out Lady Harpendene.

Miss Winton chuckled unexpectedly. 'Oh, yes, the bath! I can promise you, ma'am, that if Mrs Pritchard was about no impropriety took place then!'

Lady Harpendene eyed her curiously. 'You treat of the matter very lightly, Miss Winton.'

'Yes, because I know Damien – Shalford, so well. At bottom he's a gentleman, despite his rakish ways. He would never lay a finger on a lady of Miss Devenish's quality.'

Lady Harpendene gave her a long appraising look and decided that only frankness would answer in this case. 'How deeply are your affections engaged with his lordship?' she asked.

'Not at all,' replied Miss Winton cheerfully. 'We are old friends; His Grace is anxious to see his son married and – ' She hesitated as if uncertain of the wisdom of saying more.

'And?' prompted Lady Harpendene who was not going to be denied the truth of the matter.

'And I have twenty thousand pounds a year,' concluded Miss Winton with a deprecatory gesture of the hand, as if in apology for such a circumstance.

'But, surely, money cannot be a first consideration with the Evesham's?' Her ladyship was plainly startled. 'Though I allow the late Duke was a heavy gamester and rattled through his rents. Is Shalford cast in the same mould?'

'No, though he is no pinchpurse. But his grandfather did more damage to the estates than was generally supposed and – well, the whole story is not mine to divulge, ma'am, but be assured that Lord Shalford must marry where money is.'

'His mother?'

Miss Winton grimaced slightly. 'You are shrewd in your conjecture, ma'am, but he'll not hear a word against her.'

'Aye, Lucilla Cavendish ever held the gentlemen on a leading rein,' nodded her ladyship. 'But her own son? What kind of young man is he?'

Miss Winton smiled almost fondly. 'Not half as black as he is painted, I promise you. I fancy you would like him, ma'am. I do.'

If this sounded to be an odd statement, coming from the gentleman's betrothed, Lady Harpendene did not regard it as such.

'Even had you no particular liking for his lordship,' she said slowly, 'if Sir Quentin's tittle-tattle should get about, your mortification must be near as great as my granddaughter's. What can be his object, do you suppose?'

'I collect he believes Miss Devenish to have considerable expectations.' Miss Winton did not phrase her reply as a question, nor did she permit any note of interrogation to be apparent in her voice.

'What? Is he short in the wind also?' rapped out her ladyship.

'I cannot be sure of that, but he lives high and I have no doubt that a wife with a comfortable portion would not come amiss.'

Lady Harpendene was lost in thought for a few moments while Miss Winton regarded her expectantly. Then she reached out a hand to the bell-pull. 'It will afford me great pleasure to have you as my guest,' she announced. 'I will have a room made ready for you at once. We can dine at whatever hour pleases you since my grandson, who is staying with me, is eating his meat with close neighbours of mine, the Ryders.'

Miss Winton's rather pale cheeks became delicately tinged with colour, but she replied in her usual calm way. 'Of course. The parents of Captain Jeremy Ryder, I collect?'

'Yes. The captain is home on furlough and assisted at the rescue from the quarry yesterday.'

That piece of intelligence clearly came as a shock to Miss Winton, but the entry of Metchett to receive his mistress's instructions saved her from having to respond. Lady Harpendene, however, had not failed to observe the whitening of her guest's knuckles as her hands closed convulsively over her reticule, and was satisfied that she had read the portents aright. Having seen a glass of sherry set by Miss Winton and holding her own favoured Madeira in her hand, she settled back in her chair to exchange pleasantries until Metchett should have withdrawn. Then she said abruptly:

'Am I to understand, Miss Winton, that you are establishing yourself here as a sort of – of shield against any indiscretions my granddaughter and your fiancé may have committed?'

'It seemed to me to be the best notion,' said Honoria. 'If I show myself to be well disposed towards Miss Devenish much of the sting is drawn from Sir Quentin's spite.'

'She does not wish to marry him,' commented Lady Harpendene, sipping her wine reflectively.

'I could not suppose she would. Has she, do you know, a tendre for Shalford?'

'I suspect she may have.' Lady Harpendene was not committing herself further.

'Then what we must arrive at is the state of Shalford's feelings,' mused Miss Winton. 'That will be no easy task because of his devotion to his mama and his determination to do all in his power to aid his father.'

Lady Harpendene pulled open the drawer of the Davenport near to her and handed Miss Winton the Marquis's letter. 'His Grace is very unwell,' she said briefly.

'This makes things even more difficult.' Miss Winton, having absorbed its contents, folded the single sheet and tapped it thoughtfully against her cheek. 'I need an ally here, ma'am. Will you stand my friend?'

'I shall be happy to, my dear,' said Lady Harpendene who had taken Honoria in considerable respect, despite the brevity of their acquaintance. 'What have you in mind to do?'

*   *   *

The next morning, when Miss Devenish opened her eyes to perceive Miss Winton sitting by her bedside she began seriously to wonder if she was not suffering from a recurrence of her fever.

'Why – how – ?' she began in confusion, but Miss Winton only smiled sweetly upon her.

'Forget the whys and wherefores,' she advised, 'and drink a little of this cordial. There, that's better. I have sent your good Bridie to bed, she is quite worn down with watching over you. Now, what is all this about you and Damien?'

It really was most unfair, thought Miss Devenish bitterly, to have such a question thrown at one when recovering from fever, shock and sundry other things, not to mention heartbreak. But

Miss Winton, a calculating general, knew the value of surprise, and was not to be deflected from her purpose.

'I understand from Lady Harpendene that you met him at Winterslow, where you shot him,' she went on smoothly.

'From grandmama? How did she – oh, Sir Quentin, I suppose,' concluded Cherryanne miserably. 'Miss Winton, it was not at all as – as you might think. I do assure you – '

Just what she would have assured Honoria was never made clear because at that moment Lady Harpendene entered the room and exclaimed in satisfaction at seeing the patient sitting up in bed, apparently in full possession of her senses.

'And now, miss, if you please, can you tell us just how you came to find yourself at the bottom of a quarry?'

Her grandmother's not unreasonable query had the startling effect of reducing Cherryanne to tears. 'It was none of my fault, I promise you,' she sobbed. 'F-first there was the lioness, and – and th-then the bath – and it wasn't D-Damien's fault, either!'

'Oh, so it's Damien, is it?' said Lady Harpendene grimly.

'N-no, it's not!' retorted Miss Devenish, recalling to mind her extreme dislike of the Marquis. 'It – it's Lord Shalford, and he is the most odious, overbearing creature I have ever met!'

'He risked his life to save you,' her grandmother thought fit to mention.

'I daresay he would have done the same for his pet dog!' sniffed Miss Devenish and then realized how improper it was to be saying such a thing before Miss Winton. 'I do beg your pardon, ma'am, but his lordship has made it so plain that he considers me to be quite beneath his touch that I can only suppose he had no notion of who I might be when he made the descent into the quarry, else he would certainly not have put himself to such trouble.'

This revealing piece of absurdity was received by the two ladies in very different wise. Miss Winton folded her lips firmly as if endeavouring to repress a smile, while Lady Harpendene, raising her eyes to heaven, exclaimed: 'Hoity-toity! And did he consider you beneath his touch at the Winterslow Hut so that you were obliged to shoot him?'

'Grandmama, that was an accident,' lied Cherryanne earnestly. 'He had laid down his pistol, since the lioness had moved too far away for him to shoot at her, and – and I picked it up and it went off.'

She was unhappily conscious in the silence that followed that her explanation had rung a trifle hollow but, somehow, she felt she must convince Miss Winton that the Marquis had not been guilty of any misdemeanour. Arrogant and ill-mannered he might be, yet she could not reconcile it with her conscience to blacken his name. Her memories of their night spent together in the quarry were disagreeably hazy, perhaps fortunately so, but she seemed to recall that he had been kind and gentle. He had even spoken of offering for her – but how could he do that when still bound to Miss Winton? – and then he had said that unforgivable thing about such an outcome breaking his father's heart.

Wearily, she put a hand to her aching head and, at once, Lady Harpendene declared that that was enough of talking for the time. 'Sleep is what you need,' said her ladyship and, having satisfied herself that her niece was as comfortable as was possible, she bore Miss Winton away.

Left to herself, Miss Devenish made no attempt to check her sobs. If Sir Quentin had already poured his malevolent fabrications into her grandmother's and Miss Winton's ears it was plain that his threat to spread it generally abroad was no idle one. Miss Winton seemed not to be unduly impressed by it. No doubt she was so deeply attached to the Marquis as to be blind to any defect in his character. Sighing heavily, Miss Devenish closed her eyes in a praiseworthy endeavour to dismiss from her visual memory the recollection of a pair of green eyes that could mock or caress at their owner's whim.

Belowstairs, Lady Harpendene and Miss Winton sat at breakfast where they were joined by Mr George Marsden, whose astonishment at seeing Honoria and total lack of understanding of the reason for her presence earned him a sharp set-down from his grandmother.

Miss Winton confessed herself to be deeply concerned about the Duke. 'He is in none too good case,' she declared, 'and such alarming intelligence about Damien being at the bottom of a quarry – for I doubt Quentin would have had the kindness to wrap it up in soft linen – may well have brought on another of his heart spasms. I am persuaded I ought to drive over to Studleigh to see how things are with him.'

'George can do that for you,' said her ladyship. 'He'll ride over in half the time it will take you in a carriage.'

Mr Marsden expressed himself as being delighted to be of service and was presently on his way. He had completed nearly half his journey when he remembered that Captain Ryder had expressed his intention of paying a call at Chilcomb Manor that morning. And had not Ryder once been betrothed to Miss Winton?

'Oh, the devil!' muttered George irritably. 'They'll have to meet some time, so the soonest done the better. None of my affair, when all's said.'

With which comfortable reflection he forgot all about Jeremy and Honoria and fell to thinking of Jeremy's sister who, as Miss Devenish had suspected, was in a fair way to supplanting Miss Wharton in his affections.

Finding the fields to be heavy going, he took to the road for a time and was fortunate enough to encounter Lord Shalford's curricle proceeding towards him at a spanking pace, being handled very capably by his lordship's groom, while the Marquis, his left wrist resting in a sling, sat beside him.

'Hey, Shal! Whither away, old fellow?'

'To call upon your grandmother, to be sure. And you?'

'To call upon you and enquire for His Grace. Miss Winton is mighty concerned for him.'

'Miss Winton?' echoed the Marquis in amazement.

'Yes, she's at Chilcomb. Don't ask me the ins and outs of it, but she is as close as inkle-weavers with m'grandmother.'

A reluctant grin spread over the Marquis's face. 'Well, I'll be – !' he said appreciatively. 'Come, George, turn in your tracks and let us proceed to Chilcomb. I have a notion we may find something there to interest us.'

CHAPTER
THIRTEEN

'Have no fear, ma'am, she'll do very well now!' boomed Dr Arbuthnot in what Lady Harpendene considered to be an odiously patronizing way as he took his leave of her. ' 'Twill be a little irksome for her until the bone mends but, apart from that, there is no reason why she should not be up and about after her usual fashion in a couple of days.'

'Pompous idiot!' stated her ladyship succinctly as she watched the doctor climb into his gig and drive away. 'I wonder why I bear with him. I vow I know as much of medicine as he!'

Miss Winton, to whom she had addressed herself, thought this last remark to be very likely true, but deemed it prudent to change the subject to discussion of what might be devised for Miss Devenish's entertainment.

'Is she a great reader, ma'am? For, if so, I shall request Shalford to put the resources of the Studleigh library at her convenience.'

Lady Harpendene snorted. 'Reader – yes, of rubbishy novels, like all you young people today!'

She would very likely have gone on to lament in time-honoured fashion that she did not know what the world was coming to had not Metchett chosen that moment to usher in Captain Ryder. The scene then presented took on all the appearance of a set piece. The captain, standing transfixed in the doorway, his eyes upon Honoria; that young lady, equally immobile, returning his regard in a manner which would have earned her a very sharp rebuke from her mama had she been present to witness it; the butler, aware of the tension but not of its cause, looking from one to the other; and Lady Harpendene, all too conscious of the delicacy of the moment, cudgelling her brains to think of some unexceptionable remark with which to pass off the situation.

'Ah, Jeremy, you will be looking for George, no doubt. He

has ridden over to Studleigh on Miss Winton's behalf – I have no need to present the captain to you, I believe, Miss Winton? – I had promised myself the pleasure of calling at Cobblers this afternoon to make another arrangement for you all to dine here in place of the one that had to be cancelled the other evening. Will your mother be at home, do you suppose?'

'To tell truth, ma'am, she is not in very high form, else she would have accompanied me this morning. Oh, nothing too serious, a slight cold, no more, but she felt it unwise to visit a household already stricken by injury. Your most obedient, Miss Winton.'

The captain was being very correct; Miss Winton returned his bow with an equally formal acknowledgement, and Lady Harpendene rushed again into speech.

'Daffy's Elixir, that's the thing!' she declared. 'Always sets me up when I am out of sorts. Come close to the fire, Jeremy, it is a raw day, as cold as any this winter, for all we are well into March.'

The weather provided a safe topic for conversation until Metchett brought in sherry, by which time Miss Winton had recovered her poise and was talking away as easily as her ladyship. Captain Ryder, having said all that was proper, was about to make his adieux when the door burst open to admit Mr Marsden, followed more soberly by the Marquis.

'Met Shal on the road,' announced George triumphantly. 'He says the Duke's all right and tight and – morning, Ryder. Thought I'd find you here.'

'Honoria,' began the Marquis, 'just what are you – '

'Damien,' she interrupted him swiftly. 'I believe you are not acquainted with our hostess. Ma'am, may I present Lord Shalford?'

Not one detail of his lordship's appearance escaped Lady Harpendene's keen scrutiny as he bowed over her hand. 'As like to your mother as can be imagined,' she remarked, in a tone that made it plain she did not consider such a likeness to be any great thing in his favour.

'You do me too much honour, ma'am,' he murmured, a fleeting gleam of amusement lighting up his dark eyes.

'I have to thank you for your care of my granddaughter, my lord. On several occasions.'

A slight quiver at the corner of Damien's mouth acknowledged the hit. 'Fate has indeed taken a hand in our affairs, ma'am,' he agreed.

She was not deceived by his mild manner but deemed it not to be the moment to pursue the matter. 'I am glad to learn that His Grace is feeling more the thing.'

For an instant his face hardened and she was brought to realize that, however much he favoured his mother in looks, he did not share the same easy temperament. 'No thanks to my cousin for that,' he said curtly.

'Damien, Quentin has never been spinning his nonsense into the Duke's ears?' cried Honoria in dismay.

'Don't know what you mean by "his nonsense", but he painted so lurid a picture of me, lying broken in a quarry, that His Grace was thrown into such a state of anxiety as to endanger his health. For that, if for nothing else,' he added grimly, 'he will answer to me.'

'Now, Damien,' said his betrothed on a minatory note, 'you know you cannot be at outs with Quentin because – '

'Because what?' he flashed.

'Well, think of my position if he talks of your – your connection with another lady,' she said demurely. He eyed her angrily.

'I am thinking of your position, Honoria, and thinking it is time and enough it was made clear!' He looked directly at Captain Ryder who stood, rigid as a statue, grey eyes smouldering, fists clenched behind his back. 'Let us have done with this betrothal of ours.'

'No, no, that would never do, Damien,' she protested. 'Cannot you see, if I were to throw you over now it would lend an air of verisimilitude to Quentin's tattling?'

'The devil it would!' growled his lordship. 'Yes, I suppose you are right, we'll have to stay rivetted until this blows over.' Much of the anger faded from Captain Ryder's eyes as he looked, bewildered, from one to the other. The Marquis took pity on him. 'She ain't going to marry me, Ryder,' he explained kindly. 'Well, how could she when all her heart is – '

'Damien!' implored the now scarlet-cheeked and not at all composed Miss Winton, but his lordship was not to be deflected from his purpose.

'No, I'll not be silent. It was a cucumberish scheme, anyway, and I'm no nearer to finding my heiress.'

'I imagined you to have found her, my lord!' said Captain Ryder in a stifled sort of voice.

'What – Honoria? Good God, man, she don't give the snap of her fingers for me! You'd be a fool not to have her, she's as game as a pebble – a real Trojan!' This rousing encomium had the effect of putting Miss Winton in mind of the fact that they were forgetting poor Miss Devenish and she must see to her comfort. 'I'm for Bath tomorrow, do you wish to accompany me, Honoria?' went on the Marquis, then, glancing from her flushed face to the captain's intent one, he added quickly, 'No? Well, perhaps you don't care for the idea.'

Miss Winton opened her lips as if to reply, then, thinking better of it, cast him a very speaking look and hastily left the room.

'And I had best be off, ma'am,' said Captain Ryder, starting as one coming out of a trance and making his bow to her ladyship. 'Servant, m'lord.' He hesitated, then took the hand the Marquis held out to him. 'I hardly know what to say.'

'Then say nothing,' advised his lordship sensibly. 'She's a bit hot at hand but you'll know how to deal with that, I daresay. The thing is, she's right. We cannot break the engagement just yet or we'll have all the tabbies saying it was because of Miss Devenish.'

'Your delicacy of feeling does you credit, my lord. But why did you ever –' He caught the warning expression in the Marquis's eye and turned to Mr Marsden. 'I rode over on my new mare for you to see her paces. She's a prime bit of blood – well up to your weight, I'd say.'

George's face lit up with pleasure. Horses he could understand, simple uncomplicated creatures that gave you their loyalty and had no finicking notions about honour and propriety.

'Something slap, is she? Then, if you'll excuse me, ma'am, I'll just step outside and look over her points. Coming, Shal?'

'Lord Shalford and I have things to discuss,' said his grandmother in a very repressive tone.

'What? Oh – er, yes, yes of course. Well, I – I shan't be long.'

'Don't hurry on my account,' returned her ladyship, seating herself with great deliberation and arranging her numerous scarves to her satisfaction. 'My regards to your mother, Jeremy. I hope she will soon be in better spirits.' As the door closed behind the captain, she motioned to Damien to take a chair beside her. 'And now, my lord, may I know what precisely has been going on between you and my granddaughter?'

'Nothing that she need be ashamed of, ma'am. I wish my conscience was as clear.'

His patent sincerity impressed her in spite of her doubts, and she watched him closely while he told her of his meetings with Cherryanne, observing the softening of his expression when he uttered her granddaughter's name and the way he presented Cherryanne's behaviour to her in the best possible light. When he had finished she nodded, as if satisfied.

'And what do you propose to do about all this, my lord?'

'What can I do, ma'am?' he asked simply.

'Nothing until Sir Quentin shows his hand,' she agreed. 'But should he do so and Miss Winton's kindly offices be insufficient to check a scandal, would you be prepared to redeem my granddaughter's character?'

'If needs be, yes, ma'am, but – '

Her eyebrows went up. 'But, my lord?'

'I doubt she'd have me!' Much though he strove to conceal his feelings, the hurt in his voice betrayed him.

'Let us be plain with one another, my lord. Miss Winton has given me to understand that your affairs are in so poor a way that you must marry for money.'

The Marquis flushed with annoyance. 'She had no right to discuss such a thing with anyone!'

'You discussed her affairs with even less discretion just now.' she reminded him. 'She would make you a good wife, Shalford.'

'She loves Ryder,' he returned shortly.

'In my day, love was never considered a necessary concomitant for a marriage such as yours.'

'What? Marry her and be a complaisant husband? Not in my style, ma'am, I assure you! But I won't disappoint you. When I marry my heiress, my affections will be centred solely on her money-bags! And now, if you will excuse me, I must return to Studleigh, for I intend to journey to Bath tomorrow there to confront my cousin.'

'You are never going to offer him a challenge? That, if you will forgive my saying so, would be a lamentable indiscretion, my lord.'

'I'd liefer horsewhip him!'

'What – with one hand? I am obliged to confess that I think that very unlikely. You could, however, inform him that if he persists in his intentions you have my permission to marry my granddaughter yourself. That should bring him to a stand.'

'I told you, ma'am, I doubt she'd have me.'

'Well, he's not to know that, is he?' she pointed out, very reasonably.

'True enough!' He rose to take her hand. 'My thanks for your understanding, Lady Harpendene. Rest assured Miss Devenish will not suffer through any act of mine.'

She smiled up at him almost impishly. 'Yes, my lord, I think I understand very well. Take care how you go on.'

After he had left her she sat alone for some time with her thoughts until joined by Miss Winton.

'Oh, has Damien gone? I did want a word with him. Is he, do you know, resolved to go to Bath tomorrow?'

'I believe so, but I have impressed upon him the imprudence of putting a period to Sir Quentin's life.'

'He won't do that,' said Honoria confidently, 'because Quentin won't be there. He goes to London today.'

'And it would not suit Shalford's dignity to be chasing him all over the country?'

'More than that. It will give Damien time to think and, when his first wrath has cooled, he will begin to comprehend that Quentin should be allowed to make the first move.'

Lady Harpendene rose, gathering her scarves about her. 'I must have a word with Charity. Shalford is prepared to cast you off and marry her should it become necessary.'

'Very proper of him,' assented Miss Winton.

'But he fears she will have none of him '

'Now, why, I wonder?' marvelled Miss Winton.

'This, I mean to discover,' said Lady Harpendene and went upstairs to her granddaughter's bedroom.

Here she learned with no loss of time that Miss Devenish, while very sensible of his lordship's condescension in offering for her, found herself quite unable to contemplate such an outcome.

'I assure you, dear grandmama, he is merely doing what he thinks he ought. It is prodigious kind of him but such an alliance would be most distasteful to me. In any case, it is quite – quite unnecessary. I am sorry to learn that he and Miss Winton are not to be wed, but I have no doubt she will find greater happiness as Captain Ryder's wife than as the Marchioness of Shalford. As for his lordship, he has but to crook his little finger and half the ladies of the ton will fall at his feet. He'll not lack a wife for very long.'

Wondering what Damien could possibly have done to put himself so far beyond forgiveness, Lady Harpendene wisely said no more but advised her granddaughter to have a little sleep and left her. This Cherryanne, having first cried her fill, obediently did. Her grandmother's last words to her had made small impression on her unhappy state of mind.

'In two or three weeks' time, when you are better, my dear,' had said Lady Harpendene, 'I have the notion of carrying you off to London. You will remember that I spoke to you when first you came here of my hopes of Amelia Caldwell taking you on for a season, but then she went off to Brussels with her husband. I had a letter from her this morning, telling me she expects to be back in St James's Square by the end of this month and would be delighted to receive you a week or so after that. It all fits in most admirably and I myself will accompany you for a time. I should like to see London just once more. They say Almacks is as full of starch as ever – I cannot understand what people see in the place. In my opinion, it is not to be compared with Mrs Cornelys' assemblies at Carlisle House in my young days. But it is all the go, I suppose, and if Amelia can procure vouchers for you you will be well set up.'

She later disclosed her intention to Miss Winton, who gave it her full approval. 'That would be just the thing,' she exclaimed.

'It would distract her mind and allow time for all this to blow over.'

'Presuming that it does blow over,' warned Lady Harpendene. 'Now, about my other plan.'

'I think I had better accompany you,' said Miss Winton, not altogether happily.

'No.' Her ladyship was quite decided. 'Shalford has declared his intention of going to Bath tomorrow, he could come by Winchester. I would be easier in my mind if you were here.'

Miss Winton had to smile. 'To stand guard? Ma'am, I beg of you, what are you going to *say* tomorrow?'

'I don't know,' confessed Lady Harpendene, 'but my tongue has never yet failed me.'

Miss Winton breathed a silent prayer to whatever gods might be concerning themselves in the matter, but no hint of her apprehension was apparent in her untroubled countenance as she saw her hostess comfortably disposed in her chaise the following morning.

Her ladyship, resplendent in a shoulder-caped pelisse of pale grey wool, ornamented and lined with violet satin and trimmed with swansdown, with imposing turban of matching satin, indicated to the awe-struck Kenyon that he might proceed.

'W-where to, m'lady?' he ventured to enquire.

'To Studleigh, if you please, and as I wish to be there not later than midday, you'd best get over the ground without delay.'

Calling upon Romulus and Remus to give of their best, the deeply impressed Kenyon urged them away in rattling style, leaving Miss Winton waving encouragingly after the departing vehicle.

As she turned to go into the house, it occurred to her to wonder if Sir Quentin had indeed left Bath for London. While she had no love for the gentleman nor particular concern for his welfare, neither did she wish to see Damien forced to flee the country for an ill-judged attack upon his cousin, and she knew her betrothed well enough to understand that should the two men meet before his choler had abated then almost anything might happen.

Lady Harpendene, in her solitary state, was thinking much the same thoughts. She had ever had a kindness for handsome young rakes and Damien had aroused it.

F

'I dare swear he's vastly taken with her, but he'll not marry to disoblige his parents,' she muttered, banging on the floor of the chaise with her stick to emphasize her deliberations so loudly as to cause Kenyon to rein in his pair and look round in alarm. 'No, no, go on! Spring 'em, man, spring 'em!'

'Yes, m'lady!' gasped the scandalized groom and pushed the greys to unheard of efforts so that they arrived, lathered and trembling at such unaccustomed ill-use, a good fifteen minutes in hand, before the front entrance of Studleigh.

The elderly butler who admitted her seemed less than appreciative of his unlooked-for visitor. 'I doubt if His Grace is receiving, m'lady.'

'Then I'll wait until he is!' she snapped. 'Pray inform His Grace that I have something of moment to impart to him and will not waste either his time or my own. Also be so good as to inform him that I was known to him many years ago as Alicia Douglas.'

That took the trick. The butler knew who the Hon. Alicia Douglas had been as well as he knew whose grandmother Lady Harpendene was and, ushering her into a small saloon where a good fire was burning, he hastened in search of His Grace's valet, a gentleman as venerable as he himself, to whom he declared that he had known all along how it would be and Master Damien had cut line just once too often.

'Not a bit of it!' said that worthy cheerfully. 'Offer her ladyship every civility while I get His Grace into good pin. I have a notion that this will cook Sir Quentin's goose for him!'

For, unbelievable as it may seem to their employers, servants have their own ways of discovering things and, in the opinion of the staff at Studleigh, Sir Quentin had behaved in a very scaly fashion. To have spun a tale of disaster about the Marquis to his father and then not even wait to see if all was well with him seemed to them to be the outside of anything. Even were they not informed about the Winterslow Hut affair, Miss Devenish's visit to Studleigh had not passed unnoticed and this, added to his lordship's gallant attempt to rescue her, had aroused great speculation. While Miss Winton was accorded general approval, should the Marquis change horses in mid-stream as it were, it could not in the opinion of his faithful retainers be held to be of any great significance, since any lady he honoured with his attentions would serve to make the possibility of Sir Quentin's inheriting the title a shade more remote – a circumstance which could not fail to afford gratification to all.

CHAPTER
FOURTEEN

'Damien,' said his mother plaintively, 'you cannot be pursuing Quentin up to London to call him to account – and for what, pray? After all, he hasn't said anything to anyone outside the family, has he? Nor will he if he intends to marry Miss Devenish.'

'What if she won't have him?' The Marquis was standing by the window, looking out on Royal Crescent and toying with the cords of the curtain drapes.

'She would be mad not to,' said the Duchess simply. 'Unless you – she – oh, do stop playing with that cord or you will have the curtains down atop of you! I should have thought for a house supposed to be furbished in the first style of fashion that those outdated festoons would have been replaced long since.'

'Mama,' said his lordship, taking no notice of Her Grace's petulant outburst, indicative of her agitated frame of mind, 'if she don't take Quentin there'll be no holding his resentment. I cannot allow Miss Devenish to suffer from it without making a push to rescue her.'

'But – but Honoria?' she protested weakly, sinking on to the sofa and having recourse to her aromatic vinegar. 'Yes, I know she said she was not going to marry you, but could you not persuade her?'

'Not a chance in the world,' he said curtly. 'Honoria is going to marry Jeremy Ryder – but do not, I beg of you, be telling Lady Braidestone that!'

'All that money!' she murmured wistfully. 'I cannot see that Captain Ryder is any more deserving than we are! I – Damien! What nodcocks we are, to be sure!' He eyed her suspiciously and requested to be further enlightened. 'Why, Miss Devenish, of course! Quentin seems well pleased with her prospects and the Harpendenes, as I recall, were never short of a penny.'

Her son sighed. 'No doubt, mama, but there is a world of difference between a genteel fortune and a great one.'

Her face fell like that of a disappointed child. 'And we need a great one?'

'Yes, my love, if we are to keep Studleigh.'

'For myself,' said the Duchess largely, 'I care nothing for the place. But your father –'

'Just so. If he was forced to sell it after all his efforts to get us off handsomely, it would be the end of him.' He flicked the curtain cord from him and turned to face her. 'What d'you say, mama, shall I put a notice in *The Gentleman's Magazine* or the *Morning Chronicle*, d'you think? Impoverished peer, sound in wind and limb, with crumbling family seat and heavily mortgaged estates to offer, seeks well-heeled wife. Her consequence need not signify, since his should be great enough to ensure her being accepted in all but the most stiff-necked circles!'

At the bitterness in his voice his mother cried out in protest. 'Oh, no, Damien! Your father would never ask it of you!'

'I know it, ma'am. But it is the least I can do for him who has worn himself out in my service.'

'But – if you feel you must offer for Miss Devenish?' she faltered.

'Oh, she won't have me,' he returned shortly.

The disclosure that there were two ladies in the world who did not wish to marry her beloved son so shocked Her Grace that she was momentarily deprived of speech. Finally, she got out: 'What a very unusual young woman she must be!'

'Unusual?' He rolled the word upon his tongue as if savouring it. 'Yes, you could say she is unusual. She is also hot-tempered, self-willed, impertinent – nay, rude! – full of pluck and spirit and – and quite adorable!'

'Oh, Damien!' The Duchess's eyes filled with ready tears. 'You're in love with her!'

He came to sit beside her and take her hand. 'Now, mama, don't be getting any romantical notions into your pretty head. Love is not a necessary concomitant to a marriage such as mine, or so I am informed upon good authority.'

'Whose authority?' she demanded to be told.

'Lady Harpendene's.'

'That old – did you speak to her, then?'

'I put myself in her hands. She is aware of my difficulties.'

'You mean you told her we were all to pieces and you could not marry her granddaughter?'

'I obtained her permission to offer for Miss Devenish should the necessity arise.'

'But,' protested the bewildered Duchess, 'I don't understand you, Damien. With one breath you say you must marry a great heiress, then you talk of offering for Miss Devenish who, you tell me, won't have you – and why not, I should like to know? She is not likely ever to receive a more favourable offer! What do you hope to achieve?'

He patted her hand soothingly. 'To silence Quentin, of course. He knows well I am a far greater catch than he – pockets to let or not. No more than yourself could he conceive of my being turned down. Or so Lady Harpendene believes.'

'She is quite right,' said the Duchess after a little consideration. 'But I doubt it will silence Quentin for he is going to be very angry if he cannot have Miss Devenish.'

'What can he do?' asked the Marquis scornfully. 'To be spreading scandalous reports about the future Duchess of Evesham would not be at all to his taste for it would reflect upon the family. He has a great sense of what is due to the Strattons, has cousin Quentin.'

'And a great capacity for vindictiveness,' said Her Grace with unusual insight. 'Have a care, Damien, he may well do you a mischief.'

But he only laughed and told her not to be fanciful, Quentin would not be so ill-advised. In which happy conviction he was to be shown to be quite at fault, for Sir Quentin was devoting considerable thought to the problem of how to remove that apparently insurmountable obstacle from the path of his ambition, his noble cousin of Shalford.

His prime object in making generally known the dubious connection between the Marquis and Miss Devenish was two-fold; the first essential being to press the lady into marriage with himself and secure her presumed fortune; the second and scarcely less urgent aim was to open Miss Winton's eyes very fully to the nature of the man she was engaged to marry.

Miss Winton, now, he mused, as he sat watching his valet change the dressing on his swollen ankle, a strange young woman, to be sure. She had accepted his tactfully worded story with as little concern as if she had heard it all beforehand. Could it be that Shalford, fearful of the tale getting about, had told her as much as he thought fit for her to know? Sir Quentin uttered a sharp expletive, indicative of his annoyance, and Harding looked up in question.

'It is not giving you pain, sir?'

'No, no,' said his master irritably. 'It does very well, the swelling would appear to be subsiding.'

'Indeed, sir, I think it greatly improved. I venture to foretell that, within a week, you will be walking easily on it.'

'No, Harding,' said Sir Quentin softly. 'I will not. You will please to remember that this ankle is destined to trouble me for several weeks.'

'As you say, sir,' agreed Harding, drawing up a stocking over his handiwork. 'And if his lordship should call to see you?'

Sir Quentin smiled approvingly at the man's quick understanding. 'I shall receive him with my foot bound up upon a gout-stool. I doubt even his hasty temper would vent itself upon so helpless an object!'

Harding was of the same opinion but it had him quite at a loss to know what his master had in mind. Capricious and unscrupulous he might be, yet he did not lack courage. Doubtless he had no wish to cross swords with the Marquis and, indeed, it would not be at all seemly for cousins to be at each other with the buttons off. Such reflections, however, were best left unvoiced and Harding contented himself with saying:

'Then it would be best, sir, if you maintained the pretence for the benefit of all the household.'

'Lest my mother should remark that she had seen me walking about as brisk as an eel? Yes, you have a point there, and – my potion, Harding? I'll be needing more.'

'Yes, sir, but I had every expectation of your calling upon the doctor for your regular bleeding and thought to remind you then.'

'I cannot see him until I am afoot again, else he will require to look at my injury. Nor do I wish my mother to know anything of this overheating of my blood which gives the good doctor such concern. I will pen a note for him; be so good as to call at his house this afternoon.'

Harding bowed and, collecting up his cloths, withdrew, leaving Sir Quentin to ponder on just how great a length of time should elapse before he presented himself again to Lady Harpendene's notice. Three weeks, he thought, should be sufficient for her to talk sense into the girl and, once having secured his bride, then he could turn his attention to the Marquis. Several schemes had presented themselves to his ready imagination, but his cousin's dexterity with sword and pistol, allied to a tendency to land on his feet like a cat in any misadventure, had prohibited the taking of undue risk. There was no denying that an end must be made of the Marquis before he married and produced an heir, and all in the most innocent-seeming way.

Sir Quentin sighed in the manner of one who regrets having to perform so disagreeable a duty. It was all very unfortunate, and would undoubtedly hasten the Duke's demise, but the thought of literally killing two birds with one stone appeared to afford him great satisfaction and presently, smiling contentedly at such an agreeable prospect, he closed his eyes and composed himself for sleep. A moment later he opened them again very wide and sat up in his chair.

'I wonder have I been at fault in not examining the affair at the Winterslow Hut more closely,' he debated aloud. 'Odds on't the tale could be improved upon by the judicious bestowal of a guinea or two and her ladyship's doubts quite set at rest.'

Harding, entering the room quietly to see if his master required anything further, was startled to hear him laugh and the sound was enough to cause the valet to retreat again as noiselessly as he had entered, for well he knew that what might afford amusement to Sir Quentin could bode little good for some some other.

*   *   *

When due time had passed Sir Quentin did not, as might have

been expected, go directly to Winterslow, but called first at Chilcomb Manor to be received by Metchett with the unwelcome intelligence that her ladyship and Miss Devenish had left a few days before for London. Thereafter, Sir Quentin's movements became even more unpredictable for he went north towards Marlborough. Once there, instead of seeking lodging at the Castle, he pressed on to Beckhampton where he was not known, and put up at the Wagon and Horses for a night and a day, using an assumed name and laying aside the dress and bearing of a gentleman of quality. Harding, who was much astonished at this proceeding, was instructed to remove himself and the phaeton to the Bear at Devizes, at which renowned hostelry his master would join him when his business was completed.

Sir Quentin, meantime, had further established himself as a person of modest means by declining to order a private dinner and partaking of the Ordinary. This meal was substantial enough to attract a number of persons and, for a small sum, the guests ate as much as they pleased of several dishes. Sir Quentin fell into conversation in the most genial manner with his fellow diners, so that it was not at all remarkable when he repaired with two of them to the taproom and sat with them for some time, finally allowing himself to be persuaded to join them in going to view a cockfight that was being held locally.

Once there, these two tidy ones, now seemingly in merry pin, became very free with their money in placing bets, until a gentle hint from Sir Quentin cautioned them that such prodigality was attracting attention, whereupon the one proclaimed himself to have not a feather left to fly with, while the other informed the company at large that they were more accustomed to matching their tykes at Jem Rolfe's amphitheatre than setting the cocks. After which ingenuous confession, they withdrew, followed by scornful laughter and a few coarse and idiomatic remarks from the local enthusiasts.

Once outside, however, after a few quiet exchanges which sounded to be in the nature of last-minute instructions from Sir Quentin and acquiescence from his now strangely sober companions, they parted company. Sir Quentin returned to the inn where he engaged the services of a carriage to bear him to Devizes on the following day and went to bed, there to sleep the sleep of one satisfied that his plans had been laid with scrupulous attention to the smallest detail.

Harding was taken aback to receive his master at an early hour the next morning and to be ordered to assist him into his usual natty attire with no loss of time. Then, after a hurried breakfast, they set out, giving the general impression that their destination was Bath, but no sooner were they clear of the town than they wheeled south of the Bath road and made for Winterslow.

So gratified was Sir Quentin with his arrangements and so hasty had been his removal from the vicinity of Beckhampton that, upon perceiving a pleasing tavern set fairly amid trees just off the road, he decided to stop for a meal and a rest. Harding, who had been observing his master's high colour and air of suppressed elation with no little unease, ventured to suggest that he availed himself of some of Dr Vernon's potion, but the advice was angrily waved away.

'Fiddle! I'm in prime order! Stop cossetting me like an old woman!'

And, as if to prove his ability to do without any medical stimulant, he consumed two bottles of wine with his meal and topped that off with several glasses of brandy.

Alarmed at this excessive indulgence on the part of his normally abstemious employer, Harding dared to offer to handle the phaeton for the remainder of their journey but got a sharp set-down for his pains, and they proceeded at a cracking pace.

At last, to the valet's profound relief, the end of the journey came in sight but not before they had courted disaster on at least two occasions. The first of these came about when they encountered an on-coming curricle and pair, holding well to their side of the road. Just as they drew near, both at full stretch, Sir Quentin seemed to loose his hold upon the reins and drew one hand across his forehead as if bemused. His team plunged and wavered and, had it not been for the superb driving of the gentleman in the curricle, there was little doubt that both vehicles would have smashed into each other, with what result at such speed can be left to the imagination.

Somehow, Sir Quentin had regained control of his cattle and

they careered on, but Harding, looking over his shoulder, saw the
curricle drawn up and the gentleman staring after them. Captain
Gronow it was, he could swear to it, and a greater rattle there was
not in all London. Soon it would be about that that notable whip,
Sir Quentin Stratton, was no more fit to handle a phaeton-and-
four than was a babe in arms. Never had Harding seen his master
in such case, driving like a man possessed, cheeks flushed, eyes
glittering, teeth showing in a strange, fixed smile.

The second incident was scarce less alarming. They had come
up with an Accommodation coach on a narrow stretch of road and,
once again, Sir Quentin's judgement seemed to fail him. The
coach was lurching about and proceeding at a dangerous speed
for so cumbersome a vehicle and Harding perceived that it was
being driven by a young fop who, doubtless, had bribed the
coachman to let him take the ribbons for a stage, to the great
discomfort of the passengers.

As the phaeton drew level a lady put her head out of the window
and gave vent to a shrill scream of alarm, while an unhappy outside
passenger shouted: 'For God's sake, don't attempt it, sir, or we'll
all be in the ditch!'

But Sir Quentin's inborn skill did not desert him at the last
moment and they squeezed by, though Harding was prepared to
swear that their offside wheels did not touch ground at the moment
of passing. Urged on by the shouts and imprecations of the self-
appointed coachman and his companions, they sped forward once
again and no further alarms hindered their progress until they
approached the Winterslow Hut.

The sky had been heavy and overcast all day, the light had
faded early and, because of Sir Quentin's protracted lunch and
the nap which he had felt necessary for his well-being afterwards,
dusk combined with a light mist was already falling. Harding,
mentally determined to have his master laid upon his bed with a
double dose of Dr Vernon's potion inside him within minutes of
their arrival, was preparing to spring down quickly and hand the
phaeton over to the first ostler who offered, when a sudden whirl
of mist across their nostrils caused the leaders to jib and hesitate
just as they were swinging into the forecourt of the inn. Once
again, it appeared beyond Sir Quentin's power to check them, the

reins went slack and the team plunged out of control. Then from the side of the inn, almost out of the mist, or so it looked to Harding's fascinated gaze, a yellow beast seemed to rise from the ground and hurl itself towards the phaeton. The already agitated leaders reared and kicked; Sir Quentin stood up, relinquishing all hold on the reins, one hand clutching his throat, the other pressed to his chest.

'The lioness!' he cried out, and then, 'Shoot her, man, shoot her!'

The frail vehicle rocked and swayed and, before the horrified valet could lay hold of his master, Sir Quentin was flung violently from it to the ground.

*   *   *

'I cannot understand it, my lord, though I allow myself to have been much at fault in not ensuring that the young dog was shut up. We had him to replace th'other one that the lioness slew and there's no doubt that he's a big, yellow creature. In the mist and failing light, perhaps, to one who knew the story it might well appear that — '

'Don't hold yourself to blame, landlord.' Damien laid a re-assuring hand on the man's shoulder. 'My cousin was of a full-blooded habit. I am informed he had been receiving treatment for it. He died of an apoplexy. To judge of what his man told me, he had been in poor case all day and had indulged himself unwisely. To mistake the dog for a lioness, even in bad visual conditions, was not to be expected of a man in full command of his senses.' He paused, thinking deeply. 'Now I had best go on to Bath to acquaint my mother with the sad tale. The conveyance should arrive from Studleigh tomorrow to carry my cousin's body thence, where he will be interred in the family vault.'

'You will have some food before you go, my lord,' begged the landlord.

'Yes, a bite perhaps, but I may not linger. I must push on at least as far as Amesbury tonight.'

'At once, my lord. I'll set it for you upstairs in the front room where you may be private.'

The Marquis was about to protest that he would prefer to eat in the coffee-room but changed his mind and, with a wry smile, went upstairs to the chamber where first he had spoken to Miss Devenish. Standing by the window, looking down into the fore-court, he thought to himself of the tragedy and near tragedy it had witnessed and turned over in his mind what Harding had told him when he had arrived at Studleigh that morning, his horse close to foundering under him and he as shaken and wan as if he had been meeting with ghosts.

'Out of all reason excited he was,' the valet had explained, shaking his head in bewilderment. 'Nor I haven't seen him eat nor drink like that in many a month, for the doctor said 'twas not good for him. It was as if – as if he had come to a turning-point and made a decision, whether for good or bad is not for me to say, my lord, but I'd the notion it was bad for someone.'

'Bad for someone, was it?' mused Damien. 'I wonder who? Ah, well, best not to brood over that for whatever mischief he was planning will come to nothing now.'

It so happened, however, that the news of Sir Quentin's un-happy fate did not reach the ears of two somewhat dubious gentle-men lodging in a tavern near Beckhampton. Nor, indeed, if it had would it have meant anything to them, for the smoothly spoken toff who was paying them handsomely to carry out his wishes had not seen fit to disclose his true identity, a not unusual precaution in such circumstances.

CHAPTER
FIFTEEN

Lady Caldwell's well-appointed house in St James's Square was as elegant and stylish an establishment as could be found anywhere in London, and her ladyship was a sprightly matron who could scarce believe that she had a daughter already married and was like to become a grandmother before the year was out.

'Too ageing, my dear Lady Harpendene!' she declared, rolling her expressive dark eyes Heavenward. 'I vow nothing ever fell out half as well as your bringing Miss Devenish to support my spirits, for my younger girls, as you know, are still in the schoolroom. it will be quite two years before the elder is ready for her come-out, and long before then I should surely have lapsed into the dismals and be thinking of nothing more stimulating than which lace cap to tie on under my chin – *such* a lowering reflection!'

Lady Harpendene permitted herself a thin smile. Though from anyone else she would have treated such a frivolous expression of opinion with contempt, Amelia Caldwell stood in the unique position of being daughter to her oldest friend, and when she looked at her she saw not Amelia but Deborah, her mother, so like her deceased parent was Lady Caldwell.

Miss Devenish, sitting primly on a chair beside Lady Harpendene, nibbling a Naples biscuit, said nothing, and even when her enthusiastic hostess began to outline a few of the pleasures in store for her, she merely interposed a few shy words to remind her that it would be a little time before her collar-bone would be perfectly mended.

'Oh, indeed, my dear, I would not dream of bustling you about until you are feeling more the thing. For the present, our days will be well spent in seeing to your apparel, for so taking a young lady must be set off to the best advantage!' One sweeping glance informed Miss Devenish that what had passed for the first style of fashion in Bath would never do for London. 'And I can promise you a truly brilliant season for the Princess Charlotte and her husband are now entering into the social scene. She is quite the ragamuffin still, you know, despite her married state, but of such a warm and generous disposition one cannot help but like her.'

As she was speaking Lady Caldwell was taking stock of her young protégée. The girl looked rather pale and downcast but that, to be sure, could be attributed to her recent unfortunate experiences, of which her grandmother had supplied as detailed an account as she considered advisable. She was undoubtedly a Beauty, and one who would repay the attention her ladyship intended to lavish upon her. A lovely face, of course, was not everything, but Lady Caldwell was of the opinion that quite a modest competence would serve to get the young lady off her hands before the season was over and reminded herself to have a word with Lady Harpendene on that subject without loss of time.

'I leave the business of dress entirely to you, Amelia. You will do as you think best.'

Even as she spoke, Lady Harpendene recollected that to be giving such a carte blanche to Lady Caldwell was little short of lunacy, and resolved to qualify her statement when they were private together.

'Oh, to be sure, it will afford me the greatest pleasure!' Lady Caldwell looked her delight at the prospect of spending someone else's money. 'Dear mama was ever saying that if I did not find myself to be in the latest mode I was thrown so utterly out of spirits as to be quite beyond anything!' She then regaled them with a lively account of Lady Cholmondeley's ball at which the Regent had appeared, 'dressed in black trousers, if you please! Depend upon it, he will set a new fashion, though I cannot but wonder if dear Mr Brummell would have approved.' She sighed gustily and fell to considering George Brummell's unhappy situation for quite ten seconds before continuing. 'Just as soon as Miss Devenish is ready for it, I propose to give a small ton party to launch her into society. Have you any acquaintance among young ladies of your own age in town, my dear?'

Miss Devenish was about to disclaim any such hopeful connection when Lady Harpendene broke in. 'There is Miss Honoria

Winton, though she may still be at Bath with Her Grace of Evesham, yet she informed me she has the intention of returning to London before long.'

'Oh, you know Honoria? She would be just the person for you to be seen with for she is of the first consequence, being betrothed to Shalford, and like to put you in the way of meeting all the fashionables.' Then, catching an eloquent glance from Lady Harpendene, she went on with scarcely a pause for breath. 'And now – I may call you Cherryanne, may I not? Such a charming name! – you will be wishing to put off your bonnet and see your room. It was Phoebe's – my eldest daughter, now Lady Phillimore – and I have had it made over for you. I will summon my abigail to take you upstairs while your grandmama and I have a comfortable cose.'

Murmuring her thanks, Cherryanne permitted herself to be led away and was greeted by an enthusiastic Bridie in the throes of unpacking her valises.

'Sure, miss, 'tis like a princess her ladyship means to be treating you! Everything of the best and them all so kind with it! Now you be sitting down there with your feet up on that chair for I know by the white little face on you that you have the headache. And if I read the signs aright, you'll be needing all the rest you can get to keep abreast of my lady's plans!'

Miss Hanrahan proved to be perfectly accurate in her prognostications for thereafter Miss Devenish's days were so filled with visits to silk and lace merchants, to dressmakers and hairdressers, to perfumers and mantua-makers; with driving in the Park when once her hostess was satisfied that her appearance was complete to a shade; and with seeing every sight in London from the Elgin Marbles in a wooden shed at the British Museum to the waxworks in Water Lane, that she had little time for thought upon any other subject. For, although nursing a broken heart and therefore incapable of being moved by the simple pleasures enjoyed by more fortunate beings, Miss Devenish could not but be sensible of the admiration her beauty commanded which, when set off by the tasteful wardrobe recommended by Lady Caldwell, bid fair to establish her as one of the Toasts of the town. Truth to tell, in spite of her misfortunes, Miss

Devenish found herself to be not utterly indifferent to a nicely turned compliment or a gathering where the company was generally pleasing, though, too often, she lay disconsolate upon a damp pillow until dawn to awake heavy-eyed and low in spirits to Bridie's voluble distress.

The news, conveyed to her by Miss Winton when she accompanied the Duchess on her visit to London to commiserate with the unhappy Lady Stratton, of Sir Quentin's demise, at first so shocked her that she was unable to take in its full significance. When she did, she most unaccountably burst into tears, while her grandmother and Miss Winton, one on either side of her, patted her hands and commended her extreme sensibility in lamenting the death of one who had been so ill disposed towards her.

Sniffing into her handkerchief, Miss Devenish felt she could hardly inform the ladies that it was not so much the fact of Sir Quentin being no more that occasioned her tears as the realization that now the Marquis need not feel obliged to offer for her and she, of course, would be deprived of the pleasure of turning him down. The mere thought of his lordship brought on a fresh paroxysm, and she was easily persuaded to retire to her room and have her cry out.

'Shock, no doubt,' said Lady Harpendene in a perfectly expressionless voice. 'It does take people in the strangest ways, or so I am given to understand.'

Miss Winton agreed that it could be so, though each lady carefully avoided catching the other's eye.

'Callous though it may seem to be taking thought for myself at such a time,' said Honoria, 'I think it proper to inform your ladyship that I intend to terminate my engagement to Shalford at once.'

Lady Harpendene raised her eyebrows in well-simulated disapproval. 'And he so recently bereaved? Miss Winton, I had not thought you capable of such unkindness!'

'I have written to him to this effect,' went on Honoria blithely, ignoring this satirical shaft, 'and I have suggested that he comes to town as soon as may be so that the thing may be done in a proper style. In just four weeks I shall be twenty-one and – well, a decent interval must elapse before – er, before I – '

'Before you can accept the addresses of another gentleman?' suggested Lady Harpendene helpfully. 'But I thought it was arranged that Shalford was to renounce you in the most affecting manner and nobly thrust you into Captain Ryder's embrace?'

'Oh, no, that won't answer.' Miss Winton was looking rarely confused. 'Jer – Captain Ryder don't care for the notion and Damien says he'd never carry it off. Besides, well – '

'There is no need for such subterfuge, is there?' asked Lady Harpendene, who perceived that certain confidences had been exchanged during Miss Winton's stay at Chilcomb. 'When do you expect Shalford?'

'At any time for he should have received my letter by today at latest.'

'And how do you propose to jilt him?' enquired Lady Harpendene curiously.

'I have not quite decided but I dare say it will not prove difficult. He is of such a fiery temperament that a quarrel will occasion no surprise.'

'I am almost beginning to pity his lordship,' commented Lady Harpendene, the twinkle in her eye belying her words.

'I do pity him,' declared Miss Winton roundly, 'torn as he is, poor boy, between his duty and his love.'

'If I could be certain of that – but he must make the decision himself.' Her ladyship sounded to be at her most forbidding but Miss Winton was not deceived.

'I feel sure it will be the right one, ma'am,' she said, smiling. 'Now, I am proposing to arrange a visit to Kew Gardens for I am persuaded that they are truly at their best at this time of the year. It would please me greatly if Miss Devenish could bear me company – and Mr Marsden, too, if it should be convenient for him.'

'I'll answer for it that they will both be delighted.'

Miss Winton was not so confident on that head, but she had no doubt that Lady Harpendene's grandchildren would do as she directed them. George had waited dutifully upon his cousin since her coming to town, though, since his grandmother had informed him bluntly that, as he appeared to be the tail runner of three claimants to Miss Devenish's hand, he had best look elsewhere for a wife, his attendances in St James's Square had fallen off to a marked degree and he showed lamentable signs of reverting to his old habits of frequenting such places as Cribb's Parlour and the Westminster Pit, to mention but two of his more reputable haunts. However, since his grandmother's opposition to his union with Cherryanne had put him in an unassailable position where his father was concerned, he assented willingly enough to her ladyship's commands, only lamenting the fact that Shalford was not in town to join their party at Kew.

Damien, who had made an excellent recovery from the injuries he had sustained in the quarry, had received his betrothed's letter and was considering the implications of it. Though he had been anticipating his dismissal since the threat of disclosure by Sir Quentin had been removed, yet he was concerned about how his father would take this further piece of unwelcome news. The Duke liked Honoria, as much for herself as for the relief her fortune would give to his straightened circumstances and, as they sat together at dinner in the vast, gloomy dining-room at Studleigh, Damien wondered just how greatly the knowledge that she was not to be his daughter-in-law would affect His Grace.

After the covers had been removed and they were installed on either side of the considerable fire which was, even in the mildest of weather, necessary for their comfort, he tentatively broached the subject by remarking that, if his father could spare him, he felt the need to pay a short visit to London.

'But, of course.' The Duke's gentle acceptance of his wishes made Damien feel more than ever guilty for the blow he was about to deal him. 'I had not hoped to keep you tied by the leg down here for ever. I only pray you have not found it too great a bore.'

'No, sir, that I have not,' replied the Marquis and, to his surprise, found that he meant it. He rose to kick back a log that had fallen forward from the fire with a sublime disregard for the tender care Foster had lavished on his superbly polished Hessians, and so did not observe the affectionately quizzical glance His Grace directed at him. 'I have had a letter from Honoria, sir, informing me that she proposes to release me from our engagement. I think it best that I go to town to discuss this with her.'

'So Honoria is going to throw you over, is she? Hmm, yes. I had a feeling you might not suit.'

'You had, sir?' The Marquis was so astonished at this calm acceptance of what he had expected would be a severe shock to his parent that he was almost bereft of words.

'I fancy she will marry Ryder after all,' went on the Duke in his quiet way.

'Y-yes, sir, I fancy she will.' Now where the devil had His Grace got that information from, wondered his son.

'But it will all be a shade uncomfortable for you, will it not?' went on the Duke, savouring his brandy as if it was of infinitely greater importance than his son's future happiness.

'If you mean Honoria's throwing me over, I don't care anything for that,' said the Marquis carefully, 'but heiresses do not grow on every bush, sir.'

'No, to be sure they do not,' agreed his father placidly, 'but I am persuaded you will discover a solution to our problem, Damien.'

The Marquis wished he could share His Grace's optimism, and it was in a very troubled frame of mind that he set out for London the next day. He was travelling light since he did not anticipate being away above a se'ennight, taking only Lawson, his groom, to attend him. He had elected to drive his team by easy stages to Speenhamland, where he kept a change of horses at the Pelican – an extravagance, he reminded himself, he would be forced to dispense with in the future – and then on the main Bath road into London.

Once at the Pelican and half the journey behind him, the Marquis ordered his disappointed groom to have the fresh team poled up and they were on the road again within the hour.

While awaiting his master, Lawson had fallen into conversation with two down-the-road looking fellows, who had proclaimed their intention of being in London that evening, but when he looked around for them they were nowhere to be seen and, as they were riding a likely-looking pair of tits, he supposed them to be well on their way.

The new team were four blood chestnuts, very much on the go through lack of exercise. The Marquis handled them gently, baiting them at Colnbrook to give them a good breathing space for the run across the Heath to Hounslow, and so on through

Isleworth and Chiswick to his ultimate destination, the Clarendon in Bond Street. This fashionable hostelry had been honoured by Her Grace's patronage, since she had declared that to open up the ducal town house for her call upon the bereaved Lady Stratton was a needless extravagance and not to be thought on. Damien was grinning to himself at this diverting notion as he drove across the Heath, for the Clarendon, which kept one of the most expensive tables in London, was hardly the place for his mama to practise her economies.

The day was warm with the sun shining mistily through a thin layer of cloud. The Marquis had thrown off his riding-coat and was sitting, hat tilted to the back of his head, whistling meditatively to himself and tooling his cattle along as easily as if he was driving in the Park. He looked at Lawson, thinking that the man had been rather silent for the latter part of the journey, and noticed the groom take out a handkerchief and furtively press it to his brow.

'Too hot for you? Ease open your coat if you wish. There'll be few to notice on the road.'

'No, m'lord, quite the contrary.' The man shivered uncontrollably. 'I feel strangely chilled and bemused. Doubtless I have taken a cold.'

'Then put my driving-coat about your shoulders. I'll not be needing it.'

'Thank you, m'lord.' Lawson pulled on the many-caped drab coat and cleared his throat hesitantly. 'Beg pardon, m'lord, but you have primed your pistols, I take it?'

'What? No, I have not. Damnation! I'd better, I suppose, though nowadays the Heath in broad daylight is as unlikely a place as any to be accosted. Still we had best be on the safe side of chance. D'you feel equal to taking them for a spell while I see to it?'

Lawson, who knew better than to suggest he should prime his master's pistols for him, agreed that such a task should not be beyond his powers, but his strained expression as he changed places with the Marquis caused the latter to ask sharply: 'Did you eat anything while at the Pelican?'

'No, m'lord, but I accepted a pot of home-brewed from two

other travellers who were making for London. I thought it tasted a bit brackish so I emptied out the most of it while their attention was diverted.'

'Not like the Pelican to serve ale that is not in prime condition,' commented the Marquis, concentrating on his pistols. He had just completed his task as they rounded a bend and came upon a gig, half across the road, with a young woman standing up in it exhorting the driver, an even more youthful country lad, to get out and give her the reins. At once Lawson drew the curricle to a stand, eyeing the space available for passing the gig with some apprehension.

'I'd not attempt it, m'lord. Not with that cob lurching about in that fashion. It's no place to be turning a vehicle.'

'Not the best, I allow.' Damien prepared to spring down from the curricle. 'And if I don't lend a hand we'll be here for ever. That chawbacon's but sawing at the poor brute's mouth – there! The wheel's in the ditch. Hold 'em steady.'

'Don't go, m'lord!' The groom's hand on his sleeve checked him. 'There's someone lurking in the bushes yonder – d'you see? It could be a trap.'

'Yes, I see.' The Marquis slid his pistols into his pockets. 'Maybe your ill-tasting home-brewed was no fault of the Pelican's, after all. I'll keep the gig between me and the bushes and the moment I have control of the cob do you drive past. That should bring our lurker out of his hiding and I'll have a fair shot at him.'

'I don't like it, m'lord. He could have a fair shot at you first.'

'I doubt that.' The Marquis took his signet ring off his finger and slipped it into his fob. 'My green coat and black beaver are like enough to your livery – I'm playing the groom, carrying out his master's commands! Now, be ready to spring 'em when I sign to you.' So saying, he alighted nimbly and approached the gig. 'Permit me, ma'am,' said he with easy courtesy, going to the head of the stout but flustered cob, that now had his ears set back and his eyes wildly rolling as he perceived the four pawing, resty chestnuts awaiting his pleasure. The young woman looked at her saviour with an odd mixture of relief and pity in her regard, while the driver of the gig sat lumpishly, doing nothing at all. This conduct went far to confirm the Marquis's suspicions that it was a plot to slow the curricle and hold up its occupants at leisure, but he allowed no sign of his unease to show in his voice as he went on cheerfully: 'What did you think you were about, lad, to be turning in a place like this and a mile of straight road on either side of you?'

As he spoke he was gently coaxing the cob to the side of the road, for it was no part of his intention to do other than make space for the curricle to pass. A muttered reply that sounded remarkably like: 'Ye'll soon find out, my buck!' made him even more convinced that the trap was ready to be sprung. Raising his arm in signal to Lawson, he backed the gig further into the ditch to the alarm of its occupants, the boy crying out: 'Hey, what be you a-doin' of, a-trapesin' about like 'at?'

The Marquis did not enlighten him for he was too occupied with holding the cob steady, while Lawson urged the chestnuts past. As he did so, a horseman burst from the cover of the bushes and galloped forward, pistol drawn upon the curricle and its driver. Damien spun round, leaving the cob to his own devices and, in the same movement, drew his own weapon and fired. A moment later a riderless horse bolted across the road and Damien, his second pistol in his hand, was kneeling by the fallen rider. One look was sufficient to tell him he had done his work well and no further trouble was to be expected from that quarter, but the sound of another shot brought his head up to look where Lawson was drawing the curricle to a halt and, to his dismay, he saw the figure of his groom slide down to the floor of the vehicle. A movement in the brushwood caught his attention and, although the distance was too great to be certain of a good result, he fired again lest Lawson's attacker should entertain any ideas of emerging to deliver a *coup de grâce*. Then, picking up his recent assailant's undischarged weapon, he hastened towards the curricle with complete disregard for his own safety, but anxious only for Lawson. As he reached the vehicle another bullet crashed into it, but so wild was the aim that he was encouraged to walk into the bushes, calling out: 'All right, you have loosed off both your barkers. Now come out and let us have a sight of you!'

A low groan answered him and when he almost stumbled over a recumbent body he realized that his aim had been truer than he knew. He was also beginning to understand that this attack had some unusual aspects and, as he bent down to loose the footpad's neckcloth, he looked about him keenly for signs of any further trouble.

'Now, tell me, as you value your life, who set you on to this?'

The fellow, having no notion that his life was not worth a farthing dip, was only too ready to confess anything that might save him from the gallows. The Marquis, though desperately anxious to see how Lawson did, bore with him patiently until the weak voice faltered and ceased; then, with a very sombre face, he rose and returned to the curricle.

At first he thought it was all up with Lawson too, but a swift examination showed the damage to be no worse than a smashed shoulder. 'Ruined my driving coat, too!' he muttered as he unstrapped his valise from the back of the vehicle and, pulling out a shirt, ripped it up into a rough bandage to staunch the bleeding. 'By God, yes! No doubt they mistook him for me in that rig!'

Wedging the half-insensible man into his seat as best he could, he gathered up the reins and was about to give the fretting chestnuts the office to start when he thought of the gig and, looking back, was rewarded by the sight of it disappearing rapidly in the opposite direction. Shrugging resignedly, he decided to leave it at that. Doubtless they were only a couple of youngsters who had been tempted by a bribe; they most likely had no notion that their employers had any intent other than robbery. His first concern was to get Lawson to a doctor and, whipping up his team, he set them off at full stretch, wishing the sun would not beat quite so strongly upon his unprotected head for, at some time during the mêlée, he had parted company with his handsome beaver.

*   *   *

The sun was also shining warmly upon Kew as Miss Winton's party explored the gardens in every direction. Their numbers had been augmented by a friend of George's, an agreeable enough young gentleman who, regrettably, did not display that admiration for the beauties of Nature to be expected from one engaged upon such an expedition. In fact, it shortly became clear that all his admiration was directed upon Miss Devenish and that he had basely taken advantage of his friendship with George to insinuate himself into the party in order to be near the object of his adulation.

As the gardens were about four miles in circumference, extending from Kew southward along the Thames towards Richmond, he had ample opportunity to further his aims. Very soon, however, George had become aware of his friend's perfidy and, insinuating his person between that of the over-attentive gentleman and Miss Devenish, he remarked in a very daunting way that it was time and enough that they made their way to Kew else they would be finding themselves to be excessively late for their dinner.

Since it was scarce four o'clock and Mr Marsden had ever been insistent that no gentleman sat down to his dinner before seven, Miss Devenish was hard put to it to keep her countenance, being irresistibly reminded of a dog with a bone who, having no wish for it himself, refuses to yield it up to any other. So through the fields towards Kew they went at a brisk pace, pausing at the village for a light refreshment of Rhenish wine and Banbury cakes, before returning by water to London.

Once upon dry land again, Mr Marsden depressed his friend's pretensions still further by bidding him a somewhat curt farewell and calling up a hackney to convey the ladies and himself to Park Place, during the course of which journey he severely tried his companions' composure by his strictures upon the behaviour of bucks and others of like character.

On arrival at their destination, they found Lady Braidestone in a state of agitation and his lordship nowhere to be found. 'Why, Honoria, must you be for ever taking after your father and absenting yourself when most needed?' her ladyship required to be informed. Miss Winton, ignoring this undeserved animadversion upon her character, asked what might be the trouble.

'Trouble? Why none at all, save that Shalford has been waylaid on Hounslow Heath and, not wishing to inflict a gravely injured man upon Her Grace at the Clarendon, came directly here in search of you.'

'Gravely injured?'

'Shalford?'

The simultaneous exclamations from the two young ladies and George's chiming in with: 'Old Shal? Good God, ma'am, how does he go on?' made Lady Braidestone realize that she could have phrased her explanation more explicitly.

'It is not Shalford that is wounded,' she hastened to assure them, 'but his groom who was apparently wearing his driving-coat – for what reason I could not discover – and the miscreants mistook the man for the master, or so I understand to be the case. But he shall tell you the tale himself for, unless I am mistaken, here he is returned from the Clarendon with Her Grace.'

Miss Devenish, despite her detestation of his lordship, could not restrain a low sob of relief which passed unobserved as the doors opened once more to admit the Duchess, and behind her the tall figure of the Marquis, immaculate in pantaloons and long-tailed coat and apparently in perfect health.

'My dear Lady Braidestone, was there ever anything so tiresome?' burst forth the Duchess. 'I cannot thank you enough for taking in poor Lawson. To be sure, the Clarendon would not have cared for it above half had Damien deposited him on their doorstep. Hotels, even the best of them, lack understanding in such matters, don't you find? And, of course, there would have been all kinds of questions which, in the rather odd circumstances which Damien assures me obtain in this affair – '

The Marquis checked his mother's outpourings with upraised hand. 'Of that we cannot be certain, mama, so let us presume it was no more than a regular hold-up for purposes of gain.'

'If that was all it was, why pick on a sporting curricle and not a laden carriage?' she retorted spiritedly. 'Anyway, the footpad told you – '

'The footpad, mama, was at his last prayers, and could well have been addled in his head.'

'You shot him, then?' enquired George with eager interest.

'Shot 'em both,' said the Marquis briefly.

'What did you do with – ' began George and then remembered the presence of ladies. 'Har – humph! Yes, of course!'

'Informed a magistrate at Hounslow while Lawson was being patched up by a doctor. They'll deal with the matter.' As he spoke, Damien's eyes were on Cherryanne and, to her extreme mortification, she found herself blushing vividly when he addressed himself to her. 'I hope I see you well, Miss Devenish, and that you are quite recovered from your dreadful experiences of our last meeting.'

'I thank you, my lord,' she heard herself make formal reply. 'And may I also express my gratitude for your care of me upon that occasion, and your disregard for your own safety.' Of a sudden she was aware that the eyes of everyone in the room were upon them, Miss Winton's in amusement, Lady Braidestone's in interested speculation, the Duchess's with solicitude, and George's with an expression of dawning comprehension. 'I – you will have so many things to attend to,' she stumbled on, wishing that he would release her hand and stop looking at her in quite that way, 'I feel it only right that George and I should take ourselves off. George, if you would be so kind as to escort me back to St James's Square?'

George opened his mouth but shut it again when the Marquis said gently: 'Allow me to be your escort, Miss Devenish. I have a carriage waiting outside.'

'Yes, Damien, take the barouche,' said Her Grace, swooping upon Cherryanne and kissing her upon either cheek. 'And don't hurry! Give my kindest to your grandmother, my dear, and tell her I shall be calling upon her tomorrow or the day following.'

Somehow, quite how she did not know, Miss Devenish found herself being handed into the Duchess's barouche, while his lordship seated himself opposite her, his dark eyes fixed upon her downcast face with such intensity of feeling as made her heart turn over in the most alarming fashion. No sooner had the door closed upon them than he reached forward to take her hands.

'Cherryanne,' he said in an oddly choked voice. 'It's no good. I love you. I have loved you, I think, from the moment I first saw you, standing at that window of the Winterslow Hut.'

Miss Devenish, although in a very confused state of mind, yet refused to allow herself to be taken in by this declaration. So he loved her, did he, but he was not going to offer her marriage because such a mesalliance would break his father's heart! The Duke might even disinherit his son and, unfeeling creature though he might be, Miss Devenish was not going to be party to any such disaster befalling the Marquis. In her misery, she forgot all reason and the hauteur in her voice when next she spoke would have done justice to her grandmother.

'Have you forgotten, my lord, that you are betrothed to Miss Winton?'

'No longer, I assure you,' he said almost gaily. 'Honoria has cast me off. But, my love, how we are to contrive the Lord only knows!'

So that was it and her instincts had not failed her!

'Pray do not trouble yourself on my account, my lord,' she flung at him. 'No contriving will be necessary!'

'Listen to me!' he commanded so imperiously that she longed to hit him. 'I cannot explain it all now, but there must be some way – I cannot let you go.'

'I fancy, my lord,' said she, trying hard to keep hold of her temper, 'that you will be truly thankful to know that I decline to entertain or – even listen to any sort of proposal you may be thinking of making me!'

'What d'you mean – any sort of proposal?' He was so taken aback that he relaxed his grasp and she snatched her hands away. 'I am speaking of marriage – what else did you imagine?'

It was Cherryanne's turn to be taken aback, but she quickly rallied. 'And break your father's heart, my lord?' she asked sweetly.

At that there was a short silence, then the Marquis said painfully: 'I can only pray that it will not.'

'You may rest easy on that score, my lord,' she returned with the calmness of desperation. 'Nothing would induce me to accept your very condescending offer.'

'Condescending?' he exploded. 'You little gapeseed! I adore you!'

Being called a gapeseed did nothing to improve the lady's temper, and she whiled away the few remaining minutes before they drew up before Lady Caldwell's door in delivering a detailed dissertation upon his lordship's character, or lack of it, with sundry animadversions upon his failure to display even the most rudimentary consideration for others, his total lack of manners, and any other observations of a derogatory nature that came to her mind.

When the carriage stopped, Damien, who had heard her out in silence, alighted and, letting down the steps with his own hands, escorted his fulminating love to the door, directing the coachman to take the barouche back to Park Place.

'I must thank you again, my lord, for your great kindness to me upon another occasion,' she continued with affecting dignity. 'I would not wish to appear ungracious despite all that has passed, and most sincerely wish you well.'

'I am coming in to see Lady Harpendene,' said he, taking not the least notice of this touching little speech.

'To see grandmama? You cannot – I do not wish – but why?'

She stopped hastily for the door was opened and Lady Caldwell's butler was eyeing them in some surprise. Short of entering into a brangle upon the doorstep, Miss Devenish saw no way of dissuading her escort from his intention, so she stepped inside, closely followed by the Marquis and, as they did so, Lady Harpendene crossed the hall from the drawing-room.

'Back so soon, my dear? I had not looked for you this early,' she greeted her granddaughter. 'Good evening, Shalford. Pray join me in a glass of wine. I was about to sit down to a solitary dinner for my host and hostess have been swept up into some unexpected festivity.' So saying, she led the way back to the drawing-room. 'I had word from Miss Winton of your possible arrival, my lord,' she went on, settling herself into a handsome winged chair. 'Had you a comfortable journey?'

'Hardly that, ma'am,' he said, and told her about it while Miss Devenish stood, plucking at her gloves and wondering how she could extricate herself from so awkward a situation. Her grandmother, whose sharp eyes missed nothing of her confusion, solved the problem for her.

'Charity, be so good as to run upstairs and fetch me my fan,' she requested peremptorily. 'I find it oppressively hot this evening.'

The Marquis held the door for Miss Devenish, who vouchsafed him the merest nod in passing, and returned to her ladyship's side.

'I offered for her, ma'am, and she won't have me,' he said in a tone of near despair.

Lady Harpendene pursed her lips thoughtfully. 'You offered for her, knowing it would mean giving up Studleigh?'

'You knew that? Oh – Honoria, I suppose. I can't help it, I love her.'

'You foolish boy!' she said, but very kindly. 'And you would throw your heritage away because of my wilful little grand-daughter?' He looked so downcast that she was moved to put him out of his misery. 'Let me assure you, however, that though she may not be as great an heiress as Miss Winton, your father is of the opinion that she will do very well!'

'M-my father?' gasped the Marquis, looking as stunned as if he had been planted a facer by one of the more talented members of the Fancy.

'Yes, we had a lengthy discussion upon your future,' she informed him. 'Our acquaintance is of some standing, you know. But why does the girl rebuff you?'

'She said something about breaking my father's heart – my God, I believe I said that to her in the quarry! But I meant – oh, not what she thought! Lord, what a wretched business I've made of it.'

'Yes, you have, haven't you?' agreed Lady Harpendene. 'The assumption that your father could not accept her for his daughter-in-law would touch her pride. Yes, that must be it, for I swear she knows nothing of your other troubles.' She watched his face, grown suddenly vulnerable with understanding. 'Be patient with her, Shalford. She's a spirited filly.'

He grinned ruefully. 'She's all of that! I'll not break her, ma'am. More like she'll break me!'

Her ladyship did not venture to express an opinion on this point of view. 'If you would be counselled by me,' said she, inspecting her rings as if she had never properly seen them before, 'not a word about being able to marry her because of the settlement I am making on her.'

'I was ready to marry her without it!' he protested.

'Yes, yes, I know that,' she soothed him. 'But in her present capricious temper, would the silly child believe it?'

'Very likely not,' he was obliged to agree. 'But, ma'am, is she – are you – is she really an heiress?'

'Ten thousand a year when you marry her and another five or six with my possessions when I am gone!' she informed him. 'Your father seemed quite satisfied – sssh! Here she comes.' As Miss Devenish entered, her ladyship rose. 'Shalford is dining with us,' she announced. 'Give me a little time to make ready,' and, removing the fan from her granddaughter's nerveless fingers, she left them alone.

'May I pour you a glass of wine, Miss Devenish?'

'N-nothing at all, I thank you. I, too, m-must make ready. I cannot sit down to dinner looking like this,' she stammered, not knowing which way to turn in her confusion.

'I think you look beautiful,' he said simply. 'I have your grand-mother's consent to pay my addresses to you.'

'You – you have?' she quavered, feeling such reply to be remarkably inadequate. 'But – your father?'

'Lady Harpendene has explained to His Grace how it is that he will not break his heart if we were to be married.'

Cherryanne's eyes opened very wide indeed. 'Grandmama? But how could she – ?'

'She knew him years ago,' said the Marquis, very sensibly offering no other explanation but taking her firmly in his arms.

'But – ' she tried again, making a gallant attempt to marshal her forces against so determined an assault.

'No buts, my darling!' he whispered, and kissed her until she cried out for mercy yet clung to him the more as if in apology for her lack of fortitude.

'Damien,' she breathed when it was possible.

'Yes, my love?' he murmured, playing with a lock of her dark hair and watching her with so wistfully tender an expression as made her long to throw her arms around his neck and cherish him. But before such weakness could be contemplated, something had to be said.

'Are you quite sure your father won't cast you off for marrying me?'

'Not he!' promised Damien, resuming his attentions so that she quite forgot any further objections she might have raised in her more lucid moments, and contented herself with assuring him that she had not meant any one of the terrible things that she had said to him in the barouche, and would he ever forgive her?

The Marquis, drawing her closer, found it remarkably easy to forgive her and, satisfied that his sentiments were fully reciprocated, with great presence of mind he put a stop to any unnecessary conversation by continuing to make love to her. Miss Devenish thereupon abandoned all attempts at explanation, for the time being at least, and did everything in her power to respond to his lordship's most gratifying civilities.